A VIOLENT END

By the same author

FINAL MOMENTS
SCENT OF DEATH
COLD LIGHT OF DAY
LAST WALK HOME
EVERY SECOND THURSDAY
ELEMENT OF CHANCE
A FORTNIGHT BY THE SEA
FAMILY AND FRIENDS
IN LOVING MEMORY

A VIOLENT END

EMMA PAGE

A CRIME CLUB BOOK
DOUBLEDAY
NEW YORK   LONDON   TORONTO   SYDNEY   AUCKLAND

A Crime Club Book
Published by Doubleday, a division of
Bantam Doubleday Dell Publishing Group, Inc.
666 Fifth Avenue, New York, New York 10103

DOUBLEDAY and the portrayal of a man
with a gun are trademarks of
Doubleday, a division of Bantam Doubleday Dell
Publishing Group, Inc.

All of the characters in this book are fictitious,
and any resemblance to actual persons, living or
dead, is purely coincidental.

Library of Congress Cataloging-in-Publication Data

Page, Emma.
    A violent end / Emma Page. — 1st ed. in the
U.S.
        p.   cm.
    "A Crime Club book."
    I. Title.
PR6066.A29V56   1990
823'.914—dc20   89-38242
                                                    CIP

ISBN 0-385-41094-8

For Christopher
with much love
(To say: Well done!)

A VIOLENT END

1

On this Friday morning in mid-November the long spell of golden autumn weather showed signs of coming to an end. Swirls of cloud, gunmetal grey, slipped along through the lower sky, the freshening wind held a threat of rain.

In the scattered hamlet of Overmead, a mile or two to the east of Cannonbridge, lights shone out from isolated homesteads. Three-quarters of a mile beyond the silent, shadowy expanses of Overmead Wood, a neglected stretch of open woodland, a side road, scarcely more than a glorified lane, branched northwards from the main thoroughfare running out of Cannonbridge. Some five hundred yards along the side road stood Jubilee Cottage, the home of Ian and Christine Wilmot, in a sizable garden still bright with Michaelmas daisies, chrysanthemums, yellow poppies.

The cottage had been converted a few years ago from a pair of semi-detached Edwardian dwellings set at right angles to each other. It was now a handsome, substantial, many-gabled residence with ornamental windows and ornate chimneystacks, its mellow, rosy brick elegantly set off by cream-coloured paintwork, brilliant swags of scarlet pyracantha berries round the doors and windows.

In her comfortable bedroom on the first floor, furnished, like the rest of the house, with carefully chosen Edwardian furniture bought from auctions and salerooms, Karen Boland, a cousin of Christine Wilmot, was up and dressed, washed and groomed, ready for her day's studies at the Cannonbridge College of Further Education. She had been a student at the college since September, following a full-time course in general education.

Karen was sixteen years old, slightly built, delicately pretty, with small, soft features and a smooth, rounded forehead that gave her a lingering look of childhood innocence, a little at variance with the veiled expression of her wide hazel eyes; they held a suggestion of wary containment, the look of one who has already learned some of the harsher lessons of life.

She was dressed in a sweater and slacks, ankle boots. She wore no make-up; her fine, clear skin had a peachy bloom. Her wavy, shoulder-length hair, a shining golden brown, was taken back and secured with a fashionable clip on the crown of her head.

Across the landing she heard her cousin Christine leave the bedroom she shared with her husband, Ian, and go downstairs. Karen crossed to the door of her own room and opened it a fraction. She could hear the muted tones of the kitchen radio giving out the morning's information and opinions, the sounds of Christine preparing breakfast. Along the corridor she could hear Ian splashing in the bathroom.

She closed her door quietly and went to her desk. On a shelf above her books were neatly ranged. She took down an old maths textbook and opened it. The last few pages had been pasted to the back cover along the outside and bottom edges, forming a concealed pocket.

She fingered a snapshot out from the pocket and sat down at the desk, gazing intently at the likeness. After some moments she opened a desk drawer and took out a magnifying glass. She sat closely studying the photograph.

Along the corridor the bathroom door opened, she heard Ian's footsteps going back to the bedroom. Karen at once replaced the photograph, restored the book to the shelf and put the magnifying glass away in the drawer.

A delicious fragrance of percolating coffee greeted her as she entered the kitchen. On the radio a weatherman spoke of lowering skies, falling temperatures, strong winds springing up, scattered showers and rainstorms later in the day, some of them heavy.

"That sounds like the end of the fine weather," Christine said with a grimace. She was a markedly competent-looking woman of thirty-four, with an air of vigorous health, of all her energies being strongly directed towards clearly defined ends. She ran a mail-order agency and also acted as a party organizer for more than one enterprise.

She cut bread for the toaster. Everything done swiftly, with economy of movement. She was sturdily built, somewhat above average height. Her naturally straight hair, of an indeterminate brown, was becomingly curled, cut in a trouble-free, up-to-the-minute style. She was trimly dressed in distinctive casual clothes of good quality. She had few natural advantages in the way of features or colouring but where another woman, less determined, would have appeared decidedly ordinary, Christine achieved a result attractive to the eye.

Karen set about laying the table. Christine was her first cousin. Both Karen's parents were dead and she was in the care of the Social Services Department of the local authority. She had come to live at Jubilee Cottage in July, when the school year ended. She had previously been living with foster-parents in Wychford, a small town ten miles to the west of Cannonbridge. Difficulties had arisen and the foster-parents had refused to keep her. She had been returned to the residential children's home in Wychford from which she had originally been sent to the foster-parents. It was from this residential home that she had been transferred at the end of term into the care of the Wilmots.

As Karen took plates from the dresser Ian Wilmot came down the stairs and into the kitchen. Easy and unhurried, with his usual amiable, half-smiling expression. Good-looking, with fair hair and blue eyes; four years older than his wife. He worked as a planning assistant for the Cannonbridge Council.

He spoke a few good-humoured words to Karen and Christine, picked up a newspaper and glanced through it as Christine set a packet of muesli on the table. "There's a cold chicken in the fridge for this evening," she told them. She wouldn't be in for supper herself, Friday was always her busiest day, she would be out from shortly after lunch. Always important on a Friday to make sure she got her dues from the pay-packets before the weekend spending began in earnest. And there were always a couple of evening parties she must look in on, sales parties she had helped to organize: clothes, lingerie, kitchenware, jewellery, make-up, toys, children's wear.

Ian looked up from his paper. "I've got that meeting at seven-thirty," he reminded her. The meeting, to be held in a school hall in Cannonbridge, had been organized by a local action group drumming up opposition to a proposed building development. Ian had to attend as an observer for the Council.

Christine glanced across at Karen. "What about you? Will you be going to Lynn's after college?" Lynn Musgrove was a fellow student of Karen's, on the same course. She lived close to the college and Karen sometimes went home with her after classes; they did their homework together.

"I'm not sure what I'll be doing." Karen reached cups and saucers down from the dresser. "I might go along to the library." The public library stayed open till eight on Friday evenings. "It depends what homework I have."

"Are you making any more friends at the college?" Ian asked in an easy tone from behind his newspaper. She seemed to be settling into the course well enough but she hadn't so far brought any friend home, not even Lynn Musgrove.

Karen shrugged. "There's no one special." She took knives and spoons from a drawer. "You've no need to worry. I'm getting on fine."

"You know you're always more than welcome to bring anyone here. For a meal, or to stay the night. For a weekend, if you like."

"Yes, I do know that. Thank you."

Ian gave her a little nod by way of reply, an encouraging smile. Christine didn't smile. She stood watching as Karen went into the larder and came out again with honey and marmalade.

"Has Paul Clayton been in touch with you at all?" Christine asked suddenly.

Karen came to an abrupt halt. She stood staring at Christine, holding the jars in a tight clasp. A bright flush rose in her face.

"Has he been in touch with you since you've been here?" Christine persisted. "Has he attempted any kind of contact?"

Karen drew a long, quavering breath. She moved again, went to the table and set down the pots. She didn't look at Christine.

"No, of course not." She put a hand up to her forehead, shielding her face. Clayton was a married man with a young family, a neighbour of Karen's foster-parents in Wychford. An association had formed between Karen and Clayton and had inevitably come to light; this was why the foster-parents had refused to keep her, why she had been sent back to the children's home.

"You're quite sure?" Christine pressed her. "He's made no attempt at all to get in touch with you?"

The colour ebbed from Karen's cheeks. She remained motionless by the table. "Yes, of course, I'm sure." She still didn't look at Christine, still kept her hand up to her brow. "He's made no attempt."

Ian folded his paper and put it down. "You would be sensible and tell us if Clayton did make any approach?" he said gently.

Karen lowered her hand and grasped the back of a chair. Her head drooped. "Yes, of course I would."

"You know we're only thinking of what's best for you," Ian added in the same gentle tone.

"Yes, I know that."

"You do realize," Christine put in with a quick frown, "that if you were foolish enough to start seeing Clayton again and it came out, the Social Services would consider we weren't exercising proper control over you. You'd probably be moved from here, very likely back into another residential home. You wouldn't want that, would you?"

Karen raised her head and looked her full in the face.

"No, I would not." She spoke with fervour. "That's the last thing I'd want."

Ten miles away, in an exclusive, expensively landscaped development on the edge of Wychford, the Clayton family sat at breakfast. The house was large, as modern houses go, set among tall old trees, smoothly sculptured lawns, still emerald green.

In the big breakfast kitchen the four Claytons ate almost in silence at a central table under the glow diffused from an up-to-date light fitting. The entire house was done out in the same impersonal, businesslike way: Scandinavian-type styling, clean lines, new materials, everything of good quality, functional, hard-wearing, trouble-free. As if someone had chosen the lot in a single rapid swoop on a high-class furniture store—which was indeed precisely what had happened, the someone in question being Paul Clayton, his wife Joan remaining at home, feeling herself unfitted to take part in the foray.

The Claytons were eating a cooked breakfast. Joan Clayton punctiliously cooked a good breakfast for them every morning, winter and summer, one area of endeavour in which she could feel in control.

Paul Clayton was an electronics engineer, with his own prospering, expanding business. He was just turned forty, a tall, handsome man with a rangy figure, chiselled features, thick dark hair, grey eyes. His look was intent, unsmiling, the look of a man with a quick temper, who didn't suffer fools gladly. Beside his plate lay his usual pile of newspapers. As he dealt with his breakfast he glanced rapidly over the financial pages of each paper in turn, here and there marking something with his pen.

Opposite him, anticipating every need of her husband and two children, Joan Clayton sat drinking her coffee with a tense, frowning air, watching in simmering silence Paul's brisk manoeuvres with the newspapers.

The children ate their breakfast as always, without fuss or complaint. Ten-year-old twins, boy and girl, they carried on their customary running mealtime conversation with each other in subdued undertones. Well-disciplined and well-behaved, they knew better than to try any larking about in front of their father.

Clayton drained his cup and pushed it forward without so much as a glance at his wife. She at once refilled the cup and pushed it back to him, watchful that not a drop spilled into the saucer.

She was a plain woman, the same age as her husband to within a few weeks. She looked every year of her age and more, with her despondent, anxious air. Carefully dressed and groomed, but without any natural feel for clothes, the end result was invariably the same: dowdiness.

She had known Paul all her life. They had grown up next door to each other in a working-class street of small, rented terrace houses in Wychford. They had attended the same school, sat in the same class. Paul was the son of a factory hand with little money to spare, Joan the daughter of a building labourer content to drink his pint of beer in the pub at the end of his day's work, invest his weekly few shillings in the football pools, an occasional flutter on a horse or dog.

By nature Paul was a clever, hard-working, ambitious lad with an interest in science, always experimenting in the garden shed. Joan was neither clever nor ambitious and she had no interest in any form of science. She was a plain, hefty child, asking no more than to run errands for Paul, clear up his many and varied messes, her greatest pleasure to be permitted to help in an actual experiment.

When Paul was ten years old his father died. There was now even less money to spare. It became very clear to him that his path in life was to work still harder, help his mother as much as possible, make his way in the world as best he could. He left school at the earliest opportunity, got a job in his father's old workplace, went to night school, studied hard, but still spent many hours in the garden shed experimenting. Over the next few years he had several bright ideas which he passed on to his firm, receiving modest lump sums by way of token recognition.

As soon as Joan left school she went to work as a kitchen-hand in a working man's café nearby. She still thought the sun rose and set with Paul Clayton, she was still ready to fetch and carry, lend a hand, in the evenings and at weekends. They never courted or dated in any conventional sense but neither of them ever had any other dates. Paul had no interest in any kind of social activity. He was interested only in getting on. His mother died when he was twenty but his goals and ambitions were undiminished. He remained in the same house, on his own now; he continued to live the same kind of life.

The years slipped by. Then, one evening in his garden shed, Paul had an exceptionally bright idea. He knew at once he was on to a winner. This one he didn't pass on to his firm, this one he hung on to. He was by now twenty-eight; if he was ever going to amount to anything he must make a start soon. Joan knew what was in the wind. She took it for granted he would pass the idea on as before, but he told her no; this one he was going to develop himself.

He called on more than one bank manager, he approached other conventional sources of capital, but without success. The world was sunk in recession, it was no time for a young man from the back streets to be welcomed through the portals of finance houses, no one wanted to know.

And then one winter Saturday some months later, Joan's father won a substantial sum on the football pools he had unsuccessfully patronized for decades. His immediate reaction was that he would give up work and enjoy himself, but Joan thought otherwise. She said not a word about the win to Paul but sat talking long and earnestly, first to her mother and then to her father; she talked more in the next few days than she had ever talked in her life.

At the end of this sustained onslaught her father caved in. He put on a clean shirt and went next door. He was a simple, direct man, anxious for his daughter's welfare and future happiness; he put his proposition to Paul simply and directly: if Paul would marry Joan he could count on a good chunk of the winnings—at a fair rate of interest—to set up in business. It was by no means a fortune but he could at least make a modest start.

It took Paul thirty seconds to make up his mind. The wedding took place at a register office four weeks later. Joan moved into the little house next door and Paul began operations in a small rented unit on the local industrial estate.

Joan was overjoyed. She remained overjoyed for some years. After two years the twins were born and she was even happier and busier. Paul worked harder than ever, still going to evening classes, still studying, still spending hours in his shed, although she no longer joined him there but sat contentedly knitting or sewing in front of the living-room fire when the twins were in bed. She never felt herself neglected or lonely.

The business prospered. Paul moved into larger premises. The twins went to school. Paul decided that the time had come to leave the little house, move somewhere more suited to their improved position. Joan would have been happy to stay where they were but she fell in as always with whatever Paul decided. The new house was fitted out with every kind of labour-saving device; there was a good deal more leisure now for Joan, a good deal more money to spend.

She had nursed hopes that Paul might at long last begin to relax, they might branch out into a more social life together. But Paul brushed aside all such tentative suggestions. He looked on social life with contempt as the shallow activity of vain people without enough to do or to think about. "Find some outside interests," he told her. "Spend some money on yourself. Take things easy, enjoy yourself."

She did her best. She joined the Parent-Teacher Association, took part in church activities, went to classes in cookery and flower-arranging. She made an effort to do something about her appearance, bought new clothes in the latest fashions at prices she could scarcely credit. But they never felt right on her. She settled in the end for upmarket versions of the plain, functional, serviceable garments she had always worn.

And still there remained a wilderness of leisure she didn't know how to fill. Paul didn't appear to notice as she began a slow slide into depression, punctuated by unnerving, seemingly random attacks of panic.

Now, on this November morning, she glanced about and saw that the children had finished breakfast. She sent them upstairs as usual to wash their hands and faces, brush their teeth, make themselves ready for school. It was always she who drove them to school; Paul's works lay in the opposite direction.

She sat watching her husband with tense concentration. He looked at his watch, drained his cup and pushed back his chair. At once she nerved herself, launching precipitately into speech.

"Will you be coming with me to the musical evening next week?"

He paused, surprised.

"In the church hall," she added rapidly. "Tuesday, half past seven, it's for Third World charities. I mentioned it to you last week. You promised to think about it and let me know."

"I'm afraid I forgot all about it," he told her amiably.

She twisted her hands together. "It's a good programme, in a very good cause."

"I'm sorry." His tone was still easy and amiable. "I simply haven't the time. We've got a rush on just now." He stood up, smiled down at her. "Anyway, it's hardly my style. But don't let me stop you going. You get out and enjoy yourself. There must be some woman from the church you can go with." He gathered up his newspapers. "I may be late this evening. Don't bother about any supper for me, I can get a bite somewhere. If I want anything when I come in I can get it myself."

She sat gazing up at him, her hands tightly clasped. "That's three times this week you've been late home."

He made a comical grimace. "Is that so?" He patted his pockets, checked his keys. "You know how it is, the business won't run itself. If there's work to do, it's got to be done." He kept impatience from his voice, kept his expression friendly and smiling. "Competition's fiercer than ever these days. If you don't keep pushing forward you very soon grind to a halt." He went round the table, stooped and gave her a perfunctory kiss on the cheek, straightened up, turned to go.

She suddenly overflowed with anger and resentment. "You're seeing that girl again! That's why you're late!"

The muscles tensed along his jaw. He didn't turn back to look at her. "What girl?" he asked lightly.

"What girl?" she echoed fiercely. She was on the edge of tears, but she kept her voice low because of the children. She had an air of being astounded at her own temerity but she pressed resolutely on. "Have you got half a dozen girls on the go, then, that you don't know who I'm talking about? I'm talking about Karen Boland."

"You're talking nonsense," he said soothingly. He half turned, half smiled. "You're upsetting yourself for nothing. I haven't laid eyes on Karen since she left Wychford, months ago."

There was a brief silence. "Is that the truth?" She looked beseechingly up at him.

He patted her shoulder. "Of course it is." He glanced again at his watch. "I may have been a fool but I'm not a damned lunatic. That's all water under the bridge, best forgotten." He gave her shoulder another encouraging pat and left the room. She heard the front door open and shut, his car starting up, moving off down the drive.

She got slowly to her feet, shaken and trembling. From force of habit she began to gather up the breakfast things, set them down on the draining-board. She stood beside it with her head lowered and her eyes closed, fighting back tears.

When the children came running downstairs again a few minutes later she looked her normal self. She cast an eye over them, gathered up her purse and shopping-bag. "Come along, then," she said in her everyday tones. "Mustn't be late for school."

In Jubilee Cottage also breakfast was coming to an end. Ian Wilmot was pouring himself a last cup of coffee when he heard the postman. He rose with controlled haste and went into the hall, coming back with a handful of mail which he put down in front of his wife. "All for you again," he remarked cheerfully.

Christine glanced quickly through the post and laid it aside. All business mail, to be dealt with later. She looked up at Ian. "Nothing from your application?" He had applied for a better job in the South.

He picked up his cup. He remained standing by his chair, drinking the coffee. He shook his head, smiling. "No, not yet."

She continued to gaze up at him. "If you're on the short list, surely you'd have heard by now?"

"Possibly." He kept his amiable look, his light, dismissive tone.

She frowned. "You had real hopes of this one." Until six months ago he'd been confident of promotion in due course in his own department in Cannonbridge where he'd worked for the last twelve years. He believed he'd given satisfaction, he'd always got on well with his head of department. But six months ago the head had died suddenly and a new man had been brought in. The easygoing atmosphere altered overnight. The new man was a good deal younger than his predecessor, a good deal sharper, far more critical. He began a relentless drive for efficiency, singling out in uncomfortable ways those members of staff whose performance struck him as less than satisfactory. Ian's name figured well up on this list.

Christine tilted back her head. "That's the fifth job you've applied for in the last few months," she observed.

He moved his shoulders but said nothing.

"Is there anything else on the cards?" she pursued.

He drank his coffee. "Not at the moment." He smiled again. "Something will come along one of these days."

She made no reply but sat gazing up at him.

He finished his coffee. "Are you nearly ready?" he asked Karen.

She nodded, ate her last morsel of toast, drained her cup.

Ian went into the hall to put on his outdoor things. Christine stood up and began to clear the table.

Karen followed Ian into the hall. She reached down her brown quilted jacket from the hall-stand and slipped it on. She gathered up the long tresses of her wavy gold-brown hair, twisting it loosely into a coil on top of her head before pulling on over it a knitted woollen cap of bright daffodil yellow.

Ian took her long matching scarf from its peg. "You'll need this," he warned. "It'll be a cold day." He draped the scarf round her neck and shoulders, tucking in the ends as if she were a child, smiling tenderly down at her. She stood in docile silence, smiling up at him.

In the kitchen Christine, returning from the fridge, paused by the door leading into the hallway, left slightly ajar. She caught sight of the two of them through the narrow aperture. She stood motionless, watching as Ian adjusted Karen's woollen cap, touched her cheek, bent his head and kissed her lightly on the lips.

"Ready, then?" he asked.

"Yes, I'm ready." She picked up her shoulder-bag, a fashionable affair of cream-coloured macramé, pulled on a pair of woollen gloves. She suddenly paused and exclaimed, "Oh—I was forgetting. The theatre scrapbook. I borrowed it from one of the students. I promised faithfully I'd return it today. It's up in my room. I'll run up and get it, I won't be a moment."

Behind the kitchen door Christine remained silent and motionless, studying the expression on her husband's face as he stood watching Karen run swiftly up the stairs.

2

The morning was now a little more advanced. The carriage clock on the study mantelpiece at Hawthorn Lodge showed nine twenty-five. The lodge was a pleasant Victorian villa not far from Overmead Wood, half a mile from the Wilmots' cottage. It stood in an attractive rambling garden full of twists and turns, unexpected vistas.

The study was a cosy room on the ground floor, furnished with unpretentious comfort and due regard for the period of the house. The walls were hung with old theatrical mementoes; the book-shelves were filled with theatrical biographies, memoirs, reminiscences, histories, texts of plays, postcard albums of the Victorian beauties of the old music halls.

Desmond Hallam stood before his desk with a pen in his hand, nervously glancing through the essay on the nineteenth-century novel he had written yesterday evening, making minor alterations as he read.

Sill a few years from fifty, of medium height, sparely built; a mild-looking man with nondescript features, thinning hair of uncertain brown brushed back from a lined forehead, hesitant eyes of the same indeterminate brown. He was nattily dressed, carefully groomed.

He had begun attending classes at the Cannonbridge College of Further Education in September. He had worked as a personnel clerk in the town until the takeover of his firm by a large national group at the beginning of the year. The negotiations leading up to the takeover had been a well-kept secret until the last possible moment and Desmond had been taken totally by surprise when the news broke. Not that he had been harshly dealt with; like all the other redundant employees he had been put out to grass on generous terms.

He had lived at Hawthorn Lodge a good ten years. His father had been the manager of a high-class menswear shop in a town some distance from Cannonbridge. After his death Desmond's mother suggested joining forces with her son; she had been left well provided for.

The arrangement suited them both. Desmond was more than happy to leave his Cannonbridge lodgings to set up house with his mother, with whom he had always got on well. Mrs. Hallam bought Hawthorn Lodge and the two of them lived a tranquil, self-contained life in harmony and content until Mrs. Hallam's death a few months after Desmond had been made redundant by his firm.

The clock struck the half-hour. Desmond blew out a resigned breath and laid down his pen. Good or bad, the essay would have to stand now. The literature class was at ten and he wouldn't dream of being late. Better go up and see if Aunt Ivy was ready—he was giving her a lift into Cannonbridge. She rode in with him three or four times a week to do the shopping, making her own way back by bus.

He put the essay into his briefcase. His aunt, Miss Ivy Jebb, was his mother's older sister, a retired assistant nurse. She had been staying at Hawthorn Lodge since the late spring when she had been urgently summoned by Desmond, alarmed at the lowered state of his mother's health after a bout of influenza.

The two sisters had never been on close terms, Desmond's mother finding Ivy bossy and manipulative. Over the years Desmond had laid eyes on his aunt barely half a dozen times. But his alarm at the deteriorating condition of his mother swept aside such minor considerations.

"I'll be along on the next train," Aunt Ivy had at once assured him. She had been delighted to leave her bed-sitter in the northern town—eighty miles from Cannonbridge—where she had spent her working life, delighted to step out of the restricted existence that was all she could manage on her pension and dwindling savings, delighted to entrain for the rural peace of Overmead, the substantial comforts of Hawthorn Lodge. What was a little nursing in return for such rewards? She would have her sister on her feet in no time at all.

She had immediately taken over the running of the house. She nursed her sister with energy and competence and for some time Mrs. Hallam appeared set on the road to recovery, but her weakened heart suddenly gave way.

Desmond had been devastated by his mother's death. Coming so soon on top of his unexpected redundancy, it had thrown him completely off balance. There was now not even the familiar nine-to-five routine of work to distract his mind and he fell into a state of despairing grief.

Ivy Jebb was more than willing to stay on to deal with everything, take care of him, look after the house when he finally ended up for a short stay in the psychiatric unit of a local hospital, in a condition of total collapse.

"You must make a new beginning," the psychiatrist advised him when he began to mend. "Enlarge your horizons, broaden your mind, find new interests."

Desmond had dutifully nerved himself in due course to enrol at the college, choosing classes in local history, literature, play-reading. He broke his days up into segments, creating tiny points of interest to get him through the next hour or two, a book to be returned to the library, a cup of coffee in the college canteen, weaving little by little a web of activities that might gradually expand to fill the days and weeks, the months and years, warding off emptiness, bleakness and desperation.

Now he left the study, went up the stairs and gave a light tap on the door of Aunt Ivy's bedroom.

"I'm just coming," she called back. A moment later she threw open the door. A short, dumpy woman with a good deal of curly white hair and a soft, pink-and-white, indoor skin; she wore fashionably rimmed bifocal spectacles. She was dressed in a fawn-coloured jumper and skirt.

She greeted Desmond with the wide smile of determined motherliness which had been her most constant expression since she had walked in through the front door of Hawthorn Lodge, a smile somewhat at odds with the shrewd, detached assessing regard of her pale blue eyes behind the lenses. Desmond gave her in return his nervous, placatory grin.

Ivy stepped back into her room and picked up a lightweight jacket of navy-blue woollen material from the back of a chair. She put it on, tugging a matching beret over her curls, picked up her gloves and shopping basket. She glanced out at the overcast sky.

"I could do with my good Harris tweed coat, now the weather's turning cold," she observed as she came out on to the landing and closed the door behind her. They set off down the stairs. "I think it's time I went back to fetch my winter things." She rather liked that remark, it set exactly the right tone of being in charge.

Desmond made no reply, he felt his heart give a nasty lurch. A couple of months ago, shortly after he had left hospital, he had casually raised the matter of when Ivy might be thinking of returning home. He had had no particular reason for mentioning the subject, there was no thought in his head other than that she wasn't likely to be staying with him much longer.

To his immense astonishment—and consternation—Ivy had blandly informed him that she had given up her bed-sitter just after he had gone into hospital. She had phoned her landlady who had quite understood that Ivy's place was now with her nephew. The landlady had obligingly agreed to store Ivy's belongings until Ivy could deal with them.

Desmond had all at once realized the inescapable truth: having got herself nicely bedded down in Hawthorn Lodge, Aunt Ivy hadn't the slightest intention of ever letting herself be uprooted again.

"I could pop there and back by train," Ivy mused aloud as they reached the foot of the stairs. "I could sort through my things, decide what to keep, give the rest to Oxfam. I shan't want to keep a great deal, clothes mainly, a couple of pictures, a few books and ornaments." She gave him her open, guileless smile. "There's no point in bringing any bedding, any pots and pans, crockery or cutlery, you're more than well supplied with all that kind of thing here."

He could manage only a vague murmur in reply. He felt himself borne along on an irresistible current.

They went out through the front door into the sharply scented autumn air. As he locked the door behind them he was assailed by a surge of guilt. He had cause to be eternally grateful to Aunt Ivy, she had been indispensable during the last few terrible months. But to live with him here for good—and she gave every sign of having a good many sprightly years left to her—that was something he hadn't bargained for.

He backed his car out of the garage.

"I'd have to stay overnight, of course," Ivy pondered as she got in beside him. "I couldn't manage both journeys in one day, not by train."

Still he could find nothing to say. She settled herself in beside him, fastened her seat-belt. "It would be a lot quicker by car, of course. But it would be a dreadful imposition to ask you to take me, I wouldn't even think of suggesting it." She gave him her resolutely maternal smile. Behind her glasses her eyes gleamed like pale blue gimlets. "If only I could drive, I'd hire a little van myself and shoot up there and back. I'd quite enjoy it."

Still he said nothing but started up the engine. She flicked a glance at his face in the mirror. She could see her shots had gone home; he looked wretched, guilty, indecisive.

She turned her head and looked out at the blowy morning. She need say nothing more, it could all stew quietly on its own, she was totally confident of the outcome.

The day grew steadily colder, with a gusting wind. Rain fell intermittently across the region.

The clock over the impressive entrance to the Cannonbridge College of Further Education showed twenty minutes to six. The college was housed in a tall turn-of-the-century building near the town centre, not far from the public library.

Much of the building lay in darkness; most of the daytime classes were over by this time and the evening classes weren't due to begin for the best part of two hours.

Light shone out from a second-floor room where a class in English language was being held for the first-year General Studies group. In the third row Karen Boland sat beside Lynn Musgrove, chewing her lip over a particularly tricky grammar question.

The classroom door opened and a middle-aged woman clerk came softly in. She went up to the desk and spoke to the lecturer in a low murmur; the class worked diligently on. By way of reply the lecturer gave a nod and a jerk of his head at where Karen sat.

The woman went over to Karen, stooped and spoke to her in the same subdued tone. Karen laid down her pen, rose and followed her from the room.

A few minutes later Karen returned and resumed her seat. Before she again began to wrestle with the grammar questions she scribbled something on a scrap of paper and slid it across to Lynn Musgrove who ran her eye over it and then slipped it into her pocket.

3

Ten minutes past seven on Saturday morning, not yet daylight. Sounds began to penetrate Christine Wilmot's sleep: the rattle of a wheelbarrow, footsteps on gravel. She stirred and rolled over, glanced across at the other bed. It was empty, the covers thrown back.

She switched on the bedside lamp and looked at the clock. After a moment or two she got slowly out of bed, yawning. She put on her slippers and housecoat and went over to the window.

She drew back the flowered curtains. The morning was quiet and still after yesterday evening's wind and rain. Along the skyline lay a band of deep grey cloud, shading into silvery grey above; frail streaks of carmine rayed out over the horizon.

Down below, light streamed out over the garden from the kitchen window. The evening's stormy lashings had stripped leaves from trees, the last scarlet and yellow roses from the bushes, flattening dahlias in the beds, golden rod along the borders.

Ian was busy dealing with the havoc. He turned his head and saw her standing at the window, raised a hand in salutation and resumed his task.

Christine left the window and crossed to the dressing-table, peered at her face in the glass, ran a comb through her hair. She went slowly downstairs and made a start on the breakfast. She always cooked a substantial fry-up on Saturday morning. However busy the day might be, Saturday always retained something of a holiday air, a hangover from childhood schooldays. And there was time to enjoy and digest a good breakfast. Christine never shopped on Saturdays when the stores were crowded; she got all that out of the way on Thursday morning before her own busy time began. On Saturdays she drove out around the hamlets and villages to the north of Overmead, a prosperous rural area where she had by now built up a highly satisfactory trade.

The kitchen was warm from the heat of the all-night stove. She put the coffee on to percolate, took bacon and sausages from the fridge. She heard Ian come in through the back door a few minutes later as she was rinsing mushrooms and tomatoes under the tap. Ian went into the utility room, coming through into the kitchen a little later when she was back at the cooker again.

"You're an early bird," she greeted him. "How long have you been up? I never heard you."

He didn't answer her question. "I tried not to wake you. I didn't sleep too well, I had a touch of indigestion. I went along with some of the committee last night, after the meeting. We went to the chairman's house, his wife had laid on some refreshments. I thought I might as well get up and get going, instead of lying in bed, tossing and turning." He gestured out at the garden. "Plenty to be done after the storm."

She stirred the contents of the frying-pan. "Do you want fried bread with your breakfast?"

He made a grimace. "No, thank you."

"Too much booze last night?" No edge of censure in her tone.

"No, very little booze, as a matter of fact." And no defensiveness in his tone. "It must have been the sandwiches that upset me. Lobster. Very good, but a bit too rich for that time of night."

She lowered the heat under the pan and set about making toast. "It was almost twelve when I got in myself. These sales parties can be a bit too much of a good thing sometimes. Some of these house-wives don't know where to draw the line when they start letting their hair down. I was absolutely exhausted, I went flat out the moment my head hit the pillow. I never heard you come in." She paused as she was about to cut more bread and looked up at him. "How much toast can you eat?"

"Actually, I don't think I want anything to eat," he said with apology. "Just some coffee, that'll do me."

She wasn't at all put out. "You could try something to eat, a piece of dry toast, perhaps. It might do you good, put a lining on your stomach."

He shook his head with emphasis. "No, thanks. Just the coffee, good and strong, that's all I want."

"Not to worry," she assured him. "The food won't be wasted. I haven't started cooking Karen's breakfast yet, so she can have yours. Give her a shout, tell her to come down right away, her breakfast's ready."

He went into the hall and called loudly up the stairs. Without waiting for an answer he went along to the utility room, coming back into the kitchen a minute or two later.

Christine was pouring his coffee. He began to drink it at once, scalding hot, black, very strong. Christine switched on the radio, giving it half an ear. She finished laying the table and returned to the cooker where the contents of the pan were ready for dishing up.

"Where's that girl?" she exclaimed on a note of irritation. "I don't hear her moving."

"Perhaps she wants a lie-in," Ian suggested. "She may have gone to bed late."

"She certainly wasn't up when I got in." Christine moved to the kitchen door. "And I know she doesn't want to be up late this morning. She told me she wants to go to the Amnesty book sale."

In the hall she called sharply up the stairs. There was no reply.

She clicked her tongue, muttered something and went rapidly up to Karen's bedroom. She beat a loud tattoo on the door.

No reply, no sound from within.

She thrust the door open and marched in. She came to a sudden halt.

The room was empty. The bed had not been disturbed, the covers lay smoothly in place. The curtains were drawn back, the window closed. Everything neat and orderly.

She stood staring round, frowning down at the carpet. Then she went along the corridor to the bathroom and looked in. She opened every door upstairs and glanced inside, then she went slowly downstairs again.

Ian was pouring himself more coffee. He became aware of her silent presence in the kitchen doorway and turned his head.

"She's not here," Christine said flatly.

He frowned. "Not here?"

"Her bed's not been slept in. She's not anywhere upstairs. I've looked."

He stared blankly at her.

She burst out: "I know where she is! She's with that Paul Clayton!"

"Clayton?" he echoed in incredulous tones. "You don't think she's run off with him?"

"Run off?" she repeated with a startled face. "No, that wasn't what I meant. I never thought of that."

She turned and went running up the stairs again. He heard her moving noisily about, opening and shutting drawers and cupboards.

She came down again a few minutes later. "She hasn't taken any of her things."

Ian drank his coffee. "I don't see why you should jump to the conclusion that she's with Clayton. She could easily have stayed the night with some girl from college."

"Then why hasn't she let us know?"

"She probably tried to, and couldn't. There was no one here to answer the phone. She could have gone to a disco or a club, or a party maybe, with some students from the college. She could have missed the last bus, decided to stay the night with one of the girls. She's probably still in bed, fast asleep." He glanced at the clock. "It's only just gone half past seven." He took another drink of his coffee. "I can't honestly see there's any real need to worry. She'll phone us as soon as she gets up."

She gazed at him in silence, then she said slowly, "Yes, I suppose you're right. That could be what happened."

"I'm sure it is," he said heartily. "She'll be here by the time you get back from your round. If she phones, I'll be here to answer it. Now stop worrying and forget it. Sit down and eat your breakfast. We could give the Musgroves a ring after you've eaten, see if Karen's there, or if Lynn knows where she might be. We can't very well ring them yet, it's too early."

It was by now broad daylight, the sky still flamed a brilliant orange-gold from the sunrise. On the northernmost edge of Overmead a lad of thirteen let himself out of the back door of the cottage where he lived, took his bicycle from the shed and loaded it up with his fishing tackle, his sandwiches and flask, a folded macintosh in case of any more storms of rain.

But the morning looked fine enough as he set off down the lane. A minute or two later he entered a side road running south. It would take him to the main road which he would cross, continuing south, headed for the river.

He whistled cheerfully as he pedalled along. There was as yet scarcely any traffic. The birds sang, sunlight glittered on yesterday's puddles of rain.

As he came into sight of the main road the rough tracts of Overmead Wood stretched out before him on his right. He looked over at the wood with old affection; he had spent many a happy hour there with his mates, playing Robin Hood.

Something caught his eye among the trees, a long, bright loop of yellow, dangling from a branch. He slowed his pace. A broad grass verge, still muddy from the rain, overgrown with weeds and brambles, ran along the edge of the wood. A number of books were scattered over the ground. A fancy, light-coloured bag or satchel lay among the reedy grass and dead thistles, spilling its contents.

A long-tailed pheasant rose from the verge and flew away as he halted and laid his bike down on a little rising mound, comparatively clean. Mindful of his clothes and footwear, he picked his way to inspect the books, the bag with its contents: notebooks, pens, pencils, a case of mathematical instruments, all soaking wet. He touched nothing, he left everything where it lay. Then he straightened up and made his way along a narrow track, treacherous and slippery, meandering between oaks and chestnuts, sycamores and birches, to where the long yellow scarf hung from its bough, drenched with rain, the yarn snagged and snarled where the wind had flung it against rough bark.

He glanced about, peered into the recesses of the wood. On the ground, some distance away, a flash of the same bright colour caught his eye. He moved gingerly towards it.

When he was still a little way off he stopped suddenly and put a hand up to his mouth. The vague blur of colour had all at once resolved itself into a tattered yellow cap on the head of someone lying sprawled face down in a muddied clearing between the trees.

4

Detective-Chief Inspector Kelsey, a big, solid rock of a man with a freckled face and shrewd green eyes, a head of thickly-springing carroty hair, left the woodland clearing and made his way towards his car, followed by Detective-Sergeant Lambert. A minute search of the area was already under way.

It was plain from the scatter of books on the grass verge that the dead girl was Karen Boland, a student at the Cannonbridge College of Further Education. A library ticket in an inside pocket of her jacket supplied her address.

The police doctor had made a preliminary estimate of the time of death, setting it at between five and eight on the previous evening, Friday, November 13. The body was fully clothed and there was no sign of any sexual assault.

Karen's right ankle had been violently wrenched, possibly broken, some minutes before her death. The wrench had in all probability happened in the course of her headlong flight from her attacker over the uneven ground. She could have caught her foot and been sent flying, pitching heavily down, unable to rise, with her assailant crashing along behind her.

As she lay prostrate, shaken and winded, in considerable pain from the injured ankle, her attacker had knelt on her back, producing severe and deep contusions, pressing her head down with force into the mud and leaf-mould. Her face had been massively bruised, abraded and lacerated, her left cheekbone fractured by counter-pressure from a tree root. She had been held down for some time; she had died from asphyxia.

But to make assurance doubly sure her assailant had then viciously bludgeoned her, striking several savage blows on the back of her head, shattering the skull. A few feet from the body lay a heavy billet of wood, a piece of broken bough, clearly the weapon used in the clubbing. Caught up in the bark were strands of yellow wool, long gold-brown hairs, fragments of tissue, tiny embedded splinters of bone.

If Karen had at any stage been able to strike out at her killer her hands could give no evidence of it. She had worn woollen gloves, soaked and filthy now, ripped and snagged. The skin of her killer's hands, Kelsey pondered, must surely—unless similarly protected by gloves—be scratched and marked, possibly deeply, from a swift passage through the wood.

The nylon material of Karen's quilted jacket, the dark stuff of her slacks, showed rents and tears from thorns and spines, projecting boughs. Her ankle boots were caked in thick yellow mud. The clothes and footwear of her killer must also bear this kind of witness. And the thorns and spines, the projecting boughs, carried threads and fibres, ripped from the clothing of pursued and pursuer.

The two men reached the car and Sergeant Lambert opened the door. "Jubilee Cottage," Kelsey directed as he got in. They approached the dwelling a few minutes later. The gates were standing open and Lambert turned the car into the neatly gravelled driveway.

A car was drawn up at one side of the house. A ladder with a bucket suspended from a rung had been set up against the guttering at the front of the house. At the foot of the ladder stood a wheelbarrow half full of garden refuse. On the ground close by lay a pair of stout work gloves, a hand brush and trowel, a pair of secateurs.

At the sound of the car the front door on the left jerked open and Christine Wilmot came flying out, her face puckered in alarm. At the sight of the two men she halted abruptly, knowing them instantly for policemen. "Karen!" she cried. "What's happened to her?"

"Mrs. Boland?" Kelsey asked. Though she looked scarcely old enough to be the girl's mother.

She gave her head an impatient shake. "I'm Mrs. Wilmot," she said rapidly. "Christine Wilmot, Karen's cousin. She lives here. What's happened to her? Has there been an accident?"

Ian Wilmot came running out through the same open door, looking from one to the other, his face full of concern. "Is it Karen?" he blurted out. "Has something happened to her?"

"Mr. Wilmot?" Kelsey asked.

He gave a nod. "Ian Wilmot." He gestured at Christine. "My wife." He thrust his hands together. "What's happened to Karen?"

Kelsey disclosed his identity. "I think we'd better go inside." At his words the other two fell silent, then Christine began to utter little trembling sobs, her head drooping. Ian put an arm round her shoulders, and steered her into the house.

He led the way into a sitting-room on the right of the hall. They all sat down, Ian on the arm of his wife's chair, his hand resting on her shoulder. She had by now fallen silent. She sat on the edge of her seat, clasping her hands tightly together.

"I'm afraid I bring bad news," Kelsey said gently. "Very bad news." Christine set up a tiny whimpering sound. Ian stared at the Chief.

"I'm very sorry to have to tell you," Kelsey said, "that Karen is dead."

Christine gave a loud cry and put both hands up to her face.

"Was it an accident?" Ian asked. "A road accident?"

The Chief shook his head. "Her body has been found in Overmead Wood. I'm afraid there's no doubt about it: she's been murdered."

Christine broke into unrestrained sobs.

"Murdered?" Ian echoed with incredulous horror. "Was it a sex attack?"

"Not on the face of it," Kelsey told him. "We'll know more about it after the post-mortem."

"When did it happen?"

But the Chief wasn't prepared at this juncture to give an answer, however approximate, to that question. "We'll know more after the post-mortem," he repeated. He glanced at Christine, rocking and sobbing. "I think some tea—"

"Yes, of course." Ian got to his feet but the Chief waved him down again. "Sergeant Lambert will see to it."

Lambert went across the hall and through an open door into the kitchen. A woman's outdoor jacket had been thrown carelessly over the back of a chair, with a shoulder-bag, a headscarf, a pair of woollen gloves lying close by on the table. He filled the kettle and put it on to boil.

In the sitting-room Christine had regained some degree of composure. She sat up and took a handkerchief from her pocket, she dabbed at her eyes.

"I was trying to ring Karen's foster-parents, over in Wychford, just now, when you arrived," Ian told the Chief, "but I couldn't get any reply. Karen lived with them until fairly recently. When she didn't turn up this morning, or phone, I suddenly thought she might have taken it into her head for some reason to go over there to see them."

The Chief asked him how long Karen had lived at Jubilee Cottage.

"It was getting on for the end of July when she came here," Ian told him. "She came to us from a children's home in Wychford, but she'd only been back there a short time. Before that she'd been living with the foster-parents in Wychford, the people I was trying to phone just now." He supplied their name and address.

"Why did she leave the foster-parents?" Kelsey asked.

"There was some trouble with a neighbour and the Social Services thought it best if she was moved from there."

"How did she come to be living here with you?"

"It was Karen's own idea," Christine put in. She seemed a good deal steadier now. "I hadn't seen her since she was a child, our families were never close. But I was the only living relative she knew of, so she wrote to me—entirely off her own bat—and asked if we'd be willing to have her live here. She'd already made inquiries and discovered there was a course at the Cannonbridge college that she could take. She seemed very anxious to be part of a family again, to live with someone she was related to.

"So we met her, we had her over here for a weekend once or twice." She drew a shivering breath. "We liked her, we felt sorry for her. We talked it over and agreed to take her. It was settled that she would finish the school year where she was, and then come to us."

"We were very pleased at the way it was working out," Ian added. "She was settling down, working hard, doing well at the college."

"What was the trouble with the neighbour over in Wychford?"

"He's a married man, his name's Paul Clayton. We've never met him. It seems the Claytons know Karen's foster-parents and Karen used to go to the Claytons sometimes to keep an eye on their children when the parents were out in the evening. The parents wouldn't always be out together, he'd be working late—he has his own business in Wychford, something to do with electronics—and his wife would be out on some interest of her own. Mrs. Clayton came home unexpectedly early one evening and found her husband and Karen together." He grimaced. "The balloon went up."

"Was there any contact between Clayton and Karen while she was living here with you?"

"Not that we know of," Christine answered. "I asked her once or twice if Clayton had been in touch with her but she was most emphatic that there'd been no contact of any kind. This morning, when we discovered she hadn't been here all night, my first thought was that she might have met him yesterday, spent the night with him somewhere. I wanted to phone him but Ian wouldn't let me."

"I couldn't believe she was with Clayton," Ian explained. "I couldn't believe she'd be such a fool, not after the sensible way she'd behaved all the time she'd been living here. I was sure she was

with some girlfriend from the college, that she'd walk in or phone at
any moment. I thought it would be madness to ring the Claytons. It
could start up all kinds of trouble for them again, very probably all
for nothing."

"Why was Karen in care in the first place?" Kelsey wanted to
know. "What happened to her parents?"

"They're both dead," Christine told him. Her face began to dis-
solve again. "I'm sorry." She put her handkerchief to her eyes. "It's
been such a shock."

Sergeant Lambert came in with a tray of tea. "I can give you the
bare bones of Karen's history," Ian told Kelsey as Lambert handed
round the cups. "Christine doesn't know anymore than I do, we
only know what the Social Services told us. We never talked about
the past with Karen. We thought it best if she put it all behind her
and made a fresh start."

"What kind of past was it?"

"Her parents lived in Okeshot, that was where Karen was born."
Okeshot was a prosperous market town roughly the same size as
Cannonbridge, eighteen miles to the south-west. "Her mother died
when Karen was a small child, and her father didn't remarry for
some years. He died not long after the second marriage. That left
Karen with her stepmother." He recited the string of facts in a flat
monotone.

"After a time the stepmother remarried, a man called Lorimer.
Lorimer abused Karen and she became pregnant. The whole thing
came out and Karen was taken into care. She had an abortion. There
was a court case and Lorimer went to prison. He's still there, as far
as I know."

Christine appeared by now to have recovered complete control.
She sat sipping her tea, her face wiped clear of expression.

Ian took up the story again. "The stepmother stood by Lorimer.
What it came down to was that she had to choose between him and
Karen. The Social Services wouldn't allow Karen to live in the same
house as Lorimer again and the stepmother told them she intended
to take Lorimer back when he'd served his sentence. So Karen had
to remain in care."

"To get back to yesterday," Kelsey said. "When did you first miss
Karen?"

"We didn't miss her till this morning," Ian told him. "When we saw that her bed hadn't been slept in. We were both out yesterday evening." He explained about Christine's catalogue round, the sales parties, the action-group meeting he had attended, the refreshments afterwards at the chairman's house. "It was late by the time I got back here, getting on for one o'clock. Christine was already in bed, asleep. I never gave a thought to Karen. I took it for granted she was here, safe and sound, in her bed."

"I got home at about a quarter to twelve," Christine put in. "I assumed Karen was in bed, she was always in bed long before that. I went straight to bed myself."

"Had you expected Karen to spend yesterday evening here?" Kelsey asked her.

"I asked her at breakfast what she would be doing after college but she said she wasn't sure, she might go along to the public library. There's a girl at college she was friendly with, a girl called Lynn Musgrove, she's the only friend Karen ever mentioned. I tried to ring Lynn this morning to see if Karen was there or if she had any idea where Karen might be. Lynn wasn't in, she'd gone out early, running, she belongs to an athletics club. I spoke to Mrs. Musgrove. She told me Karen hadn't been there at all yesterday evening. Ian was sure Karen was perfectly all right, that she'd turn up at any moment, so I went off on my rounds as usual. But I couldn't get Karen out of my head, I was so worried about her. I decided to come back here to see if she'd come home, and if not, try to decide what to do. I'd only been back a few minutes when you arrived."

Kelsey asked what the Musgrove household consisted of.

"We haven't met either Lynn or her mother," Ian explained. "All we know is what Karen told us. Mrs. Musgrove's a widow, they're not well off. Mrs. Musgrove works an evening shift at a plastics factory. There's a younger child and Lynn has to keep an eye on her while the mother's at work—that's why Lynn was never able to come over here in the evenings, it was always Karen who went there."

"Is there any man around?"

"Karen never mentioned any man. From all she said, Mrs. Musgrove seems to be a quiet, hard-working, respectable woman, struggling to bring up her family. I didn't get the impression she'd have the time or the money for much social life. And Lynn sounds a sensible, steady girl, not in the least flighty."

"Did Karen have any boyfriends at the college?"

"Not as far as we know."

Kelsey looked at Ian. "What about friends or colleagues of your own? Is there anyone who might have met her here, taken a fancy to her? Is there anything you recall? Anything you noticed?"

Both Ian and Christine shook their heads.

"Did she ever mention anyone from the college? Someone who was a nuisance perhaps, pestering her, making a pass, trying it on? Some male member of staff, maybe, or a mature student? Or maybe someone she came across on her way to or from the college?"

Again they shook their heads. Karen had never mentioned anything like that.

"What was her relationship with you?" Kelsey asked Ian.

"She was always pleasant and friendly, always cooperative, wanting to do anything she could to help round the house. There was never any problem. She treated me like a brother, or a friend."

"Did she have a crush on you?"

"No, not in the least."

"Did you find her attractive?"

He looked steadily back at the Chief. "She was a very pretty girl, but I never regarded her in that way. I looked on her as someone in our care, like a daughter or a younger sister."

Kelsey asked how Karen usually made her way to and from the college.

"I took her in the car in the mornings," Ian told him. "She came home on the bus." The time of the bus she caught varied according to the day of the week, the time of her last class, if she was staying on at the college for a club or a meeting, if she was going to the library or to Lynn's house. Karen always got off the bus by Overmead Wood, a few yards from the junction of the main road with the side road.

"Did you ever give her a lift home?" Kelsey asked Ian.

"No, never."

"Did she ever get a lift home from anyone else?"

She had never mentioned a lift to either of them.

"What would she normally do if she missed her bus? Would she set off to walk home?"

Ian shook his head. "It's a fair distance, especially when you're carrying books. There's a good hour between buses, so she couldn't expect the next one to come along and pick her up on the way. And she'd think walking home would be a waste of time—especially on a cold, wet evening like yesterday—when she could be getting on with her homework in comfort, at the college or in the public library."

"I'm positive she wouldn't try to thumb a lift," Christine said with energy. "She was well aware of the dangers, we'd warned her about it more than once, and she always agreed it would be a very foolish thing to do."

"If she did miss her bus," Kelsey persisted, "and she did decide to set off walking home, and someone she knew, or knew slightly, pulled up beside her and offered her a lift, someone living in Overmead, perhaps, maybe someone she knew only by sight, do you think she'd be likely to accept the lift?"

"Yes, I think she probably would," Christine answered after a moment.

"Then again," Kelsey said to Ian in an easy tone, "if she'd set off walking and you happened to come along, on your way home, and you pulled up beside her, she'd naturally get in."

Ian frowned. "Yes, of course she would, but that never happened. I never gave her a lift home, ever, and I certainly didn't give her a lift home yesterday."

"How did you spend yesterday afternoon?" Kelsey asked.

"I was out on site visits all afternoon—that's how I normally spend Friday afternoon. I drove home from the last site. I had a bath, changed, had something to eat and then went along to the meeting. It started at seven-thirty."

"Is that your car outside?"

"Yes, it is."

"Did you use it yesterday to go to work?"

"Yes, I did."

"We'd like to take a look at it."

"Certainly." Ian led the way outside. Christine followed the Chief and Sergeant Lambert. "My wife used the car this morning when she went out on her rounds," Ian told them.

Kelsey surveyed the vehicle, a smallish family saloon, claret-red in colour, some four years old. He opened the door and glanced round, opened the boot and looked inside. He returned to the interior of the car and scrutinized it with greater care, being particularly scrupulous in his examination of the pedals, the carpet by the driver's seat.

"The sites you visited yesterday," he said to Ian. "Were they muddy?"

"Yes. One or two were very muddy."

The Chief peered down again. "There's no sign of any mud here."

"I cleaned the car this morning, ready for Christine to take it out."

"You gave it a pretty good going over."

"It needs a good going over after I've been out on the sites, that's why I clean it on a Saturday morning. I've got one of those cordless electric dustettes I use on it, they're very thorough. I always give the pedals a scrub when I wash the car."

The Chief straightened up. "I'd like to see the shoes you were wearing yesterday when you drove home."

Ian stuck out one foot. "I was wearing these." Brown leather slip-ons, bearing evidence now of his morning stint in the garden. "I never wear good shoes on a Friday because of going over the sites. These are old but they're still fairly reasonable. They're strong and waterproof, they clean up well enough."

"The clothes you wore yesterday on your way home, I'd like to see those too. Not just the outdoor garments, everything: socks, underwear, handkerchief, tie, gloves, the lot."

"Yes, certainly." Ian led them back into the house, taking them first into the front hall. He opened the door of a wardrobe and showed them a jacket, oldish but still respectable, made of close-woven, proofed gabardine, medium grey, with a hood, a quilted lining. "That's my Friday jacket," he said. "It keeps the wind out." He took a pair of leather driving gloves from a shelf in the wardrobe. Newish, in good condition.

"May I see your hands?" Kelsey asked.

Ian held them out, turned them over. Very well cared for, the skin smooth, the nails neatly trimmed. "You look after your hands," the Chief observed.

Ian moved his shoulders. "I have to, in my job. Can't go to the office looking like a navvy."

He took them upstairs into a large double bedroom. He opened a wardrobe and took out a hanger with a pair of dark grey trousers, spotlessly clean, undamaged, carefully pressed. He pulled open drawers in a chest and showed them a set of underwear, socks, a shirt, a polo-necked sweater, all immaculately laundered. From a pile of handkerchiefs, carefully ironed, folded in four, he picked up the top handkerchief. "That's everything," he said. "Bar the tie." He crossed again to the wardrobe and lifted a tie from a rack inside the door. "That's the one I wore yesterday to the office, but I took it off and put it in my pocket when I got into the car to go round the sites. I slipped the sweater on over my shirt. I usually take a sweater to wear on the sites, it can be pretty chilly. I can't wear it in the office, of course, it's always a collar and tie in there."

"Everything's been washed," Kelsey pointed out.

"That's right, everything except the tie. I put it all in the machine this morning, as soon as I got up. It's no bother, it's all automatic, it looks after itself while I get on with other jobs."

"Do you usually do a load of washing on a Saturday morning?"

"Yes, I do. Not just my own things, Christine's, or any household stuff that's in the basket." He raised no objection when the Chief looked carefully through all the rest of his outdoor clothing: suits, jackets, trousers, shoes.

Kelsey then asked if he could see Karen's room and Ian took them across the landing. He stood in the doorway, beside Christine, watching as the two policemen made a rapid search. Within a short time they came across the snapshot inside the back cover of the maths textbook.

The Chief studied it in silence. It showed a tall, lean, good-looking man in early middle age, standing beside a small saloon car in a deserted country lay-by. He held himself in a relaxed stance, smiling out at the camera.

The Chief held out the snapshot for the Wilmots to see. Neither of them had seen it before, neither could identify the man, or the car.

On top of a chest of drawers stood two framed photographs; Christine identified them for Kelsey. One showed Karen as a child of three or four, with her parents, a loving, happy, family group. The second had been taken a few years later. Karen stood beside her father, he had his arm round her shoulders. He smiled down at her with fond pride and she gazed out at the camera with a confident, open, trusting look.

The Chief asked if there were any recent likenesses of Karen, for use in the investigation. Christine produced a school photograph taken at the end of Karen's last term in Wychford, together with some snapshots from a trip the three of them had made to the sea one Sunday in late September.

"One other thing," Kelsey told Ian, "and I'm afraid not a very pleasant one. I have to ask you to identify the body."

Ian made no reply but gave a couple of nods. His face was calm and controlled.

But some little time later, as he came out into the mortuary corridor, white-faced, shaken and trembling, all calm had forsaken him and he was desperately struggling to retain the last vestiges of control.

5

Yellow Pages and the Wychford telephone directory between them supplied the name P.A. Clayton, a manufacturer of electronic components with a factory on the Wychford industrial estate and a private address on a modern exclusive housing development on the western edge of town. As it was a Saturday morning the Chief directed Sergeant Lambert to drive straight to the private address.

A car was drawn up in the gravelled turning-circle by the front door; a medium-sized, cream-coloured saloon, a couple of years old.

Lambert's ring at the bell was answered by Mrs. Clayton, looking tense and flustered at the sight of them. She wore an apron over expensive, dowdy clothes, she glanced uncertainly from one to the other. An enticing, savoury smell of cooking drifted out from the kitchen quarters.

The Chief disclosed his identity and her expression grew even more anxious. He asked if the P.A. Clayton listed in the phone book was in fact Paul Clayton. She told him that he was.

"You're both acquainted with a Mr. and Mrs. Roscoe who act as foster-parents for the local authority?"

She frowned. "Yes, that's right."

"I wonder if we might speak to your husband?"

"He's not here," she told them. "He's over in his office on the industrial estate. He always goes there on a Saturday morning to catch up on the paperwork." She fell silent for a moment and then burst out: "What do you want him for? What's all this about?"

Her look of anxiety deepened as Kelsey studied her without speaking. At last he said, "We're making general inquiries with reference to the death of a girl who was recently fostered by the Roscoes."

Her mouth dropped open, she took a pace back. "Karen Boland?" she asked. Her tone was agitated.

"Yes, Karen Boland. Your husband's name has been mentioned to us as someone who knew her. You will appreciate that we have to follow up every lead. We'd like to ask your husband a few questions."

"How did she die?" She clasped her hands. "How did it happen?"

"I think we'd better come inside," Kelsey said. She led the way in silence into the kitchen, turned to face them.

"How did she die?" she asked again. She appeared on the verge of tears. "When did it happen?"

"There'll be a post-mortem later today," Kelsey told her. "We'll know more about it then."

She grasped the back of a chair. "However she died it couldn't have been anything to do with Paul. He never saw her after she left the Roscoes and went back to the children's home. I'm certain of that, he gave me his sacred word he'd never see her again."

Kelsey made no reply and she burst out again with increasing agitation: "It wasn't Paul's fault that he got mixed up with her, it was all her doing. That's the kind of girl she was, sly, deceitful, absolutely no good—that's why she was taken into care in the first place. She'd been in the same kind of trouble before, only much worse, over in Okeshot. Mrs. Roscoe told me about it after the business with Paul, I never knew a word about it before. I'd never have let her set foot in the house if I'd had the faintest idea."

Her face had taken on a deep rosy tinge, her eyes looked glassy bright. "Mrs. Roscoe told me after Karen left that she was glad to see the back of her, she'd never liked the way she looked at Mr. Roscoe." She grasped the chair so hard that it swung back on its legs, almost toppling over. Without pausing in her flow she jerked the chair back into position. "Any man, any man at all, I don't care who he is, or how good a husband he is, can be led astray if a girl's determined enough." Her voice brimmed over with vehemence and animus.

Still Kelsey said nothing. "She wasn't under age," Mrs. Clayton continued in a rush, by now half sobbing. "You can't pin that on Paul. She was turned sixteen back in the spring. I know that for a fact."

She broke off suddenly, she looked disconcerted by his silence. She made a strong, visible effort to take a grip on herself. The colour remained unabated in her flaming cheeks. "Of course it's a terrible thing to have happened," she said in a voice she strove to keep level. "A young girl to die like that, all her life ahead of her."

"Like what?" Kelsey asked.

She gave him a blank stare.

"To die like what?" he repeated.

She glanced uncertainly from one to the other. "You said there's going to be a post-mortem." Thought raced behind her eyes. "That always means something's wrong. And you wouldn't be making inquiries if she'd died a natural death. Something bad must have happened to her."

She appeared to have regained some command of herself. She put a hand up to her face, smoothed her hair. She drew a long, sighing breath and glanced up at the wall clock. She seemed all at once to return to her surroundings, an awareness of the day, the hour, the next chore.

"I must go," she said in a lighter, more everyday voice, with a touch of conventional social apology. She removed her apron. "I have to pick my daughter up from her dance class, I mustn't be late. And my son's at the sports centre, I have to pick him up too."

She went into the hall and took down a camel-hair jacket from a peg. She slipped it on, tied a light blue, flowered headscarf under her chin and picked up a pair of gloves. Apart from the rosy flush still staining her cheeks she seemed perfectly in control.

Sergeant Lambert followed the Chief to the front door. "We'll get along out of your way, then," Kelsey told Mrs. Clayton. She gave a little hostessy nod and stepped aside for them to leave. She followed them out and closed the door.

She walked towards the cream-coloured car and stood beside it, watching with a detached, courteous air as the two men got into their own vehicle. She raised a hand in a gesture of farewell as Lambert drove off, then she got into her car and switched on the engine. Kelsey glanced back and saw the vehicle slip into motion after a conspicuously jerky start.

The Roscoes' house was not far away but in a neighbourhood markedly less fashionable. A modern detached house a good deal smaller than the Claytons', the paintwork fresh and gleaming, the windows sparkling in the sunlight, the small front garden smartly disciplined, the little lawn closely shorn, every last weed extirpated from regimented flower-beds still dutifully bright with carefully staked chrysanthemums, pompom dahlias.

Sergeant Lambert pressed the bell once, twice, three times, but there was no reply. No sign of life inside the house, or—when he walked round—in the back garden.

"Might be out shopping," Kelsey guessed. "We'll get along to the industrial estate, we can try again here after we've seen Clayton."

The electronics factory was on the other side of town and it was several minutes later when Lambert turned the car in through the gates. The place was silent. A handyman armed with a bucket and wash-leather was cleaning windows. He came over as the two men got out of the car.

"Mr. Clayton's in his office in the annexe," he told them. He gestured over at a small building. Kelsey walked briskly across and rapped on the door.

As soon as he laid eyes on Clayton he knew him for the man in the snapshot hidden away in Karen's bedroom. He was dressed in casual clothes. He looked poised and alert, with an energetic, highly-charged air.

Kelsey introduced himself and asked if they might go inside. Clayton took them into his office and pulled forward chairs. His manner was calm and cooperative.

"What can I do for you?" he asked when they were all seated, Clayton facing them across the desk.

The Chief came straight to the point; he asked him if he knew a girl named Karen Boland.

Clayton sat very still. The pleasant expression left his eyes, his look was cold and armoured.

"I did know her," he answered after a pause. "I haven't seen her for some time."

"When did you last see her?"

This time there was no pause. "I haven't seen her since she left the Roscoes—her foster-parents—and went back to the children's home. That was several months ago. May I ask what all this is about?"

Kelsey threw it at him without preamble. "Karen Boland is dead."

Clayton jerked back in his seat but recovered at once. "May I ask how she died?"

"We'll know more about that later today."

All at once the colour drained from Clayton's face. He put a hand up to his forehead, leaned forward and rested his elbow on the desk.

"Do you mind if I have a drink?" he asked in an unsteady voice. "It's been rather a shock." He stood up and went across to a wall cupboard, took out a bottle of whisky and a glass. He glanced back at the two men with a gesture of invitation but Kelsey gave a brief headshake.

Clayton poured himself a stiff whisky and drank half of it down in quick gulps.

"How well did you know Karen?" Kelsey asked when Clayton showed no disposition to resume his seat. Clayton took another swallow, topped up his glass and went back to the desk. The colour had begun to return to his cheeks.

"I expect you know all about the business of Karen leaving the Roscoes?" he said as he sat down again. His voice was once more firm, confident. He set down his glass with an air of challenge.

"We've heard something," Kelsey acknowledged. "We'd like to hear your side of it."

"It was nothing." Clayton made a dismissive gesture. "A silly flirtation, quite harmless. It meant nothing at all." He took another drink. "Mrs. Roscoe's a very strong churchwoman, on the puritanical side. She and my wife got together, tried to make a lot more out of it than there was, they blew it up out of all proportion—you know what women can be when they get the bit between their teeth." His tone invited understanding, the fellow-feeling of the badgered male. "They wouldn't be satisfied till they'd driven the poor kid out."

"Did you have any contact with Karen after she went to Overmead, to live with her cousin, Mrs. Wilmot?" Kelsey asked.

"None whatever. I gave my word to my wife that I wouldn't see Karen again, and I kept my word." He moved his hand. "Not that I had any wish to see her again. I was only too glad to forget the whole thing."

"Where were you yesterday afternoon and evening?"

He answered readily. He had spent the day in a large town some fifty miles to the west of Wychford. "There's been a trade exhibition on there this last week, it finished yesterday. I've got several customers over that way, so I decided to make a day of it. I called in here first, to see if there was anything important in the post." He had visited his customers during the morning, taken one of them out to lunch, spent the afternoon at the exhibition.

On the way home he had called on another customer. "I drove home from there. It was around seven-fifteen when I got in. I spent the rest of the evening in my workshop—it's in the garden, out of the way of the children. I was in the workshop till around eleven, then I went back into the house and went to bed."

"Do you often spend the evening in your workshop?"

"I spend most evenings there. I've done it all my life, ever since I was a lad." He grinned. "It was a draughty little garden shed in those days, I can afford something better now. I had it built specially. There's no phone in there, no interruptions. I'm always tinkering at something, always getting fresh ideas. I had several ideas yesterday after the exhibition, that kind of thing always sets my brain going. You can't stop it, you have to go along with it. If you don't tackle them right away they're all gone by next morning." He grinned again. "You could be kissing goodbye to a winner."

Kelsey asked what vehicle he had used yesterday.

"The one I normally use. I drove here in it this morning."

"We'd like to take a look at it."

"By all means." He took them out through a side door. The car was parked nearby on a hard standing—the car in the snapshot, Kelsey saw at once. A small, economical runabout, dark green, three or four years old. "It's all I need for calling on customers," Clayton said. "Easy on gas, nippy in traffic, no trouble to park."

The car had been freshly washed, thoroughly cleaned inside and out, polished to a high gleam. "That's been done by the handyman," Clayton said in answer to Kelsey's question. "He always does it on a Saturday morning." He offered no objection when Kelsey asked if he could speak to the man.

The Chief walked round to the other side of the factory where the handyman was busy on his windows. His manner was straightforward and cooperative. He didn't hesitate in his answers, but neither did he appear to be repeating something recently rehearsed; he showed no curiosity.

Yes, he always cleaned all the vehicles thoroughly on a Saturday morning, he always did them first thing, before he made a start on the sweeping out, the windows, the routine maintenance jobs. No, he had received no particular instructions this morning regarding Mr. Clayton's car.

Kelsey went back to where Clayton and Sergeant Lambert stood waiting and all three of them returned to Clayton's office and sat down again. Clayton now wore a passive, unresisting air, as if resigned to whatever might be going forward.

"May I see your hands?" the Chief asked him.

He held out his hands without demur, turning them over for the

Chief's inspection. Well cared for, no marks, no scratches or abrasions.

"Did you wear gloves yesterday when you drove your car?" Kelsey asked.

"Yes. I've got them here." Clayton pulled open a drawer in his desk and took them out. Tan leather, with a knitted trim; good quality, almost new. No stains, no rips or tears, the knitted trim undamaged.

"What clothes did you wear yesterday afternoon?" Kelsey asked.

"A business suit. And a car coat."

"We'd like to take a look at them."

"Yes, certainly. They're at home, of course." He glanced at his watch. "It's time I was getting off there anyway."

They followed his car back to the house. It was empty and silent. "I expect my wife's picking up the children," Clayton said as he closed the front door behind them. The Chief didn't inform him that they had already called at the house and spoken to his wife.

Clayton took them upstairs to a dressing-room and showed them a car coat of green-grey tweed, a dark grey business suit, a pair of black leather Oxford shoes. Kelsey examined them all. Everything of good quality, newish, clean and undamaged.

"And the other garments you wore yesterday?" he asked. "Shirt, underwear, socks."

Clayton gave him a startled glance. "They may still be in the laundry basket where I put them to be washed," he said after a moment. "The basket's down in the utility room." He turned to the door but Kelsey raised a hand.

"While we're up here we'll take a look at the rest of your clothes." Clayton stood watching in expressionless silence as the two men went through the contents of the wardrobe, the chest, cupboards.

When they had finished he took them downstairs again, into a very well-equipped utility room. But the laundry basket was empty. "I expect my wife did the washing this morning." Clayton waved a hand. "She's a fussy housekeeper."

"What time did you leave the house this morning to go to the office?" Kelsey asked him.

"Eight o'clock, near enough."

"What time did you arrive?"

"Ten past, quarter past, I suppose. I didn't look at my watch."

"Did anyone see you arrive?"

"Not that I know of. The handyman doesn't come till eight-thirty."

Kelsey gazed at him. Easy enough this morning to drive off a few miles in any direction, with Friday's clothes bundled into a plastic rubbish bag in the boot of his car, dump the bag on a refuse tip or in a waste skip, no one any the wiser.

6

There was the sound of a car outside. "That'll be Joan now, with the children," Clayton said.

Kelsey went to the window and looked out. Mrs. Clayton was sitting in the car, talking over her shoulder to the two children in the back seat. Telling them to go off and play in the garden till they were called, no doubt, prompted by the sight of the police car drawn up behind her husband's. The children got out of the car and ran off round the side of the house. Mrs. Clayton stepped slowly out on to the gravel and walked without haste towards the front door.

When she came in a minute or two later Clayton made to go out to speak to her but a glance from Kelsey stopped him in his tracks.

The Chief went into the front hall. Sergeant Lambert and Clayton followed him. Mrs. Clayton was taking off her headscarf, hanging up her jacket. She looked at the three of them without speaking. Her manner was nervous but controlled.

Clayton started to introduce her but she interrupted him. "We've already met." Clayton's expression altered as he took in the fact that they had already been to the house, had already spoken to his wife. He glanced from one face to the other, wary and alert.

"I'd like a word with your wife alone," Kelsey told him. Sergeant

Lambert turned back to the utility room, gesturing Clayton inside
ahead of him. Clayton went without protest and Lambert closed the
door behind them.

Kelsey took Mrs. Clayton along to the kitchen where they both sat
down. The delicious smell of cooking sharply reminded the Chief
that it was a long time since he had eaten. Outside he could hear the
children laughing, calling to each other.

He didn't mince matters, he asked Mrs. Clayton for an account of
her husband's movements the previous evening. She appeared
tense and subdued but answered in a straightforward manner.

She hadn't gone to collect the children from school as usual at the
end of the afternoon, she explained, as there was to be a rehearsal
after lessons for the Christmas play and the children were to be
collected at eight o'clock. She had therefore arranged to spend the
afternoon driving round to collect jumble contributions for a sale to
be held in aid of the Parent-Teacher Association. She had a list of
people who had phoned to say they had jumble to give. She had
taken the stuff along to the hall where it was to be stored; several
mothers were at work there, examining and sorting.

She had got back home at around seven. Paul came in not very
long afterwards, sometime between seven-fifteen and seven-thirty,
at a guess. She couldn't be more precise, she hadn't looked at the
clock. She had been relaxing in front of the television with a cup of
tea, tired after her exertions.

"Is that your husband's usual time for coming home on a Friday?"
Kelsey asked.

Her fingers plucked at her skirt. "He doesn't have any usual time.
It varies a lot. He's never home before six-thirty but often it's a good
deal later, sometimes nine or ten." She was used to it, it had been
like that ever since they were married.

Kelsey asked if Paul had appeared in any way agitated, if his
clothes were wet or dirty.

"I didn't look at him," she answered in a flat tone. "I heard the
front door, I knew it was Paul. I was watching television. I was pretty
tired, half dozing. Paul just stuck his head round the door and said
he'd be going along to the workshop after he'd had a shower. He'd
had something to eat. He sounded just as usual. I said OK. I didn't
even glance round. He closed the door and went upstairs."

"Did you see him during the rest of the evening?"

"I went off at a quarter to eight to pick the children up from school. When we got back I saw the light on in his workshop." She and the children knew better than to disturb him in there. She went to bed around ten-thirty. She didn't know what time Paul had gone to bed. They had separate rooms, had had them since they'd moved to this larger house. It saved him disturbing her when he worked late or got up early as he often did when an idea struck him and he would go down to the workshop for an hour or two before breakfast.

Kelsey asked what her husband had worn the previous day. She pondered before replying. He had gone out in the morning in a business suit, as usual. She couldn't say which one—he had several and wore them in turn, he never wore the same suit two days running. He always wore a white shirt with a business suit, plain or fine-striped, and there had been a white shirt in the laundry basket this morning, so she assumed that was the one he had worn. She had done the laundry that morning, she never let it accumulate. She couldn't say if he had worn a coat or jacket over his suit. He had said goodbye to her in the kitchen, she hadn't seen him leave. He might have picked up a coat or jacket from the hall on his way out.

She didn't accompany the Chief when he went back to the utility room. She remained where she was, sitting back now, slumped in her chair. She looked pale and tired; she seemed sunk into herself. Kelsey spoke to her as he went from the room but she didn't answer, didn't look at him.

In the utility room Sergeant Lambert had taken up his post by the door. Clayton had spent the interval sitting on a tall, padded stool, with his arms folded across his chest and his head lowered; he had made no effort to engage the sergeant in conversation. He looked up as the Chief came in but he didn't get to his feet.

"We'll need to have the name and address of the customer you called on your way home from the exhibition," Kelsey told him briskly. Clayton supplied the details.

"And the times, as exact as possible, when you arrived and left this customer."

"I arrived there at ten minutes to six," Clayton answered without hesitation. "I know that because I'd checked the time, I'd hesitated about calling in. But the customer works on his own account, he often stays late. As I drove up I saw the light on in his office, so I went in. His secretary was still there. She made us some tea and I stayed talking with the customer for half an hour or more." They had chatted about business, trade in general, the exhibition.

He had looked at his watch when he left. He had apologized, said he hadn't intended staying more than a few minutes. It was just turned six-thirty. The secretary was still there, in the outer office, he had spoken to her as he left. He had driven straight home, a distance of some twelve miles.

"Joan was watching TV when I got in," he added. "I put my head round the door and told her I was home."

A few minutes later Sergeant Lambert turned the car in for the second time through the Roscoes' gates; this time they were in luck.

Mr. Roscoe came to the door. An ordinary-looking man in his early fifties, with a respectable, petit-bourgeois air, a high, balding forehead, a manner tinged with habitual apology, hesitant, mildly affable. His face was deeply tanned, his hair greying; he wore heavy-rimmed spectacles.

The Chief introduced himself and asked if Mrs. Roscoe was in.

"Yes, she is." An expression of disquiet flitted across Roscoe's face. "But she's just going to dish up lunch. It's not very convenient at the moment."

Kelsey apologized for calling at a mealtime. "But it is important, we wouldn't have intruded otherwise." He remained obstinately on the doorstep. "We would very much appreciate the chance of a word with both you and your wife."

"Very well." Roscoe made a gesture of resigned acceptance and stepped aside for them to enter.

Mrs. Roscoe was in the kitchen; the room was warm and steamy with simmering pans. A scrawny little woman a few years younger than her husband, with an air of restless energy, a quick, darting, penetrating look from bright brown eyes. Very clean and well scrubbed, not a vestige of make-up, skin pinkly shining, seamed with lines, sandy hair sprinkled with grey, cut straight and short with a fringe. She wore a crisp nylon overall.

The table was set for lunch with three places. Properly and care-fully laid, spotless tablecloth, everything very neat, precisely squared up. A small boy, about five years old, sat docilely at the table with his hands folded in his lap. A pale, slight child, with a lost air. He slid them a blank little look as they came into the room.

Mrs. Roscoe was taking a covered bowl of salad from the fridge. Her glance was far from welcoming as her husband introduced the visitors.

"The Social Services sent you, I suppose," she said with irritation as she plonked the bowl down on the table. "What is it this time? Another emergency? Wanting me to take in some child at a moment's notice? Couldn't it have waited till after lunch?"

The Chief rehashed his apology. "We're not from the local station," he explained. "We're over here from Cannonbridge, inquiring into a very serious case. We believe you may be able to help us." He gave a nod over in the direction of the child. "We'd like to talk to you and your husband alone."

She had begun to simmer down, her interest was caught. "Oh well," she said, a shade less belligerently. "Can't be helped, I suppose. I dare say you don't go round interrupting mealtimes just for the fun of it." She suddenly assumed a seductive maternal smile, addressing the child with a honeyed voice. "Would you like to be a good boy and go up to your room for a little while to look at your picture-book while we talk to these gentlemen? It won't be for long." The child gave a jerky little nod, slipped from his chair and vanished from the room. Mrs. Roscoe crossed to the stove and adjusted the heat under the pans, turned down the oven.

"That little boy came to us a few days ago," Roscoe explained. "His mother had to go into hospital for an emergency operation."

"Gall bladder," Mrs. Roscoe interjected.

"The father's a salesman," Roscoe went on. "He's away travelling during the week, so he can't look after the boy."

The honeyed overlay had disappeared from Mrs. Roscoe's face and voice. "We only do short-term and emergency fostering now," she declared with a resolute movement of her head. "And only young children, the younger the better, far less worry than the older ones. We'd never take teenagers again—and we certainly would never take a teenage girl again."

Roscoe asked them to sit down and then suddenly bethought himself and asked if they would like something to eat or drink. Kelsey managed a polite refusal although by this time he felt both parched with thirst and hollow with hunger. He had learned very early in his career that an action as simple as accepting a cup of tea could alter the whole character of an exchange, placing the parties on a totally different footing, by no means always the most suitable or productive.

"I understand that earlier this year you were fostering a girl by the name of Karen Boland?" he said.

"That's right," Roscoe agreed. "She came to us early in the New Year."

A deep frown appeared between Mrs. Roscoe's brows.

"What's that girl been up to now? No good, I'll be bound." She made a sudden sharp gesture. "Not that it's anything to do with us any more, whatever she's been up to. We've had nothing to do with her since the day she left here back in the summer. Nor wanted to. Very pleased indeed to see the back of her. Let her own relatives have the pleasure of looking after her. Proper little slyboots. To look at her you wouldn't think butter would melt in her mouth."

Roscoe gave the two men a deprecating glance. "Is Karen in some kind of trouble?" he asked on a note of concern.

"I'm afraid we bring bad news," Kelsey said gently. "Very bad news. I'm very sorry to have to tell you that Karen is dead."

Mrs. Roscoe's eyes jerked wide open, she put a hand up to her mouth. There was a moment's shocked silence, then Roscoe asked, "How did it happen?"

"We can't go into details now," Kelsey told him. "We won't know it all till after the post-mortem. But we can tell you she died as a result of a brutal attack. Her body was found in a stretch of woodland near where she was living."

"A brutal attack?" Roscoe echoed. "Do you mean she was murdered?"

"Yes, I'm afraid I do."

"Murdered," he repeated on an incredulous, assessing note, as if testing the sound of the word.

Mrs. Roscoe seemed to have made a swift recovery. "I'm very sorry to hear it," she said with energy. "A terrible thing to happen to a young girl." She pursed her lips. "But I can't honestly say I'm all that surprised."

The Chief gave her a questioning look.

"That sort of girl," she declared with conviction. "Leading people on, teasing them. Asking for it, if you want my opinion. When the Social Services first told me about her past history I felt sorry for her, I thought she was some kind of victim. I did my level best for her, I can say that with my hand on my heart. And I never told a living soul about her past—not until the business with Mr. Clayton. I had to tell his wife then, it was only fair. It would have saved us all a lot of trouble if I'd told her about it before." There was another brief silence.

"We've heard something of the circumstances in which Karen left here." Kelsey glanced from one to the other. "We'd be interested to hear your account of it."

"We know Mrs. Clayton from the church," Roscoe told him. "And from the school. A very nice lady, very respectable. And Mr. Clayton's a very decent, hard-working man, a good family man."

"He's devoted to his wife," Mrs. Roscoe put in on a note of challenge. "Absolutely devoted. She's a wonderful wife and mother, she lives for her family. Karen led him on, there's no doubt about it, he'd never in a million years have behaved so foolishly otherwise."

"What actually happened?" Kelsey asked.

"What must have been happening," she went on with relish, "was that he was getting home earlier than he was letting on, and he and Miss Karen were having a high old time together while his poor wife was at her classes or meetings." She gave a brisk nod of her head. "But one evening the boy—the Claytons' son—came downstairs for something and saw them." She made a face. "I don't need to spell it out. He didn't speak to them, he just went back upstairs, they didn't know he'd seen them, that he'd been downstairs at all. A day or two later he told his mother what he'd seen.

"She didn't say anything to her husband, she didn't know what to do, what to make of it. She was very upset, of course. She came along to see me about it, to ask my opinion. Did I think the boy might have imagined it? Could he have had some sort of dream or nightmare and come downstairs half asleep? Got it mixed up in his mind with the dream? She couldn't credit her husband could get up to anything like that."

She sat back in her chair with the air of a hanging judge. "I advised her to say nothing, carry on as usual, but the next time

Karen went there, to make a point of getting home early, let herself in very quietly, see for herself if anything was going on."

"I knew nothing of all this," Roscoe interjected with distaste. "I wouldn't have gone along with that, not with laying traps." He looked at Kelsey with his habitual air of apology. "A young girl like that, feeling herself alone in the world, wanting affection. Easy to see how it could have happened, how it could have got out of hand without anyone really intending anything wrong."

His wife uttered a sound between a snort and an exclamation. Roscoe didn't venture a glance at her but plunged resolutely on. "I liked Karen well enough. She was never any trouble to us before. She was always very quiet, nice manners, nicely spoken, always ready to give a hand without sulking or complaining. She was well behaved at school, worked hard at her lessons." He paused. "Thought I must admit, after all the fuss"—he risked a fleeting look in the direction of his wife—"that I was relieved when she left. I was glad later on when I heard from the Social Services that she'd gone to relatives, that she'd chosen to go there herself. I felt that was what she needed, to be part of a family again."

"She could have been part of a family here," Mrs. Roscoe said righteously, "if she'd chosen to behave herself. I felt as if she'd stabbed me in the back, shamed me before the whole neighbourhood. I couldn't look anyone in the face as long a she was still in the house."

"No one would have known anything about it," Roscoe said with sudden boldness, "if you and Mrs. Clayton had had the sense to keep your mouths shut."

Mrs. Roscoe was not to be put down. "You would stick up for her, of course. You men are all alike. A pretty face, that's all a man sees. It takes a woman to see through a girl like that. That sort of girl's got to be exposed. I suppose you'd have done nothing, let her get away with it."

"I'd have talked to Karen about it, talked quietly, not ranting and raving. I'd have found out if there was anything in the tale, then, if necessary, I'd have had a word with Clayton, stopped Karen going round there, kept a closer eye on her, tried to help her to make friends of her own age. No bones broken, no need for the Social Services to be dragged into it."

There was another brief silence, then Kelsey asked Mrs. Roscoe if Mrs. Clayton had taken her advice.

"She certainly did," she answered with satisfaction. "She caught them, fair and square. There could be no wriggling out of it. Of course after that there was no question of Karen staying on here. We made that very clear at once, both to her and to the Social Services."

"You made it very clear," Roscoe interposed. "I was for giving her another chance."

His wife ignored the interruption. "Everything's fine again now between the Claytons," she assured Kelsey. "He was thoroughly ashamed of himself. I'll take my oath he won't do anything like that again. He can't do enough for his wife now."

Kelsey asked if the Roscoes had ever met Karen's stepmother, Mrs. Lorimer, but they shook their heads. There had never been any attempt on the part of either of the Lorimers to contact Karen during her stay with the Roscoes.

Kelsey looked at Roscoe. "I hope you won't take this amiss," he said. "It's part of normal routine in these cases. Would you mind letting me see your hands?"

Mrs. Roscoe drew a sharp, hissing breath but Roscoe complied at once. There were a few marks and scratches, the kind any gardener or do-it-yourself householder might come by, none of them fresh-looking.

"Again, I have to ask you this," Kelsey said. "I have to ask every male in any way connected with Karen, I'm sure you understand. Could you tell us where you were yesterday evening, say, between five and seven-thirty?"

Mrs. Roscoe's lips came together in a grim line. Her eyes glinted, her face glowed with protest but her husband answered before she could say anything. "I understand perfectly, I have no objection at all. I was here all afternoon and evening yesterday. I don't go out to work any more." He had been employed as a clerk by the local gas board, had suffered a slight stroke a couple of years ago. He had made a good recovery but his illness had come at a time when the board was cutting down on staff. He had been offered early retirement and had been glad to accept. "I manage very well, all things considered," he told the Chief. "Provided I always take it easy, never rush."

He jerked his head towards the stairs. "The boy you saw just now, his father can vouch for me being here most of the time you mention. He called here at about a quarter to five yesterday evening, being Friday, and finished for the week. He had tea with us, played with the lad, put him to bed, he was here about two hours altogether. I was here all the time. He left around seven, to go home and have a wash, get along to visit his wife at seven-thirty. She's in the local hospital, here in Wychford. I'll give you his name and address, he doesn't live very far." He gave Kelsey directions. "You might catch him at home now. I know he intends going along to the hospital again this afternoon—visiting time's two-thirty."

And they did catch the boy's father at home, eating a scratch meal. He confirmed without hesitation Roscoe's account of the previous evening.

7

The inspector over in Okeshot who had been in charge of the case against Lorimer was no longer with the force but a woman constable who had worked on the case—an experienced officer who had worked on several cases of a similar nature—was waiting for Chief Inspector Kelsey when Sergeant Lambert drove him over to Okeshot after a snatched meal of coffee and sandwiches in a roadside café.

The constable was a shrewd-looking woman in her forties who managed to retain an air of good-natured tolerance towards life in general. She had worked on the Lorimer case from the beginning and was able to recall clearly the people involved.

Victor Lorimer was an only child, brought up by his mother in a village near Okeshot. His conception had brought about the forced marriage of his parents and shortly after his birth his father had deserted his wife and child, vanishing without trace, never again supplying a single penny towards the maintenance of either of them, leaving his wife to struggle on as best she might on domestic work, dressmaking, fruit-picking, anything that might turn an honest shilling. It had been a desperately hard battle but she was determined that the boy should make something of himself, that she would have reason to be proud of him, that some good would result from that early, foolish mistake.

Victor grew up to be a quiet, well-behaved, studious boy, working hard at school; he and his mother were very close to each other. In due course he left school and got a job in the Okeshot public library. His mother was delighted; it was exactly the kind of secure, respectable, white-collar job she had dreamed of for him. He went into lodgings in Okeshot, later into little flats. Every month he set aside part of his salary for his mother, he often went home to see her. He never kept company with a girl, he appeared to have no interest in them. He was a regular attender at church, he had been brought up on strict religious principles.

And then, when he was almost forty, he had got married. He had met Enid Boland at church, she was two or three years older than Lorimer. After the marriage he moved into the house where Enid was living with her stepdaughter—the house to which James Boland had taken his first wife as a bride, the house where Karen had been born. It was some six months after Lorimer's marriage to Enid that the charges against him were laid.

Kelsey asked how the case had arisen.

"It seems that Karen's schoolwork had very clearly fallen off," the constable told him. Her form teacher noticed that she looked unwell, seemed worried and unhappy. She asked Karen once or twice if anything was amiss, if she could be of any help, but got little response beyond an assurance that there was nothing the matter. "Then one afternoon at the end of lessons the form teacher came across Karen in the cloakroom, in tears." This time she wouldn't be fobbed off, she pressed the girl, and it all came out.

Karen was at once removed from home and taken into care while inquiries went forward. She was fourteen years old. A medical examination showed that she was pregnant; the pregnancy was terminated.

According to Karen she had been uncomfortable at Lorimer's attitude towards her since well before the marriage. She had feared to say anything to her stepmother, afraid that Enid would accuse her of jealousy, irrational animosity towards a new man about to be brought into the household in the place of her much-loved dead father. She had never felt close to Enid, her stepmother had never displayed warmth towards her. Since her father's death she had always felt that Enid regarded her as a burden, a responsibility, even a nuisance, although Enid had never said as much and certainly always punctiliously carried out all her duties towards her step-daughter.

After the marriage it appeared that Lorimer's attentions towards Karen became more marked. He applied various emotional and psychological pressures, told her that if she complained Enid would certainly not believe her, would be only too glad to have an excuse to be rid of her, she would speedily be sent off elsewhere. This was a very real fear to Karen. Unsatisfactory as she felt her home and her relationship with her stepmother to be, they were none the less all she had to cling to. She couldn't bear the thought of being flung out somewhere among strangers.

Kelsey asked how Lorimer had reacted to Karen's accusations.

"At first he denied them totally and strongly," the constable said. But his manner had been far from convincing. "His mother called in at the station," she added. "To speak up on behalf of his character, tell us what an upright man he was, how carefully she had brought him up, what a good boy he had been, what a devoted son, he couldn't possibly be guilty of such a terrible offence. She was in tears most of the time she was here. She was certain the whole thing was a piece of mischievous invention on Karen's part, that the truth would very soon come out and Victor would be totally cleared."

"How did Enid take all this?"

"She never altered her opinion from first to last. She refused even to consider that Lorimer might be guilty. Understandable enough. She hadn't long been married, she was very much in love." Enid had appeared to close her mind resolutely to the possibility of her hus-band's guilt, to be psychologically unable to countenance the possi-bility that the accusations might be true. Even the undeniable fact of Karen's pregnancy couldn't shake her, though she could offer no suggestion as to how the pregnancy could have come about if Lorimer hadn't been involved. She could tell them of no other man who might possibly have been responsible, she knew of no boyfriend. She was forced to admit that Karen had always been a quiet, well-behaved girl who had never given any trouble, never caused any concern. Enid had never detected her in any falsehoods, had never caught her out in devious or wayward behaviour.

The constable gave a wry smile. "Enid more or less backed herself into a corner. She ended up trying to take two contradictory positions. One: Victor was totally innocent and nothing whatever had taken place between Karen and Lorimer. Two: If Lorimer was guilty it was entirely because Karen had led him on. The seduction was wholly on her side, none of it could be set down to him." She waved a hand. "That's not unusual on the part of the wife. In these complicated family situations you tend to get complicated responses."

"You told us earlier," Kelsey said, "that Lorimer at first denied everything. Did he change his mind later?"

"Yes, he did. Word of his trouble got round the town and it became known that he was strenuously denying the charges. It wasn't long before two women called into the station, two separate women, totally unconnected. They both said that Lorimer had at some time in the past interfered with children, though neither had ever reported the matter."

The first caller was an elderly woman. She had had sole charge of her granddaughter after the death of the girl's parents. At the time of the alleged offences, some eight years previously, the girl had been thirteen years old. She had reading difficulties but was anxious to do well at school. In the course of her visits to the public library she had spoken to Lorimer, had asked his advice about which books to choose.

Lorimer had been kind and helpful, had offered to give her a little unpaid coaching. She jumped at the offer and went along to his flat several times, unknown to the grandmother who believed she was at the house of a classmate.

One day the grandmother chanced to meet the classmate in the street and the lies were revealed. The grandmother had to press the girl hard to discover where she had actually been going. The girl was very reluctant to say anything against Lorimer, she was clearly attached to him. But in the end she did admit to some intimacies, though she maintained that nothing had been done against her will.

The grandmother didn't go to the police; she was afraid that if she did so the girl might be taken into care. Instead she went to see Lorimer.

He strongly denied any impropriety, resolutely maintained that the girl had invented the whole story, there was not one shred of truth in it. The grandmother told him that if he ever had anything to do with the girl again she would at once inform both the police and the library authorities. There had been no further trouble. The girl was now grown up, married, settled down, a good, sensible young woman, living with her husband in the next county. As there would no longer be any question of involving the girl the grandmother had decided to come forward, in case, as she put it, Lorimer got off. It had often worried her that he might still be getting up to the same tricks, perhaps with more serious consequences. She couldn't bear the thought that he might able to lie his way out of court, that an innocent young girl might be pilloried as a liar, have her whole life ruined, with Lorimer going unpunished.

The second woman to call in was much younger, in her late thirties. The events she spoke of had taken place some five years earlier, not long after she had been widowed. She was in sore financial straits, having been left with a four-year-old daughter to bring up on a slender income in a run-down Victorian house bought on mortgage. Her late husband, a do-it-yourself enthusiast, had intended to restore the house himself but had died when the work was barely started. She decided to let off the basement as a flat, though she couldn't charge much of a rent, because of the state of repair and the fact that the flat wasn't self-contained.

Lorimer had called in answer to her advertisement. She was delighted to find such a quiet, well-mannered, eminently respectable tenant, with a secure income.

She had been unable to look for work because of the child and she mentioned this casually to Lorimer. Not long after he was installed in the house he told her that if she could find an evening job he would be happy to keep an ear open for the child. It would be no trouble to him; he would in any case usually be in his flat, reading or watching TV.

She had leapt at the chance. There was never any shortage of evening work in the town, in hotels, restaurants, residential care homes, factories on the industrial estate.

The arrangement appeared to work very well. Some months went by. She was beginning to feel solid ground under her feet. And then something in her daughter's prattle, in her play with her dolls, began to make her uneasy, and, very shortly, downright suspicious.

She had no proof, she didn't see how she could come by any proof. She felt unable to confront Lorimer—and she had liked him, felt grateful to him; he had, whatever his motives, very definitely helped her. It never occurred to her to go to the police. What could she tell them? How could she level such a charge without an atom of substantiation against a respectable public servant? She felt she had enough on her plate already; she had no stomach for any further hassle.

She simply told Lorimer he must leave the flat, must at once find somewhere else. She would be quitting her evening job immediately, wouldn't be going out to work again until she had made other, more suitable arrangements. She had felt deeply awkward and un-certain, she had scarcely been able to look him in the face—but she couldn't see what else she could do.

Lorimer had acquiesced without demur, had asked no questions, didn't demand to know the reasons, expressed no upset. He left the house a few days later.

The episode had always troubled her. If Lorimer was innocent, what had he made of the incident, of her attitude, after all his kindness? If he was guilty, then ought she not to have taken some more definite steps in the matter, made sure he wouldn't repeat the offence? When the rumours of an impending trial reached her ears she felt impelled to call in at the police station and unload it all, drawing no conclusions, simply relating the whole thing to the police, let them make of it what they would. At least she could at last get if off her conscience.

When Lorimer learned of the appearance of these two women, it wasn't long before he changed his tune and decided to plead guilty. "But it made no difference at all to his wife's attitude," the constable told Kelsey. The man whom Enid loved so dearly, of whom she thought so highly, could never have committed such acts, therefore

he must be innocent, therefore, by the same logic, the two women—
as well as Karen—must be lying; it was all perfectly straightforward,
blindingly clear. These so-called events hadn't been reported to the
police at the time. How could they be taken seriously now? They
were obviously nothing more than totally unsubstantiated tales,
prompted by gossip and rumour, by a desire for attention.

What did they actually amount to? Nothing more than adolescent
inventions and fantasies on the part of the granddaughter, resentment and spite on the part of the widow when her unwelcome
advances had been rebuffed by Lorimer. Enid maintained that this
was the version of past events given to her by Victor, that he swore
they were true.

He told her he had decided to plead guilty solely because of
pressure from the police, from his solicitor, pressures he felt unable
to resist any longer. "It's purely for technical reasons that he's
changed his plea," she kept repeating, able in some fashion to
protect and reassure herself with this vague, all-embracing expression, able also, like most people, to believe what she wanted or
needed to believe, however improbable. From the day Karen was
taken into care Enid obstinately refused to see or speak to her.

Kelsey asked how Karen had taken it when she learned that her
stepmother intended taking Lorimer back after his spell in gaol,
with the consequence that she herself would never be able to go
back home but must remain in care.

"By the time she was told of it officially," the constable said, "it
didn't come as such a shock. She knew the stand Enid had been
taking, she had begun to realize the way things were likely to go. I'm
sure it never occurred to her to start with that such a thing could
happen." Karen had had a youngster's black-and-white view of the
situation, of the probable course of justice: Lorimer had done
wrong, therefore he would be punished, he would be the one to be
sent away.

"In the event," the constable added with a sad little shake of her
head, "what Lorimer had threatened her with did come to pass: she
was taken into care, she did lose her home and what was left of her
immediate family."

Kelsey asked if Lorimer was still in gaol. He might very well be out

by now, the constable thought. And a phone call to the prison did
indeed reveal that Lorimer had been discharged four weeks earlier.
It appeared that Enid had visited him regularly, had been waiting
for him outside the gates. It seemed that she was no longer living in
Okeshot. Lorimer's address on release had been given as Furzebank
Cottage, in a hamlet twelve miles to the north-west of Cannonbridge.

8

The afternoon was advanced by the time they approached the hamlet where the Lorimers were now living. The sunlight was waning.
Across the fields a thin mist rose where a line of willows marked the
course of the river.

They were now in deep country. Sheep grazed in the pastures. A
green woodpecker flew across in front of their car. As they rounded
a bend a young dog-fox started out of the grassy bank a little way
ahead, his tawny coat sleekly gleaming. He glanced at the approaching car, turned and trotted back again, without haste.

There was little sign of prosperity or development. The whole
area had a gloomy, settled look, as if it had been forgotten or
bypassed, but hadn't succeeded thereby in achieving contented se-
renity, only this insidious, seeping melancholy. Trees and hedges
were thickly draped with trailing, mist-grey growths of old man's
beard. Such isolated properties as they came across looked run-
down and neglected. They encountered no traffic, saw not a single
soul.

A dilapidated wooden board, amateurishly lettered at some distant time, directed them along a winding lane to Furzebank Cottage.
The dwelling stood on rising ground behind a thick screen of red-
berried thorn-bushes. There was no other dwelling in sight. In the

field opposite, four donkeys eyed the car; crows pecked the ground between.

A broken wooden gate, permanently propped open by a large mossy stone, gave entrance to a decaying stretch of hardstanding, where they left the car. The path leading up to the house—scarcely to be dignified with the name of a drive, with its rutted, pot-holed surface overgrown with weeds—ran between crumbling banks of earth. Withered remnants of former days when someone had hoed and planted, pruned and watered, still survived among the encroaching bracken and thistles: shrivelled, blackened sprays of buddleia, desiccated heads of hydrangea faded to a harsh, mottled red, tattered plumes of pampas grass.

The house was of no great size, foursquare, sturdily built, faced with flaking, dun-coloured stucco, the paintwork blistered and peeling. The front door and all the front windows were closed but as he got out of the car Sergeant Lambert could hear the crackle of a bonfire, the sound of activity some little distance away, round the back. A smell of woodsmoke drifted to his nostrils.

They didn't bother knocking at the front door but went straight round in the direction of the sounds. They found themselves in what had clearly once been a cultivated garden, an acre or more in extent, run wild now for many a year, invaded by the prickly, yellow-flowered gorse from which the cottage took its name. The ground was enclosed by tall, straggling, neglected hedges.

Several yards away a man stood with his back to them, a tall, lean man in old jeans and pullover, energetically forking lopped branches on to a bonfire. Further on, a woman slashed at the strong, stubborn weeds with a billhook. She stood sideways on to them. As she straightened up after a sweeping stroke she suddenly caught sight of the two men. She froze for an instant, then said something to the man; Kelsey couldn't catch her words.

The man didn't at once stop what he was doing. He took up another forkful of wood and flung it on the flames, then he turned deliberately and stood leaning on his fork, regarding them in silence with an alert, wary air.

"Mr. Lorimer?" Kelsey asked as he came up. "Victor Lorimer?"

The man nodded. An unremarkable face, by no means ill-favoured. Light brown hair, light grey eyes.

The woman walked across to them. "Mrs. Lorimer?" Kelsey asked. "Enid Lorimer?"

She nodded. A slim, lithe woman, a little above average height. A quiet manner, suggesting discipline and restraint. A neat, orderly look, even in old gardening clothes. An everyday face that would never attract a second glance in the street. No make-up, no artifice. By far her best feature was her thick, lustrous, nut-brown hair, freshly washed, taken simply up in a knot.

Kelsey told them who he was. Before he had time to say more Lorimer suddenly exploded into speech.

"Can't you leave me alone? I've served my time. You've no reason to come poking your noses in here, checking up on me. Leave me alone to get on with my life."

His wife slid him a warning, quelling glance and he reluctantly fell silent. He turned and thrust savagely at the pile of branches, swept another forkload up on to the leaping scarlet flames.

"Don't put any more wood on," Kelsey said brusquely. "Let it go out."

They both stared at him in surprise. Lorimer looked as if he would make an angry rejoinder but Enid laid a hand on his arm. He said nothing but turned from the fire. He took out a packet of cigarettes, lit one and began to smoke, inhaling deeply.

The Chief didn't give any reason for his presence. "We'd like to take a look round," he told them. They digested this in silence, not looking at each other. A few moments later when there was still no response, Kelsey set off with Lambert beside him.

After a brief hesitation the Lorimers fell in behind them, following closely as the two men walked across to the hedge, right round the perimeter, then methodically set about quartering the entire area, searching, examining, peering into bushes, shrubs, parting brambles, briars, saplings, long grass, weeds.

They looked through a mouldering fowl-house, a rotting tool-shed. A three-sided timber structure in an advanced state of disrepair served as a run-in for an estate car. The vehicle was a good ten years old, very well cared for, a deep slate blue.

"This your car?" the Chief asked Lorimer.

"It's mine," Enid put in. "It belonged to my first husband."

Kelsey scrutinized the vehicle, inside and out. It was in first-class condition for its age, immaculately clean and shining. "You certainly look after it," he said to Enid.

She inclined her head. "I don't like to see a dirty car."

"How do you clean the inside?"

"I run it up to the back of the house. I use the tools from the vacuum cleaner, there's a socket just inside the back door. I did it this morning, while the weather was fine."

"You had the car out yesterday?"

She nodded. "We went over to the Fairdeal supermarket." This was a large supermarket opened a couple of months back with a good deal of trumpeting in the local press. It stood in an out-of-town setting some ten miles away to the north. It particularly prided itself on its keen pricing policy.

"What time was that?" Kelsey asked casually.

"We left here just after lunch," Enid told him. "We had some tea in the restaurant at Fairdeal after we'd finished our shopping. We got back here about half past five."

"Did you go out again?"

She shook her head.

"What did you do after you got home?"

"We put the shopping away, watched the news on television at a quarter to six, then we switched over to see the Western. Victor's fond of Westerns, he particularly wanted to be back in time for the one yesterday evening, it was an old Randolph Scott."

"And after the Western?"

"The film finished at seven-thirty. We had supper—some cold cuts we'd bought at Fairdeal. We watched some more TV, then we went to bed. That would be around ten-thirty."

At the Chief's insistence she recalled precisely which programmes they had watched after supper. Lorimer stood listening to all this without comment. He appeared to have simmered down. During his tramp round the garden on the heels of the two policemen he had spoken not a word. He appeared content now to let his wife do whatever talking was necessary. He smoked all the time, lighting each fresh cigarette from the stub of the last.

Kelsey asked him to hold out his hands. He expected Lorimer to explode into another protest but he extended his hands without any change of expression, turning them over unasked. Enid also put out her hands for the Chief's inspection, although he had clearly not included her in his request.

Neither of them had been wearing gloves during their attack on the garden. Enid's hands were basically well cared for but stained and scratched now from her gardening efforts, with little tricklets of dried blood here and there. Lorimer's hands were less carefully looked after, though far from neglected. There were a number of cuts and abrasions, scars and marks, recent and less recent, some of long standing. His fingers were lightly stained with nicotine.

"You don't bother with gardening gloves?" Kelsey asked him.

"No." Just the bare monosyllable.

"What about driving? Do you wear driving gloves then?"

"No."

"Do you possess any driving gloves?"

"No."

"We'll take a look inside the house now," Kelsey announced. Neither made any protest. Enid led the way across to the back door. Inside the dwelling the Chief went upstairs and down. Not a detailed and thorough search but more than a superficial survey. Here and there he opened a drawer or cupboard, knelt to look under a bed or a piece of furniture. Neither Lorimer nor his wife objected or asked the reason for all this, what it was they were looking for. And Kelsey volunteered no explanation.

The house appeared generally in a fair state of repair but in a very dingy condition as far as decoration was concerned. There was no cellar, no attic. The downstairs rooms had been furnished comfortably enough but wore a makeshift air as if whoever had attended to the furnishing had given it little thought, didn't intend looking on the cottage as more than a temporary halting-place.

There were three bedrooms, the largest provided with a double bed and other items. The second bedroom clearly served as a dressing room for Lorimer. The third was out of everyday use, being crammed with furniture, pictures, rolled-up carpets, rugs, blankets, curtains, a miscellany of household goods, methodically stacked. In this room Kelsey did no more than stand just inside the threshold, raking the contents with his eye.

He went downstairs again, into the living-room. "Have either of you been away from the house today?" he asked.

They both shook their heads. "We've been out in the garden all day," Enid told him. "Victor's been working hard on the garden ever since—since he came here."

Kelsey asked to see what they had bought the previous day in the supermarket. They showed him groceries in the larder, food in the fridge, tins and packets bearing Fairdeal own-brand labels, bread, fruit, vegetables. They had also bought some articles of underwear for them both, a shirt and sweater for Lorimer.

Kelsey asked to see the garments. Enid took him upstairs and opened drawers. She showed him all the articles, carefully folded away. He asked if she could produce any wrappers or price tags but she shook her head. She had dropped all those into the waste basket when she put the garments away. She had burned the contents of the basket, together with the other household refuse, this morning, in the garden bonfire. She showed him the empty waste basket. "We don't get many refuse collections out here," she explained. "We burn all we can. Victor lights a bonfire most days, when he's working in the garden."

Downstairs again, Kelsey asked if Enid could produce till receipts, which could be expected, in a new, up-to-date supermarket, to show the date and time of day. But she had similarly disposed of those.

He asked how they had paid for their purchases. In cash, she told him. He asked nevertheless to see their cheque-books. They had a joint account with an Okeshot bank. Neither cheque-book showed any cheque drawn yesterday. Nor, for that matter, within the last few days.

He asked if either had visited Cannonbridge at any time on the previous day. They were both emphatic that they had not. Their trip to the supermarket had taken them in the opposite direction; it was most definitely the only journey either had made yesterday.

It was by this time abundantly plain that the two policemen hadn't driven several miles to Furzebank Cottage to carry out some vague general check on Lorimer; their visit had clear reference to some specific offence that had taken place on the previous day. But neither of the Lorimers raised this point, nor did they ask any questions themselves. Lorimer's manner had subsided into a watchful calm although he still chain-smoked.

Kelsey asked the pair to show him the clothing they had worn on their trip yesterday. They complied without protest. Some of the garments—blouse, shirt, underwear, socks, tights and the like—had been washed earlier in the day, dried outdoors, ironed where necessary, and were now being aired in a little utility room next to the kitchen. Kelsey was shown the articles tidily arranged over a clothes rack.

The other, outer, garments were produced for his inspection. A two-piece suit of Enid's, expensive when new—a few years back. Made of dark, heathery tweed, with a close-fitting jacket and straight skirt. A pair of plain brown leather court shoes with a heel of medium height. A tan-coloured suede jacket of Lorimer's, by no means new but of excellent quality, in good condition; brown worsted trousers in a small check, roughly the same age and condition as the jacket; tan leather brogues, expensive make, some years old but very well looked after. Every article clean, undamaged—and bone dry.

The Chief pointed this out. "It rained on and off yesterday from around lunch-time over the whole of this area," he observed. "Some of the showers were very heavy." The cottage was cold and smelled of damp. There was no central heating, no obvious way to dry clothing, no trace of any fire having recently been lit in the old-fashioned grates. The only sign of heating was a radiant electric fire —not switched on—standing in a corner of the living-room.

"We didn't get wet yesterday," Lorimer said in a voice that now sounded utterly weary. "It wasn't raining when we got into the car and it wasn't raining when we got out of it again, back here." It had come on to rain, quite heavily, on the way to Fairdeal and it was still raining when they got there. But there was more than one car park at the supermarket; one of them was covered, and that was the one they had used. "You go straight from the car park into the store," he added. "You're under cover all the way. It had stopped raining by the time we left Fairdeal and it didn't rain again till some little time after we got home."

In spite of these assurances Kelsey took them both upstairs and in front of them went through all the footwear he could find, all the outdoor garments in wardrobes and chests, in both the double bedroom and the dressing-room. He then led them downstairs again and looked through the front hall and the downstairs rooms on a similar mission. His searches were fruitless.

"I put it to you that it wasn't after lunch when you left for Fairdeal," he suggested, as if the detail might somehow have slipped their minds. "I put it to you that it was after breakfast, then you were back here well before lunch, before the rain started."

Lorimer looked as if he might be coming to the end of his patience. "We left here after lunch," he asserted stubbornly, with a visible effort controlling irritation. "We got back around half past five. There's no possible doubt about it."

Kelsey regarded him for some moments. "I further put it to you that at some time yesterday afternoon you left here in the car, on your own. You didn't get back till some hours later."

Lorimer vigorously denied this, as also did Enid.

"This meal you say you had yesterday in the Fairdeal restaurant," Kelsey pursued. "What exactly did you have to eat?"

Lorimer uttered a sound of rising exasperation but Enid answered calmly. "We had toasted muffins. With butter and bramble jelly, if you must have every tiny detail." She smiled faintly. "We very much enjoyed them. You don't often see muffins these days."

The Chief doubled back on his tracks, jumping on their timings from various angles but always without result; they both remained rock-solid.

Lorimer suddenly raised a hand with an air of triumph. "I've just remembered something. We passed an accident on the way home, on the other side of the dual carriageway." He named a spot some five miles distant. "I saw a police car there, and an ambulance drove up as we went by. From what I could see it looked like a big Volvo and a Ford Cortina. It would have been about ten past, quarter past, five, something like that. I think the Cortina was grey, but I couldn't swear to it."

The Chief asked Enid if she had seen the accident.

She agreed that she had. Victor had slowed down, they had both looked across, had commented on it. It was exactly as her husband had described.

The Chief sat regarding them both in silence. They evinced no sign of discomfort now, sat waiting for him to continue—or take himself off.

"You don't ask what all this is about," he finally observed.

Lorimer moved his shoulders. "I dare say you'll tell us in your own good time—if you intend telling us at all. I've long ago given up trying to puzzle out the ways of the law."

There was another pause, then Kelsey uttered the words: "Karen Boland." Just that, the name, dropped into the silence. He felt the atmosphere in the room alter. Lorimer sat rigid in his seat, Enid drew a little sighing breath.

"When was your last contact of any kind with Karen?" the Chief asked them both.

They answered readily. Neither had seen her since the trial, neither had made any attempt to see her or contact her in any way, not even through a third party. Nor had Karen ever made any attempt to contact either of them. Enid was aware that Karen had gone to live with the Wilmots at the end of July, that she had started a course at the Cannonbridge college in September. Under James Boland's will Enid had been appointed joint guardian of the girl, the other guardian being Boland's solicitor; she was kept punctiliously informed of any such changes in her stepdaughter's life.

Again Kelsey persisted: had either of them been in any kind of contact yesterday with Karen? But again he couldn't shake them.

By the time he actually got round to breaking the news of her death they were both well prepared, fully armoured against anything he might spring on them.

"I'm afraid I'm the bearer of bad news," he said at last. Enid drooped her head, she sat looking down at her hands. Lorimer gazed expressionlessly at the Chief. "I very much regret to have to tell you that Karen is dead."

Enid put her hands up to her face and began to cry softly. Lorimer stood up and went across to her. He sat on the arm of her chair and put his arm round her shoulders. She turned to hide her face against him.

"How did it happen?" Lorimer asked.

"Her body was found this morning in a wood near Cannonbridge."

"How did she die?"

"We won't know all the answers till after the post-mortem. But she was certainly murdered."

Enid's head jerked round. "Murdered?"

"I'm afraid there's no doubt about it."

She began to cry more unrestrainedly. Kelsey suggested tea and
Lorimer nodded acquiescence. While Sergeant Lambert was in the
kitchen Kelsey didn't speak. He crossed to the window and stood
looking out at the distant landscape, the mist thickening along the
river.

By the time Lambert returned with the tea Enid had recovered
sufficiently to take the cup he offered and begin to drink it. Lorimer
disposed of his scalding hot tea in a few swift gulps.

Kelsey sat down with his own cup. He asked Enid in a conversational tone how she had got on with Karen in the years after James
Boland's death, before she had any thought of remarriage.

"Well enough, in all the circumstances," she told him. Her manner was calm and disciplined again. "We were never very close but
there was never any hostility, any arguments. Her father had doted
on her and she missed him dreadfully. Naturally, she didn't think me
much of a substitute. But I always did my best for her, I always tried
to carry out my duty towards her. I'm sure she understood that, and
appreciated it. She was never a troublesome child. Not very forthcoming as far as I was concerned, but never awkward or difficult."

Kelsey looked at his watch. Time to be getting back to Cannonbridge for the results of the post-mortem.

The light was beginning to fail as they left the house and walked
across to the remains of the bonfire. Kelsey insisted that the
Lorimers go along with them, stand watching as he and Sergeant
Lambert raked carefully through the ashes.

They found nothing of any significance.

The overhead lights in the mortuary corridor shone harshly down as
Kelsey stood talking to the pathologist. The post-mortem findings
had confirmed earlier opinion: Karen was already dead from asphyxia before the first blow struck the back of her head. Two small
bones in her right ankle had been broken as she stumbled and fell to
the ground. There had been no attempt at any sexual assault.

It was now possible to narrow the limits during which the crime
must have taken place. The contents of the stomach showed that it
was several hours since she had eaten a meal but that shortly before
her death—some sixty to ninety minutes before—she had consumed
a small quantity of chocolate, nut milk chocolate, to be precise.

The Chief asked if the assault had required an unusual degree of strength.

The pathologist shook his head. "She was no great size, disabled by the fall. Any ordinarily active, healthy man or woman, particularly in a state of frenzy, could have carried out the attack. She was in no condition to put up any kind of struggle. She would be totally at the mercy of her killer."

9

Very little of the old village life remained now in Overmead. Too small and scattered ever to have been a very close-knit community, its proximity to Cannonbridge, coupled with the ever-increasing ownership of private transport, had seen it begin to slide over the last twenty years towards the day when it would be little more than a pleasantly rural dormitory suburb of the town.

The tiny school had closed some time ago and it was many years since there had been a resident vicar, the living having been united in successive amalgamations with those of neighbouring parishes. There was still a sub post office, combined with a small general store, run by a cheerful, gossipy woman now over seventy; she had operated the dual business for the past forty years.

Early on Sunday evening Chief Inspector Kelsey sat at his desk studying the results of the investigation so far.

The detailed search of the area had continued until the light failed, an hour or so earlier; it had thrown up nothing fresh. He had checked if there had been a road accident at the time and place mentioned by Victor Lorimer. There had indeed been such an accident, between a Volvo estate car and a Ford Cortina. And yes, the Cortina was grey.

A police appeal had gone out earlier in the day over the local radio, asking for anyone to come forward who had been in or near the wood during during Friday afternoon or evening, or any motorist who might have noticed something unusual or suspicious. The appeal had so far produced no result.

The police had also asked any passenger to come forward who had travelled on the bus Karen was most likely to have boarded if she had left college after her last lesson and gone straight home— the bus leaving the centre of Cannonbridge at twelve minutes past six, The driver had already been contacted; he had done his best to be helpful but without conclusive result. He was not a regular driver on the route. He was suffering from a cold in the head and had been concerned with that—and the heavy rain—during the journey. To the best of his recollection he had not been required to stop at the halt by Overmead Wood but he couldn't take his oath on it.

A couple of hours after the police broadcast a woman called in at the station, a sensible, middle-aged woman who struck Kelsey as a reliable witness. She lived in a cottage on the main road, two miles beyond Overmead Wood. She worked in Cannonbridge and always caught the same bus home, the six-twelve from the town centre.

She wasn't acquainted with Karen Boland but recognized the girl from the police description on the radio. She had seen her on the bus on several occasions, knew that she always got off at the stop by the wood. She was unshakably certain that Karen had not been on the bus on Friday evening, equally positive that no one had left or boarded the bus at that point; the bus had definitely not halted there. She clearly recalled looking out at the windswept, rain-drenched expanses of the wood as the bus drove past. She had seen no one in or anywhere near the wood, no vehicle parked in the vicinity.

One report in the account of the house-to-house visits carried out in the Overmead area struck the Chief as especially interesting. There had been no answer to an officer's ring at the doorbell of one of the dwellings, a detached house by the name of Hawthorn Lodge, on Saturday afternoon or evening, no reply to further rings on Sunday morning. The officer slipped a note through the letter-box asking the householder to contact the police as soon as possible.

The lodge was a substantial villa not far from Overmead Wood, half a mile from Jubilee Cottage. There were no near neighbours;

the nearest was able to tell the police the name of the owner of the lodge: a Mr. Desmond Hallam, a bachelor in his forties, no longer employed, made redundant some little time ago, apparently comfortably off. He was not a native of the village, he had lived with his mother at the lodge for some ten years until her death earlier in the year. He didn't mix much locally, either before or after his mother's death, though always civil and pleasant enough if casually encountered. He now had an aunt staying at the lodge, whether permanently or not the neighbour couldn't say, nor did the neighbour know the aunt's name.

But the Overmead postmistress was able to supply this detail: the aunt was a Miss Ivy Jebb, a spry lady in her sixties, a retired assistant nurse, elder sister of the late Mrs. Hallam, come to the lodge in the spring to nurse her sister during what turned out to be Mrs. Hallam's last illness. The postmistress had enjoyed a number of interesting chats with Miss Jebb when the good lady had called into the post office or shop. She was able to tell the police that Miss Jebb hailed from a town some distance away to the north, that her visit to Hawthorn Lodge had started out as a temporary one but now gave every indication of becoming a permanency.

Miss Jebb hadn't actually said that she and her nephew would be going away this last weekend but the postmistress wouldn't be surprised if the two of them hadn't gone off to the town Miss Jebb had left in the spring—she had mentioned the name but the postmistress couldn't recall it. Miss Jebb had said more than once lately that she ought to be thinking of getting her warmer things, now that the weather would be turning colder. Yes, Mr. Hallam did have a car, they had in all probability gone off in that.

It was the last note in the report that particularly caught the Chief's attention, caused him to go back through the report again, sit for some time afterwards staring thoughtfully ahead, tapping his fingers on the desk. "Wherever they've gone," the postmistress had ended by saying, "I'm sure they'll be back in a day or two. Mr. Hallam won't want to miss his classes at the Cannonbridge college. He's been going there regularly over the last month or two. Ever since he came out of hospital, poor man, after that nervous breakdown he had when his mother died."

The atmosphere among the students at the Cannonbridge College of Further Education on Monday morning was both tense and subdued. They stood about in little groups before and between classes, shocked, nervous, upset—but also absorbed and excited, talking in low voices. Everyone anxious to be helpful, to tell anything they knew; with the majority of them this was very little indeed. Karen had been only a short time at the college, wasn't a native of the town, had been quiet and unobtrusive in manner and behaviour. Many students hadn't even known of her existence, let alone anything of the circumstances of her death.

The Principal confirmed what the Wilmots had told the Chief about Karen's record at the college: she was a very satisfactory student, hard-working, cooperative, well-behaved, anxious to succeed in life. He had known that her parents were dead, that she was in the care of the Social Services, that she was living with a cousin, but he had known nothing of the original reasons for her being taken into care, nothing of the case involving Victor Lorimer.

The lecturer in charge of Karen's last class on Friday afternoon told the Chief that she had behaved as usual. The only incident which had in any way drawn his attention to her was that she had been summoned to the office to take a phone call. While personal calls to the students were in no way encouraged they were permitted, as there was always the chance of a domestic or other emergency arising. The privilege was not in general abused and it was accepted that such calls must be kept as short as possible. Karen had been briefly absent from the class, had returned to her work with no sign of agitation or anxiety.

The woman clerk who had summoned Karen to the phone couldn't remember if the caller had been male or female, nor if the call had come from a public kiosk or a private phone. When she took the call she had been on the point of leaving the office with a batch of papers to return to a member of staff. After looking in at Karen's class to deliver the message she had continued on her way. By the time she got back to the office Karen had already left. She had the impression that there had been one or two previous calls for Karen but she couldn't be precise.

The Chief asked the Principal what he could tell him about a mature student named Desmond Hallam, living at Hawthorn Lodge, in Overmead.

"There's been a letter from him this morning," the Principal said. The letter had been delivered by hand, bore no date. He produced it and showed it to the Chief. A brief note to say that Hallam had been called away on family business, apologized for missing classes. He couldn't say exactly how long he'd be away; he would return as soon as possible. The Principal had no idea where this family business might have taken Hallam, nor in what town Hallam's aunt might have been living before she came to Hawthorn Lodge.

Hallam was a quiet, studious man, the Principal added. An inoffensive, courteous man, concerned with developing new interests after painful upheavals in his personal and business life. He had one class in common with Karen Boland, a play-reading class; the full-time students were encouraged to add one or two of these recreational classes to the more demanding timetable of their regular course.

The Principal consulted the records and told the Chief that Hallam had attended all his usual classes on Friday; his last class had ended at five. The Principal promised that if Hallam wrote again he would at once inform the police. And if Hallam made contact with the college by phone, he would be asked to contact the Chief without delay.

Kelsey then spoke to Karen's friend on the same course, Lynn Musgrove. Lynn was an intelligent, serious girl, very neat and clean, with no extravagances of dress or looks. Her manner was quiet and controlled though she was still clearly shocked and deeply upset by Karen's death.

She had sat beside Karen during the final class on Friday afternoon. There had been nothing unusual about Karen's behaviour that day or during recent days. In the afternoon break she and Karen had discussed their weekend homework. Karen said she would go home with Lynn at six so that they could work on it together.

When Karen came back to the class after the phone call she hadn't appeared in any way agitated, excited, anxious or overjoyed; she had seemed her normal self. She had scribbled a couple of lines on a scrap of paper and slipped it across to Lynn. Lynn still had the note, she produced it for the Chief. It read: "Can't come home with you this evening. I've got to meet someone."

Karen had worked the rest of the grammar test with her usual attention. A few moments before the lesson ended she gathered her belongings together. As the college clock struck six she stood up and handed in her paper. She was the first to leave the classroom, turning in the doorway to flash Lynn a smile of farewell.

Lynn didn't leave the building till some minutes later; she had stayed behind to speak to the lecturer. When she got outside there was no sign of Karen. Not that Lynn had spent much time looking about. It was raining heavily. She had merely glanced casually round the car park, turned up the hood of her jacket and plunged off home.

Kelsey asked if she had seen Karen eat any chocolate on Friday afternoon. "I gave her some chocolate," Lynn answered at once. It was during the couple of minutes' break between the last two lessons. As she and Karen were walking along the corridor towards their final class Karen had suddenly said she was very hungry, she'd had little lunch. "I'd bought a bar of chocolate during morning break," Lynn told the Chief. "I still had some left. I gave it to Karen and she ate it at once." Four small squares of hazelnut milk chocolate. Lynn was able to be precise about the time Karen had eaten the chocolate; it was almost five o'clock, no more than a minute or two either way.

She knew very little of Karen's past, merely that her parents were dead, that she was in the care of the Social Services, that she had recently lived at Wychford and now lived with her cousin at Jubilee Cottage; she had made no mention of the town of Okeshot. Lynn had heard nothing of any court case and Karen never spoke of anyone by the name of Lorimer. Her manner had never invited personal questions and Lynn wasn't the type to ask them.

She confirmed the Wilmots' notions of the household of which she herself formed a part. Her mother had no romantic attachments, there was no regular male visitor to the house. Lynn was positive that Karen had no boyfriend at the college, no involvement with any member of staff or adult pupil. She had been friendly in a slight, mild fashion with one of the mature students, Desmond Hallam, but there was no question of any romance. Hallam had never struck Lynn as being in that way interested in Karen, and nothing in the way Karen treated him or spoke of him ever in the remotest degree suggested such an interest on her part. Karen occasionally got a lift home from Hallam when their times coincided, and he sometimes bought her a cup of coffee in the canteen, sat chatting with her during break. Lynn had the feeling that Karen was rather sorry for him. No, she had no idea where Hallam's aunt might have lived before she went to stay at Hawthorn Lodge.

When the Chief asked if she knew of any boyfriend or man friend outside the college, Lynn hesitated before answering that she wasn't sure. Kelsey pressed her to say what she knew or guessed, however little that might be.

"It was something she said one evening at my house when we were preparing essays on *Jane Eyre,*" Lynn told him. "It's one of the set books on the literature course. I was talking about the way Jane reacted when she discovered that Rochester was a married man. I remarked how very different attitudes were today." Karen had suddenly asked her: "What would you think if I told you I was involved with a married man?"

"I just stared at her," Lynn continued. "She said, 'That's the reason I left Wychford.' I asked her if it was all finished with now. She just shrugged and said, 'Not exactly.' She never mentioned it again, and I didn't either. I had the impression she was sorry she'd said it the moment she'd spoken." The exchange had taken place some ten days earlier. Lynn did recall one or two previous phone calls Karen had received at the college. There could have been others she didn't know about; she wasn't in every class with Karen. She didn't know who the calls were from, nor could she remember Karen making any comment about any of the calls.

A few minutes after ten-thirty a canteen assistant who had just come on duty asked if she could speak to the Chief. She was a big, fat woman in her fifties, usually of a cheerful disposition, but showing today a strong tendency to lapse into tears.

She told the Chief that she normally left work at six in the evening. She was always very sharp about getting off promptly on Fridays as she liked to catch the market stalls. Last Friday it had begun to rain heavily as she came out of the college. She paused to open her umbrella and glanced round the car park, pretty empty at that time of day.

"I saw Karen Boland over on the right," she asserted. "She was hurrying—because of the rain, it seemed to me." Karen had halted beside a car, on the passenger side. No, she hadn't seen Karen get into the car. She hadn't seen her place her hand on the door, hadn't seen her stop to talk to anyone inside. She had glimpsed Karen for only a moment, then she opened her umbrella, turned and set off for the market.

"Are you quite certain it was Karen Boland you saw?" Kelsey asked.

Yes, she was absolutely certain. She wouldn't go so far as to take her oath on it in court but in her own mind she had no doubt. "She was wearing that yellow cap and scarf, and she had that pale-coloured shoulder-bag she always carried. When she stopped by the car she turned sideways on to me. I saw her face. It was Karen all right."

Kelsey asked how well she had known the girl.

"Well enough," she answered with spirit. "I always have a chat with the students while I'm serving, particularly with anyone new or shy. I noticed Karen when she first started at the college. She looked a bit lost, she seemed pleased when I spoke to her." Tears threatened. "She was a lovely girl, beautiful manners, always so nicely spoken. One day last month I scalded my hand in the kitchen here, I was off work more than a week. Karen took the trouble to find out my address. She called round at my place one lunch-time to ask how I was, if there was anything she could do for me, any shopping or cleaning. Could she make me something to eat? Had I got anyone to look after me? She could come round in the evening if I wanted, it would be no trouble."

She dabbed at her eyes. "I was really touched. I told her I wouldn't need to trouble her, I've got my sister living in the next street, she always gives me a hand if I need it."

She looked up at the Chief with swimming eyes. "To go to all that trouble on my account—" She sighed and shook her head. "To tell the truth, I always thought she looked as if she could do with a bit of mothering herself."

Kelsey asked if she had seen anyone with Karen in the car park. No, she couldn't actually say she had seen anyone, but when she glanced over she had the impression there had been someone just ahead, someone who turned the corner of the building at the instant she glanced that way. Yes, possibly someone going round to the other side of the car. No, she couldn't make any guess as to whether it had been a man or a woman, the glimpse had been too slight, too fleeting.

Could she describe the car? She was very anxious to be of help but all she could tell them was that she had seen only the edge of the vehicle, which was parked by the end of the building, in a dimly-lit area. The most she could add after racking her brains was that the vehicle could have been largish and darkish. She had glimpsed nothing to indicate any agitation or upset on Karen's part, no suggestion that Karen might have been in any way forced into going wherever it was she was going.

When the woman had gone off to the canteen a constable on the Chief Inspector's team came along to say that he had succeeded in locating a student who had seen Desmond Hallam leave the college on Friday. Kelsey questioned the student closely. He had been sitting in the common room towards the end of Friday afternoon. Hallam came into the room after his last class and sat reading newspapers and magazines, chatting to the student with whom he had occasionally exchanged a few words before.

At about a quarter to six Hallam stood up to leave. He asked if he could give the student a lift, he was going back to Overmead. The student thanked him but said he lived out in another direction, he always got a bus. They left the common room together, still chatting. Hallam walked across to his car which was parked to the left of the front entrance. As the student went out through the gates Hallam drove past him, alone in his car. He gave the student a wave and turned off in the direction of Overmead. It was then seven or eight minutes to six. The student walked to his bus stop, had a brief time to wait, caught his bus as usual at two minutes to six.

"That phone call for Karen at twenty minutes to six," Kelsey said to Sergeant Lambert as they came out of the college. "And the canteen woman's story of seeing Karen over by the car. What do those two things suggest to you?"

"They suggest Paul Clayton," Lambert answered at once.

"And to me," Kelsey said as they reached their car.

"But I don't see how he could have done it," Lambert added. It was certain that Karen had eaten the chocolate more or less spot on at five o'clock; therefore, according to the pathologist's calculations, she had been killed between six and six-thirty. She had clearly been done to death at the spot where her body was found, a spot several minutes' drive from the car park where the canteen assistant had seen her at a few minutes past six. That left a crucial period of twenty minutes or so. At some time between six-ten and six-thirty Karen was plunging through the undergrowth in Overmead Wood with her attacker on her heels. "And if Paul Clayton was sitting talking to that customer of his from ten minutes to six until six-thirty, a good hour's drive from Overmead Wood at that time of day, then there's no way he could possibly have done it."

Kelsey got into the car. "We've only Clayton's word he was with his customer."

"And presumably Braithwaite's word too," Lambert pointed out. Braithwaite was the customer's name.

Kelsey grunted. "That's presuming one hell of a lot. We'll get over there now and talk to Braithwaite."

"And his secretary," Lambert reminded him. "She was there too."

Kelsey settled back in his seat. "I've no intention of forgetting Braithwaite's secretary."

Lambert switched on the ignition. He was just about to pull out when a thought struck him. "Clayton's car," he said suddenly.

"What about it?"

"It's three or four years old."

"What of it?"

"Clayton may not actually have owned it for three or four years. He may have bought it second-hand." Clayton had come up the hard way. He struck Lambert as a man keenly aware of the value of money, not likely to go chucking it round unnecessarily, however successful the years had made him.

Kelsey chewed his lip. "It's certainly a thought. We'll find out when he bought it. We'll do it now, before we talk to Braithwaite." Lambert headed the car back to the station.

A few minutes later while Lambert was chasing up the details Kelsey sat at his desk studying under a magnifying glass every last detail of the snapshot they had found in Karen's bedroom, showing

Clayton standing beside the car in a country lay-by. He scrutinized the foliage of trees and hedging, the growth of grass and weeds, the angle of sunlight and shadow, the way Clayton was dressed.

He glanced up as Lambert came into the room and laid a piece of paper on the desk before him. "That's the date," Lambert said. "When Clayton bought the car."

They were coming down the front steps on their way out again when a car drove on to the forecourt and a couple of men from the team Kelsey had left at the college got out. The Chief went over to ask if they had turned up anything fresh.

Yes, there had been one interesting piece of information. A member of the office staff, a young married woman who worked part time, had come on duty shortly after the Chief left. When the detectives spoke to her she believed at first she could be of no help in the inquiries but a few minutes later she returned to say she had now remembered something.

There had been a phone call to the office at lunch-time on Friday; the time, as near as she could recall it, was about five or ten past one. The caller was a man, asking to speak to Karen Boland. He didn't give his name, nor did she ask for it. She told him she couldn't go looking for Karen, she was alone in the office. All the classes were over for the morning, she would have no idea where to begin to look, or even if Karen was still in the building.

He hadn't appeared in any way upset or agitated at this response, he had made no attempt to press her to go searching for Karen. He asked if she could tell him what time Karen's last class finished in the afternoon. She was able to supply the information after consulting the list of students—which gave her the course Karen Boland was taking—and then the large timetable sheet pinned up on the office wall. The caller left no message for Karen, he merely thanked her and rang off. She had no knowledge of the second call that had come for Karen at twenty minutes to six on Friday evening. She had by then finished her stint and gone home.

10

Braithwaite's works stood in a rural setting some twenty miles to the west of Cannonbridge, a small disused factory Braithwaite had taken over on borrowed capital twelve years ago in a spirit of buoyant optimism.

It was approaching noon when Sergeant Lambert drove in through the rusting iron gates. Chief Inspector Kelsey got out of the car and stood surveying the premises: flaking brickwork, peeling paint, blistered window frames, weeds thrusting up through the concrete surround, rubbish lying about, waste materials none too tidily stacked.

On the door of a small shed-like structure standing apart from the main building the word OFFICE was visible in ancient paint. The Chief knocked on the door. It was opened by an anxious-looking middle-aged woman who gave the two men a rapid, assessing glance.

Kelsey told her who he was and asked if he might have a word with Mr. Braithwaite. She vanished into an inner room, returning after some little delay to tell them yes, Mr. Braithwaite could spare them a few minutes. She took them through into his office.

Braithwaite stood up from behind a desk strewn with untidy papers. He came round to greet them, shook hands, offered them chairs, instructed his secretary to bring in coffee. A small, slight man, his clothes hanging on him, jacket unbrushed, shirt far from clean, his whole appearance seedy and run-down.

"What can I do for you, gentlemen?" he inquired when he had resumed his seat. He offered them cigarettes which they refused. He lit one himself and drew on it heavily. The ashtray in front of him was full of savagely crushed-out stubs. He was barely forty, Kelsey judged, but he looked haggard and drawn, on the verge of exhaustion.

Kelsey came straight to the point. They had spoken to a Mr. Paul Clayton in connection with inquiries they were making and he had told them in the course of his statement that he had called on Mr. Braithwaite last Friday. Could Mr. Braithwaite confirm this?

"Yes, I can," Braithwaite answered readily. He didn't ask what was the nature of the case that had prompted their inquiries but went on at once, unasked, to supply the times of Clayton's arrival and departure; these coincided exactly with what Clayton had told them. He further added that he was able to be so precise because Clayton himself had mentioned the time when he arrived and when he left.

Kelsey asked if he had seen what vehicle Clayton was driving.

Yes, he had seen it. When Clayton left he had walked out with him to his car. It was clear from his description that it was the car Clayton had shown them on Saturday morning, the dark green runabout.

Kelsey then asked if there was anyone else who could substantiate Clayton's account.

"Yes, my secretary," Braithwaite told them. Again he volunteered additional information: his secretary was a single woman, without domestic ties, she always stayed on when he worked late. She had spoken to Clayton, had made them some tea.

Straight on cue came a light knock on the door and the secretary entered with a tray of coffee. The Chief put the same questions to her. Her manner was nervous but she gave the same version of events. And yes, she had seen Clayton's car. She had looked out of the window at the sound of his arrival, not expecting anyone at that time of evening. She had seen him drive up and park. Her description tallied with what Braithwaite had said.

When she had left the room Kelsey changed tack and asked questions about the nature of Braithwaite's business, the link between himself and Clayton. It seemed that Braithwaite was a manufacturer of heating appliance control equipment and Clayton was one of his suppliers. One of his principal suppliers, he agreed reluctantly after the Chief pressed him on the point. He had known Clayton a good many years, since they were both young men employed by others. "We started out on our own at around the same time," he added.

Kelsey drank his coffee. "Clayton seems to be doing well," he observed. Braithwaite gave a nod. "Better than you," the Chief added bluntly. "Judging by appearances." He jerked his head in the direction of the dilapidated works, the weeds, the rubbish.

Braithwaite lit another cigarette. "Difficult times," he said with an attempt at lightness. "All this foreign competition. They live on peanuts out there. They've got kids of ten making the stuff. We're supposed to match their labour costs." He managed a smile of sorts. "But we get through. We have our ups and downs but we stagger along." His voice grew firmer. "As a matter of fact I've hopes of a very good order. Should hear definitely this week. That'll set us straight."

Kelsey drained his cup, refused the offer of a refill. "You're in financial difficulties," he said crisply.

Braithwaite uttered a sound of protest. "Maybe a temporary difficulty in cash flow. We can't always get our own customers to pay up promptly. You can't push them too hard or you risk losing them altogether."

"Do you owe Clayton money? Outstanding bills?"

He moved his shoulders. "Just the current invoices."

"Nothing beyond that?"

There was an appreciable pause.

"We can always get a squint at your books," Kelsey told him.

"Maybe the last invoice as well," Braithwaite conceded.

"Yes, and the one before that, I've no doubt." Kelsey struck the desk. "The truth is you're up to your eyes in debt. Clayton could put the squeeze on you, make you bankrupt."

Braithwaite looked at him with tortured eyes. "He'd never do that. We go back too far."

"Did Clayton call in here at all last Friday?"

"Yes, he did," Braithwaite answered with force. "I swear it."

"If he did call in, then it wasn't just to pass the time of day, to chat about the exhibition, about old times. It was to talk about his money, demand payment, threaten court proceedings."

Braithwaite sat with lowered gaze, shaking his head.

"It wouldn't take much effort on my part to find out," Kelsey assured him.

Braithwaite glanced up at him. "It doesn't alter what I told you about last Friday," he declared obstinately. "Every word of that was

the truth. You can check it up hill and down dale. You won't be able
to alter it." He stuck absolutely to the times he had given for Clayton. He would be happy to adhere to the same story in court, under
oath.

The Chief leaned forward. "I put it to you that if Clayton called
here at all last Friday it was in the morning, on his way to the
exhibition, not in the evening, on his way back."

Braithwaite gave an emphatic shake of his head. "That is not so.
He called here in the early evening, as I've told you."

The Chief sat regarding him without speaking. "You don't ask
why we're so interested in what Clayton was doing last Friday evening," he said at last.

Braithwaite pulled down the corners of his mouth. "It's no business of mine. If you want me to know I dare say you'll tell me. In any
case, I don't greatly care."

"I thought you and Clayton were old mates."

"Yes, but only in a strictly business way. I've never been to his
house or met his family and he's never met mine. Clayton's always
seemed to me more than capable of looking after himself. I know
nothing of his personal life."

"Why should you suppose it's his personal life that interests us?
Why shouldn't it be his business life?"

Braithwaite's eyes jerked open. "His business life?" he echoed
with an air of astonishment. "I'd be very surprised at that."

"But you wouldn't be surprised it if was his personal life?"

"I couldn't be either surprised or not surprised. I told you, I know
nothing about it." He moved a hand. "He's not a man I've ever
thought of as having much of a personal life. As long as I've known
him he's always struck me as being wrapped up in business."

Kelsey changed tack again. "When was Clayton last in touch with
you?"

Braithwaite eyed him warily. "When he called in here on Friday
evening."

"I'm asking when he last phoned you."

Braithwaite's eyes flickered but he said nothing.

"We had a good long talk with Clayton a couple of days ago,"
Kelsey remarked. "That thought might help to clear your mind."

Braithwaite answered hesitantly, "He did phone for a moment on Friday evening."

"What time was that?"

Again some hesitation. "It was after I got home. It must have been about half past nine, a quarter to ten."

"Does he often phone you at home?"

He shook his head.

"Has he ever phoned you at home before?"

"Not that I can remember."

"Why did he phone?"

Another pause. "He said he'd been thinking over what I'd said, particularly about the order I'm expecting. He was willing to give me a bit more time, see if I get the order, before doing anything."

"I put it to you," the Chief said, "that he rang to say he'd be willing to stay court proceedings against you if you agreed to tell the police when they came calling that he was indisputably here last Friday evening between ten minutes to six and six-thirty."

Braithwaite shook his head with vigour. "He said nothing of the kind. You can sit there till doomsday but you won't get me to say he did."

A few minutes later as Sergeant Lambert pulled out into the road and turned the car in the direction of Wychford the Chief said, "We can scrub Clayton's alibi, it isn't worth tuppence." He fingered his chin. "Clayton's wife tells us he got home around seven-fifteen on Friday evening. Even if he killed the girl as late as six-thirty, that still gives him time to cover the distance from Overmead Wood and be home by seven-fifteen."

They arrived at Clayton's works as the men were breaking off for lunch. The place, by contrast with the factory they had just left, seemed full of energy and bustle. Faces appeared lively, cheerful and good-tempered; there was a general air of order and cleanliness. It was easy to imagine full order books, well turned out products keenly priced.

Clayton was coming out of the main building, talking to a foreman. He broke off at the sight of Kelsey's car, he came over as Lambert was parking it. He was smartly dressed in a dark grey business suit and white shirt. He seemed in no way disconcerted at this second visitation; he looked alert and energetic, as if he had enjoyed a sound night's sleep.

He greeted the two policemen in a friendly way. His manner was tightly controlled, poised, he appeared very much in command of himself.

"One or two points in your statement we'd like to take you over again," the Chief told him. "It's best to get them properly cleared up."

"By all means." Clayton took them across to his office. His secretary was putting on her coat. Clayton introduced her. A markedly competent-looking woman in early middle age, well groomed and well dressed, with a composed, no-nonsense air. Her attitude was detached and professional. She permitted herself no glance of curiosity, no questioning looks. "I was just going off to lunch," she told Clayton, "but I'll stay if you need me." Clayton flicked an inquiring glance at the Chief, who shook his head in reply.

When she had gone Clayton took them into the inner office and sat them down. He took his own seat behind his desk, facing them.

Kelsey at once got down to brass tacks. "You told us on Saturday that you had no contact of any kind with Karen Boland after she left her foster-parents, the Roscoes, several months ago."

"That's right."

"You stand by that?"

"I do."

"You would take your oath on that in court?"

He didn't falter. "I would."

Kelsey produced the snapshot from his pocket and set it down on the desk in front of Clayton. Clayton glanced down at it. He said nothing, showed no response. He sat very still.

"Karen went to live at Overmead at the end of July." Kelsey stabbed a finger at the photograph. "Take a look at those trees, those bushes. The weeds, the grass. That picture was taken in early autumn. Most probably around the end of September." He raised a hand as Clayton opened his mouth. "To save you the trouble of arguing, we've had expert opinion on that." Clayton closed his mouth again.

The Chief dipped his hand into his pocket a second time and pulled out the piece of paper Lambert had given him earlier. He set it down beside the photograph. "That's the date you bought your car," he said. "The car in the snapshot. Two and a half months ago. September 2. More than a month after Karen went to live in Jubilee Cottage."

Still Clayton said nothing.

"Do you still maintain you had no contact with Karen after she left Wychford?"

Clayton shifted in his chair. He kept his eyes on the photograph, the piece of paper.

"I didn't see how I could tell you the truth," he said at last. His voice held a note of apology. "I was sure you'd try to make something of it. I did see her, but just the once. It wasn't by arrangement, it was purely by chance."

He raised his eyes and looked at the Chief. "It was one lunchtime, a few weeks back. I was over in Cannonbridge on business. I'd parked my car near the college. I was going back to my car and I saw Karen coming out of the college gates. She saw me and came over. She was very pleased to see me. She was on her way to a snack bar. I went with her and picked up something for us to eat. We went along to the car and I drove a few miles out into the country. We ate the food and talked, that's all. I asked how she was settling down with her cousin, how she liked the college, that sort of thing. Then I ran her back in time for her afternoon classes."

"Did you arrange to see her again?"

He shook his head. "We both knew there would be no point in that. Not after all the uproar there'd been."

"And the photograph?"

He jerked his head. "Oh yes, that was when she took the photograph. She asked if she could take it, to remember me by."

"She just happened to have the camera with her?"

He moved his shoulders but said nothing.

"She'd brought it with her on purpose," Kelsey challenged him. "It was no chance meeting, it was arranged between you. You were meeting her regularly."

Clayton shook his head several times, in silence.

"You were making business calls that day in Cannonbridge?"

He nodded.

Kelsey thrust a finger at the photograph. "In jeans? In a striped sweatshirt? I suggest we drop this pantomime. You went on seeing Karen after she left Wychford. And always by arrangement."

11

Clayton sat with his head lowered. "All right," he said at last, "I did see her by arrangement, but not several times, just that once. She kept phoning me here, at the office, saying she couldn't forget me, couldn't we meet, all that kind of thing. I told her it was finished, better let it stay that way. But she wouldn't be put off, she kept on ringing."

He raised his eyes, his tone grew more confident. "In the end there was nothing for it but to see her. I thought I could make her see reason, spell it all out, get her to accept it. I fixed to go over to Cannonbridge one Saturday morning. She got the bus into Cannonbridge and I picked her up at the bus station. We drove out into the country. We talked for about an hour. I persuaded her she had to put the whole thing behind her, forget me, find some boy her own age. She cried a bit and then she agreed it was the sensible thing to do. She'd known in her heart that was the way it would end—that was why she'd brought the camera. She wanted the snapshot as a keepsake, she knew she wouldn't be seeing me again."

"What time did you drive her back to Cannonbridge?"

"It would be about half past eleven, a quarter to twelve."

Kelsey shoved the snapshot forward. "Take a look at those shadows. That photograph was taken in late afternoon."

Clayton dropped his head again.

"Karen's girlfriend at the college tells us Karen said something recently about being mixed up with a married man," Kelsey continued. "She gave her friend the strong impression she was still in-

volved with him—and that he was the man she was mixed up with
when she was living with her foster-parents."

Clayton sat in tense silence.

"Did you kill Karen Boland?" the Chief asked suddenly.

His head jerked up. "Good God, no!"

"Then tell us the truth," Kelsey urged. "If you didn't kill her
you've nothing to fear."

A light dew broke out on Clayton's brow. "I'm not so sure about
that." He pulled out a handkerchief and dabbed at his face. "It's
what you'll read into everything that scares the hell out of me. I
wouldn't be the first innocent man to end up with a life sentence."

He pushed back his chair and got to his feet. He went over to the
drinks cupboard and poured himself a stiff drink. He stood with his
back to them. "I realize I'm in one hell of a jam," he said between
swallows. He remained silent for some moments and then appeared
to reach a decision. He swung round to face them.

"All right, I did see her several times. I kept telling myself it
couldn't last, she'd get tired of it. Every time I set off to meet her I
swore it was the last time. But I didn't see her at all last Friday. I
swear to God I didn't. I had to lie about it all. I knew the moment
you found out I'd been seeing her you'd immediately think it was me
that killed her." He gave a short bark of a laugh. "That's what I'd
think in your shoes, I'd be certain of it." He drained his glass and at
once refilled it.

Kelsey changed tack. "Do you know exactly how Karen died?"

Clayton stood motionless, staring at him, his glass frozen in his
hand. The Chief began to spell it out, every last horrific detail. Long
before he had finished Clayton had broken down into terrible, shaking sobs.

The Chief's voice ground relentlessly to its conclusion. He sat for
some time without speaking. At last Clayton fell into a trembling
silence.

"It wasn't just a silly, meaningless flirtation," Kelsey said into the
silence.

Clayton gave a tremulous shake of his head. He came slowly back
to the desk, half fell into his seat.

"I don't expect you to understand," he said in a low, faltering
voice. "I couldn't properly understand it myself. I was never young

at the right time in my life, I think that was at the root of it. It was never anything but work, work, work. That was all I ever thought about: getting on, getting somewhere."

He looked across at Kelsey, his eyes exhausted, his face drained. "One day about a year ago, a man I'd known for years, a businessman like myself, the same age as me, he was walking out to his car one morning and he fell down dead." He shook his head, expelled a wavering breath. "That pulled me up sharp, I can tell you. All that work, all that struggle, all over, finished, inside a minute. What was it all for? Why was I still working every hour God sent? I was successful enough, I had more money than I knew what to do with. I'd made more than enough provision for the future, for my family. Why couldn't I slow down, start to take things easy, think of something else for a change?"

He stared down at the desk. "Then I met Karen." He glanced briefly up. "I don't expect you to understand," he said again. "It was as if, inside, I was still a boy, I'd never grown up. I knew from the first moment it was madness but it didn't seem to matter, I was swept along. I'd never been in love before, never with anyone, never in the slightest degree." Tears ran unchecked down his face. "For her to end up like that. She was a lovely girl." He fell again into convulsive sobs.

Kelsey waited till he had regained some measure of control. "To get back to last Friday," he said. "Did you make any phone calls to Karen that day?"

Clayton sat slumped, as if he hadn't heard. The Chief repeated his question in a sharper tone. "And this time we'll have the truth first time round," he added brusquely.

Clayton made an effort to rouse himself. "No, I didn't phone her at all on Friday. I did sometimes phone her at the college but not last Friday. I was very busy all day, I had no reason to phone her. We'd already fixed to meet this week, Wednesday, most probably. She was to ring me here on Tuesday, to arrange where and when."

"I put it to you that you tried to phone her at lunch-time on Friday. You rang the college but couldn't get hold of her."

He shook his head. "No, that isn't so." His tone was immensely fatigued. "I had lunch with a customer at a hotel on Friday." He supplied the Chief with details.

"Did you phone her later on Friday, at twenty minutes to six? Asking her to meet you outside the college as soon as classes ended?"

"No, I did not." His voice was stronger now. He shifted into a more upright position. "I was nowhere near the college at that time. I didn't go to Cannonbridge at all on Friday. At six o'clock I was with Braithwaite, in his office."

"When was the last time you met Karen?"

"Last Tuesday, at lunch-time," he answered promptly. "She came out of college and went to sit on a bench in a little public garden nearby. We'd met that way before. I pulled up for a moment, she jumped in and we drove out of town for a couple of miles. I took her back in time for her next class—she didn't have one till three o'clock on Tuesday afternoons."

"This customer of yours, Braithwaite—why exactly did you call on him last Friday?"

"No special reason. I was over that way. He's a good customer, he's dealt with us for years. I always make a point of personal contact with customers, I see them as often as I can."

"Did you call on him to dun him for money? To get him to pay his bills?"

Clayton didn't appear at all put out, he answered readily. "I did mention the bills while I was there but I didn't make a song and dance about them. Braithwaite apologized for keeping me waiting for the money. He told me he was having difficulty getting some of his own bills paid but he was getting that sorted out. He had hopes of a good order that would put him straight."

"Did you put pressure on him? Threaten to bankrupt him?"

"I most certainly did not," Clayton said with a return of vigour. "We started out in business together. I had some narrow squeaks myself in the early days, I know what it is to hit a bad patch."

"Did you call on Braithwaite at all last Friday?"

"Yes, I did."

"Then I suggest it wasn't in the evening but in the morning, on your way over to the exhibition."

"I called on him in the evening. You can ask him yourself."

"We have asked him."

"Then he's confirmed what I've told you. He must have confirmed it."

"Yes, he confirmed it all right. Hardly surprising when you can bankrupt him any day you choose. Try trotting out that sort of confirmation in court and see how far it'll get you."

"It doesn't alter the fact that it's the truth," Clayton said with stubborn defiance.

"Have you been in touch with Braithwaite since last Friday evening?"

He answered readily. "Yes. I phoned him at home on Friday evening, about half past nine."

"Why did you phone him?"

"To say I'd been thinking over what he'd told me about his financial difficulties. I made one or two suggestions I thought might be of help, getting his own bills paid."

"Or did you phone to say you wouldn't take legal steps to recover the money he owed you if he would tell the police you were with him between ten to six and six-thirty on Friday evening?"

"I said nothing of the sort," Clayton maintained with heat. "It's a monstrous suggestion, not a shred of truth in it. Did you talk to Braithwaite's secretary? She was there all the time, in the outer office. She saw me arrive, she saw me leave, she spoke to me both times. She brought in tea while I was talking to Braithwaite. Am I supposed to have squared her too? Threatened her? Blackmailed her?"

"You're well aware you can leave the secretary to Braithwaite to deal with. She identifies with him. If he goes bust she loses her job. That sort of back-up story isn't a fat lot of use. Juries aren't fools."

A brief silence fell. Kelsey looked at him squarely. "I ask you again: Did you kill Karen Boland?"

Clayton drew a long, weary breath and shook his head. "Why in God's name would I want to kill her?"

"I put it to you that Karen was very far from pestering you to resume your relationship. She was thankful when it was all over, thankful she'd been forced to come to her senses when it came out into the open."

He leaned forward. "I suggest it was you who made all the running, who did all the pestering. You kept trying to see her after she'd moved, you wouldn't accept it was over. You started hanging around outside the college, you kept phoning her there. She was torn both ways, still very fond of you but knowing she mustn't let it start up again, that would spell disaster. In the end she did meet you once or twice, tried to get you to accept the fact that she wanted the whole thing finished with.

"You never went near Braithwaite last Friday. You drove straight over to Cannonbridge after you left the exhibition. You phoned the college for the second time that day. This time you spoke to Karen. You told her you'd be waiting outside, after class. She agreed to see you, but only for a moment.

"When she came out it was starting to rain. You told her to get in the car, you'd run her home, there could be no harm in that. She got in.

"On the way you began to beg and plead with her. Wouldn't she just meet you sometimes? It would be quite safe, no one need know. She was strongly tempted. She said yes, she would, then came to her senses again and told you no, she couldn't, it would be madness. If the Wilmots found out she'd be sent packing in disgrace. It was far too big a risk."

Kelsey stabbed at the air. "It was this on-again, off-again attitude, this chopping and changing as she sat beside you, that tipped you over the edge. You pulled up and made a lunge at her. She jumped out in fright and ran off, into the wood. You ran after her."

He sat back. "Afterwards you ran back to your car, jumped in and made for home."

Throughout it all Clayton had sat in trembling silence, slowly, ceaselessly, shaking his head. When the Chief had finished he made no reply but continued to shake his head.

The phone rang suddenly on his desk. He made no attempt to answer it. The sound went on. He suddenly reached out and lifted the receiver for an instant, silencing the instrument.

Kelsey glanced at his watch. Time to be getting back to the station. And he had an appointment later in the afternoon with the Social Services in Cannonbridge. He got to his feet and stood looking down at Clayton, who made no move.

"Any time you feel like changing your story," Kelsey told him, "get in touch. Any time, day or night. We'll be ready to listen."

Kelsey's appointment at the Social Services department was with the senior officer in overall charge of Karen's case after she had left Wychford and gone to live at Overmead. Also present was the young female social worker who had been responsible under his direction for visits and reports. She struck Kelsey as conscientious, dedicated to her work.

She had called at Jubilee Cottage on a number of occasions, had satisfied herself that Karen was settling in well, there were no problems. Her last visit had taken place eight days before Karen's death. She had called in the evening, had spoken to both the Wilmots as well as to Karen.

"She was very happy at the college," she told the Chief. "She liked the course, she felt confident of doing well. I asked if she had any difficulties with either of the Wilmots but she said far from it, they were both very kind, very helpful and supportive."

Neither she nor the senior officer seemed at all surprised or disconcerted when Kelsey told them he knew for a fact that Karen had had some contact with Paul Clayton in recent weeks. The department had no record of either of the Lorimers having at any time attempted to contact the girl.

Kelsey asked what the financial arrangement was between the department and the Wilmots.

"They were paid the usual fostering allowances," the senior officer told him. "In exactly the same way as her previous foster-parents were paid. The fact that Karen was related to the Wilmots didn't affect the allowances."

He turned a page in his file. "Wherever possible the department looks to the parents to reimburse at least some of these expenses. In Karen's case the trust fund paid over agreed sums to the department for her maintenance."

Kelsey sat up. "Trust fund?" he echoed.

"Yes. Her father set the fund up for her. I don't know the details but I'm sure her father's solicitor, Mr. Spedding, over in Okeshot, would tell you anything you wanted to know. He's a trustee, as well as being one of Karen's guardians. My impression is that Karen would have come into a very nice little nest-egg later on."

1 2

The inquest on Karen Boland took place on Tuesday morning, a brief, formal affair, the proceedings opened and adjourned, the body released for burial. After it was over Chief Inspector Kelsey caught up with the Wilmots as they were leaving the courthouse. He had looked in at Jubilee Cottage on Sunday morning to pass on the results of the post-mortem. He had found Ian working strenuously outdoors. Christine was upstairs in bed on doctor's orders, in a heavily sedated sleep.

Today Ian still looked shaken and shocked but Christine appeared reasonably calm and controlled—probably, the Chief guessed, still under the influence of tranquilizers.

He apologized for troubling them again but he must ask if they could tell him anything of a relationship between Karen and a mature student at the college, an Overmead resident named Desmond Hallam. He added that his inquiries at the college had indicated a slight, casual acquaintance between the two, scarcely warranting the term friendship. Did the Wilmots know of anything more?

No, they didn't. Karen had never so much as mentioned Hallam's name, they had no idea that he had sometimes given her a lift home. They did know who he was, and where he lived. They occasionally saw him or his aunt about the village; they had never exchanged more than a passing greeting with either of them. They had no idea where the aunt might have been living before she came to Hawthorn Lodge.

Kelsey continued on his way to the car park where Sergeant Lambert waited by the car. They set off at once for Okeshot where the Chief had arranged an appointment with Spedding, James Boland's solicitor.

Spedding's offices were housed in Victorian premises in a tree-line avenue a short distance from the centre of Okeshot. As the two policemen walked into the spacious reception hall the girl at the desk was talking to a man—clearly a member of staff—who stood holding a bundle of papers. He turned his head at their entrance and gave them a swift, raking glance from bright, restless eyes. A skinny, sharp-faced, youngish man, late thirties, perhaps. He stepped back a couple of paces as the Chief approached the desk. Kelsey told the girl that he had an appointment with Mr. Spedding.

"Oh yes, Chief Inspector," she said. "Mr. Spedding's expecting you. I'm sure Mr. Trewin here will take you along to his office."

Trewin sprang forward. "Certainly. If you'd like to follow me." He led them briskly along carpeted corridors, showed them into Spedding's office and took himself off.

Spedding stood up to greet them. An affable, urbane man in his sixties. Forty years of professional life had armoured him against shock and surprise, anything the vagaries of human nature might spring on him.

"This is a dreadful business," he said as they all seated themselves. "If there's anything at all I can do to help . . ." The Chief asked what he could tell him about Karen's background and history. In particular he would like details of the trust fund set up for her by her father.

"I knew James Boland for many years," Spedding told him. "Since we were both young men." He had been not only his solicitor but also his friend.

James Boland was born and bred in Okeshot, in a very run-down quarter of the town. It was a poverty-stricken, deprived background, his father a building labourer, a morose, hard-drinking man, his mother meek and downtrodden, taking refuge in piety, in hopes of a less miserable life to come.

There were two children of the marriage: James, and his brother Maurice, several years older. Maurice was very much his father's son, drifting into the same way of life, marrying a young woman as shiftless as himself, with a similar taste for public houses and betting shops.

James Boland, by sharp contrast, grew up ambitious, hard-working and thrifty, fanatically teetotal, strictly religious. He served his apprenticeship as a cabinetmaker, saved every penny he could lay his hands on, setting up in a business on his own, in a very modest way, when he was in his thirties. He married a girl from the local church, quiet and industrious, unassuming and undemanding, in every way supportive of her husband. She helped in the office side of the business, a small furniture manufactory. Nothing fancy or over-priced; sound, honest, everyday furniture, well designed, well made, long-lasting.

Boland bought a little house in Okeshot, never wanted to move to anything grander when the business prospered, never went in for formal entertaining, never developed extravagant tastes, a liking for ostentation. All the profits were ploughed back into the business.

James had one child, Karen, born after a long period of childless-ness, much wanted and loved. At the time of the birth Mrs. Boland was already forty, Boland forty-four.

When Karen was five Boland took his little family away for one of their rare seaside holidays. On the first day of the holiday Mrs. Boland bought herself a straw beach hat. As they were going back into the seafront boarding-house at lunch-time, Mrs. Boland follow-ing her husband who was holding Karen's hand, a sudden gust of breeze whisked off Mrs. Boland's hat. She turned and plunged after it, into the path of a car. Karen and Boland, half-way up the flight of steps, heard the squeal of brakes, the shouts and screams, looked back and saw her lying in the road. She died two days later in the local hospital.

"It was a tremendous shock for both of them," Spedding told the Chief. "It threw the pair of them very close together." Boland sank himself into his business, working harder than ever. He engaged a middle-aged woman, a respectable local widow who had brought up children of her own, a member of his own church congregation, to come in as a daily housekeeper. He never contemplated marrying again; he lived for Karen and the business.

A few years later he suffered a heart attack. He insisted on being given the truth and was told there was a good deal more wrong with his health than the state of his heart, there was no question of any useful surgery. He had a few months to live, a year at most.

He took the news without fuss or self-pity, his one thought was for

Karen. He thought things over thoroughly, then he sent for Spedding.

"He told me he thought of marrying his secretary," Spedding said. "He asked what I thought of the plan." The secretary—now Mrs. Enid Lorimer—was a spinster fifteen years Boland's junior; she had worked for him since leaving school. A quiet, efficient woman, loyal and conscientious, attending the same church. She had lived with her parents in a council house, had looked after them until their deaths, was now on her own in a little rented flat. Never a pretty woman—but Boland wasn't considering her for her looks—though always well groomed, always neat and presentable. She had never had any romantic attachment. Boland felt he could trust her absolutely, he would be leaving Karen in safe hands.

"We discussed the matter from every conceivable angle," Spedding continued. "I could see no objection and many advantages. So Boland went ahead and set the unadorned facts before his secretary. She took very little time to think it over, she was happy to agree. She sat in on the discussions about the setting up of a trust fund, the making of a new will. Her opinions were taken fully into account." The trustees of the fund were to be Spedding, and Boland's bank.

In the short time left to him Boland did his best to prepare Karen for the approaching marriage. Enid visited the house frequently, tried to gain the child's confidence. The ceremony was a very quiet one, in the local church; Spedding acted as best man. Boland died six months later.

"He never made a vast fortune in his business," Spedding explained. "It was always on a relatively modest scale." But Boland had always managed his finances well and in the last few years, when he had applied himself rigorously to work after the loss of his wife, he had begun to make real money. He had been approached more than once by larger concerns interested in a takeover, and there was no difficulty after his death in finding a buyer for the business at a very satisfactory price. The money released by the sale provided the basis of the trust.

Spedding summarized for the Chief the main conditions of the trust. Enid had the right to remain in the house as long as she lived. She was assured of an income for the rest of her life, sufficient to allow her the same standard of living as she had enjoyed during the time she was married to Boland.

Karen's general expenses, maintenance, education and so forth, were to be paid for from income generated by the fund. The greater part of the trust capital was to be divided into four unequal portions, the smallest to be released unconditionally to Karen at the age of eighteen, and the other three successively at twenty-one, twenty-five, and thirty.

"What happens now to the trust fund? And to the house?" Kelsey asked.

"The house passes to Enid. The trust is wound up and the capital split down the middle. One half goes to Enid, the other half to Boland's niece, Christine Wilmot."

13

Kelsey's head jerked up. "Is Christine aware of that?" he asked sharply.

Spedding spread his hands. "I have no reason to suppose so. She was certainly never informed of it by either James Boland or myself. There was no mention of her in Boland's will, no bequest. She has never made any kind of inquiry about the trust at this office. I don't imagine she's aware of its existence." As joint guardian of Karen, Spedding had had dealings with Christine at the time the approach was made to her concerning the possibility of Karen going to live at Jubilee Cottage, but Spedding had never made any mention of the existence of the trust, let alone the possibility that she could in certain circumstances benefit under it. There was no direct connection between the payments made by the trust to the Social Services for Karen's maintenance and the fostering allowances the Wilmots received from the department. All transactions under the trust were highly confidential.

"Christine's father, Maurice Boland, had made more than one attempt over the years to cadge money from his brother," Spedding continued, "but he had no success. James never wanted anything to do with his brother or sister-in-law. Maurice is dead now, and his wife, they both died before James Boland." Maurice had drunk himself into his grave, with shrieking DTs at the end. His wife followed him twelve months later. James hadn't attended either funeral.

Christine was already grown up and married at the time of James Boland's death. "She turned out a lot better than might have been expected," Spedding commented. Although James Boland had had nothing to do with the family, he was nevertheless aware of Christine's progress. He felt she showed character, had taken charge of her life in a direct and sensible fashion. The moment her schooldays were over she had left home and gone into digs, had got herself a job behind the counter in a dry-cleaner's shop, rising to manageress before she married Ian Wilmot. A couple of years after the marriage Wilmot was transferred to Cannonbridge.

"Does Wilmot come from Okeshot?" Kelsey asked.

Spedding nodded. "His parents keep a village store a few miles from here. I had some knowledge of Wilmot from when he worked in the planning department here in Okeshot. We still have occasional dealings with him now, in the Cannonbridge office. Planning applications, property development, disposals under wills and settlements, that kind of thing. It's usually Trewin who deals with Wilmot now, he goes over there to see him sometimes. He and Wilmot were at school together, here in Okeshot. You met Trewin just now, he brought you in here." He sat back in his chair. "I was able to give Wilmot a good reference to the Social Services when the question came up about Karen going to live with them at Jubilee Cottage."

Kelsey inquired about the circumstances of Enid's second marriage.

"Enid and Karen lived together for a couple of years after Boland's death before she remarried," Spedding told him. "Karen seemed to accept Enid well enough and Enid always did her best for the girl, but it was never a close relationship. Lorimer worked in the public library here in Okeshot, he was a member of the same church as Enid. She came here and talked the whole thing over with me when she first thought of marrying Lorimer. I was her solicitor after Boland's death, and of course we had dealings from time to time as joint guardians of Karen. Enid was clearly very much in love with Lorimer but she didn't rush into the marriage. She thought it over very carefully, she tried to see it from Karen's point of view as well as her own. She brought Lorimer with her one day, to introduce him to me."

He made a little downward turn of his lips. "I must admit it seemed to me a good thing all round. It's easy enough now with hindsight to wonder if Lorimer's motive in marrying Enid was to gain easy access to Karen, but such a thought never entered my head at the time. I believed he took a normal, genuine interest in Karen, that he was really fond of Enid. I knew of nothing against him. He was well mannered, well spoken, decently educated, well read and well informed, very attentive to Enid, not at all bad-looking. I was very pleased for Enid, I thought it would work out very well. I spoke to Karen about it and she expressed no objection." In due course Spedding was invited to the wedding. The marriage made no difference to Enid's financial position under the terms of the trust or of Boland's will.

"Everything appeared to go swimmingly for a time," Spedding went on. "Whenever I spoke to Karen she never gave the slightest sign that anything was wrong. And Enid seemed very happy. I never had the impression she suspected anything might be amiss." He grimaced. "Then six months later—whoosh! The whole shebang went up!"

He sighed and shook his head. "Enid simply could not accept the fact that Lorimer could possibly be guilty. She had to believe he loved her, that his only motive in marrying her was love. She couldn't tolerate the notion that the presence of a young girl in the household might have been the real reason.

"I was brought into it at an early stage, both as Karen's guardian and Enid's solicitor. Lorimer also considered me to be his solicitor by virtue of his marriage to Enid—certainly he had no other solicitor at the time. He and Enid came running to see me. Karen was inventing it all, fantasizing. She was jealous, resented the arrival of Lorimer in the household, and so on."

He shook his head again. "But there was the medical examination, the undeniable fact of the pregnancy. Enid could scarcely put that down to invention or fantasy. I spoke to Karen on her own several times. Allowing for the situation in which she found herself, she seemed reasonably steady and composed, she was certainly never hysterical. I thought she took it all very stoically for such a young girl. She never departed from her story. It all seemed to me to hang together."

He gave the Chief a look laced with significance. "Then other episodes came to light about Lorimer, about his past. It turned out he was not quite what he had seemed. There had been other young girls—but I expect you know all about that. Even in the face of that, Enid still wouldn't—or, more likely, couldn't—believe he was guilty.

"She insisted that I take on the case, that I act for Lorimer. I had to point out that as one of Karen's guardians, to say nothing of being a long-time friend of her father, I could scarcely take up a legal posture whereby I would in effect be challenging Karen in favour of Lorimer. Enid got very agitated, accused me of prejudging the case, having a closed mind, and so on.

"Neither Enid nor Lorimer had access to any sizable amount of capital and she demanded that I should release capital from the trust fund, enough to allow her to engage a top QC to defend Lorimer.

"I told her I had no such powers, even if I had wished to do such a thing, which I certainly did not. I had no doubt whatever of Lorimer's guilt and I couldn't see how anyone else could have. I very plainly told her so. In any case a top QC's fees, apart from being a total waste of money in the face of such evident guilt, would be astronomical. They wouldn't take long to extinguish the whole of the trust fund."

"How did she take that?" Kelsey asked.

"She was quite beside herself. She took violent exception to my attitude." He grimaced. "It was a great revelation to me. I'd always seen her as very disciplined, quiet, self-effacing. To find her capable of such animus, such strength of feeling . . ." He shook his head reflectively. "She ceased there and then to employ me as her solicitor. She told me she would take her business—and Lorimer's business—elsewhere. Of course she was still obliged to maintain some contact with me because of the trust and the guardianship. She always remained one of Karen's guardians, even though Karen had been taken into care. She's always been very formal with me since that day, courteous but very cold. She's never forgiven me."

"Did she find another solicitor willing to take on Lorimer's case?"

Spedding permitted himself a hint of a smile. "The legal grapevine's very efficient. I soon learned she went straight off from this office to the local Law Centre. The man she saw there isn't one of these dewy-eyed, newly-fledged young men ready to take a tilt at anything, he's an experienced, hard-nosed man. He told her bluntly that Lorimer hadn't a snowball's chance in hell of getting away with it.

"He strongly advised Lorimer to plead guilty. That way there wouldn't be the need for Karen to be put through further ordeal, and Lorimer would almost certainly get a shorter sentence." He waved a hand. "If Lorimer had any thoughts of trying to make out in court that he'd received any kind of encouragement from Karen, that she'd led him on in any way, he'd better forget them, he'd be lucky to escape being torn limb from limb by outraged females if he persisted in that kind of tale. Lorimer finally accepted the advice and pleaded guilty."

He sighed again. "I was very sorry for Enid—I still am, come to that. She had a hard time of it from start to last. In many ways the hardest time of all must be starting now, with Lorimer out of gaol, trying to make a new life. He's not going to find it easy. But at least she has Lorimer's company now. She found herself very isolated and lonely after he went to prison. She gave up what social life she had, and her charitable work. She has the temperament to feel that kind of notoriety very keenly. Some people can harden themselves to it, but she couldn't."

"When she had to choose between Karen and Lorimer, did she have any conflict?"

"As far as I could tell, none at all. She unhesitatingly chose Lorimer. I can't say I was surprised. When Karen realized she'd have to stay in care till she was old enough to be independent, she told me she'd like to be moved away from this area, she'd feel better able to make a fresh start elsewhere. It seemed the best thing in all the circumstances, so she was sent to foster-parents, the Roscoes."

He looked reflective. "I knew Karen from the day she was born. She was a merry, outgoing, trusting child. Then, one by one, things happened to her over the years. The terrible shock of her mother's death. The realization that her father was going to die. His hasty marriage to Enid. His death soon afterwards. Enid's marriage to Lorimer, with all that flowed from that. Everything served, step by step, to turn her from that merry, trusting, little girl, into the quiet, wary, reserved young woman she was the last time I saw her." Kelsey saw the glitter of a tear in his eye.

Spedding had last seen Karen some three weeks earlier. He had had business in the Cannonbridge area so he had arranged an appointment with Karen and the Wilmots at Jubilee Cottage for the early evening. He had chatted to them together and separately, had been at pains to assure himself all was well.

Kelsey asked if Spedding had spoken to Karen about the Paul Clayton episode at the time the relationship came to light.

Yes, he had spoken to her. He had gone over to the Roscoes' as soon as he heard of it, to hear Karen's side of it. He made a deprecatory gesture. "I thought the whole thing grossly exaggerated. A typical uproar on the part of virtuous females.

"I was delighted when she went to the Wilmots not long afterwards. I thought she had a good chance at last of feeling she had a real home again, of putting down some roots. Christine was hesitant at first about taking Karen. She felt it would be a great responsibility. But Ian thought it would be a good thing for the girl, that she'd fit in well. He set about persuading Christine and before long she got quite keen on the idea. I'm sure they both grew genuinely fond of Karen. I believe it was working out very well."

Kelsey asked what were the circumstances in which Enid had left the house in Okeshot and moved to Furzebank Cottage.

"She came to see me about it back in the summer," Spedding told him. "She was anxious to leave Okeshot altogether, to cut all links with the past. She wanted to have a home ready and waiting somewhere else for Lorimer when he came out of prison. She knew she had only a lifetime right to occupy the Okeshot house, she didn't own it, but she wanted to know if it would be possible under the trust for the house to be sold and another bought elsewhere, her right to occupancy being transferred to the new house."

He shook his head. "I told her that wasn't possible under the very precise terms of the trust and will, but there was nothing to stop her renting out the Okeshot house and using the money to rent another elsewhere. The Okeshot house could be rented out on a shorthold tenancy, or, if necessary, on a succession of shorthold tenancies, so that if she later changed her mind and decided to come back again to Okeshot to live, she could always regain possession."

He waved a hand. "For all I knew, her attitude to Lorimer might change completely after he came out of prison. They hadn't been married long before the trouble blew up, and Lorimer would certainly come out of prison a very different man from the one who went in." He smiled slightly. "Of course I didn't spell those thoughts out to her. She jumped at the idea of renting out the Okeshot house and asked if I knew of any suitable property for herself and Lorimer. I pointed out that tax would have to be paid on the rent received, reducing the amount available for renting another house. The Okeshot property is very modest and can't command a high rent, so she wasn't likely to find anything very grand for the money, in fact she'd be lucky to find anything at all. She said she didn't mind what it was like, old, dilapidated, small—but it must be secluded, preferably isolated. I told her I'd do my best. I found Furzebank Cottage a week or two later, and she took it at once."

There was a knock at the door and a clerk entered. She apologized for disturbing them, went over to the desk and spoke to Spedding in a low voice. He looked across at Kelsey.

"Are we likely to be much longer?" he asked. "A client has called to see me on urgent business."

Kelsey stood up. "We'll be getting along, we've just about covered everything. We very much appreciate your help, it's been most useful. We'll see ourselves out."

Outside in the corridor he glanced at his watch: twenty minutes to one. At the reception desk he asked the girl if Mr. Trewin was about. She offered to get him and a minute or two later Trewin came into the hall.

"We'd like a word with you," Kelsey told him without preamble.

Trewin's manner was far from cooperative. He was very busy, he had papers to deal with at top speed, papers a client was impatiently waiting for. Kelsey asked what time he went off for lunch.

"One o'clock," Trewin answered reluctantly.

Kelsey asked where he went, if he used a car. With even greater reluctance Trewin named a nearby pub, adding that he walked there.

Kelsey crossed to the window and jabbed a finger over at a street corner. "We'll be parked down that turning. You come over there, one o'clock sharp. We'll run you out somewhere quiet, we won't keep you many minutes. We'll drop you back at your pub after we've had a talk."

Trewin glanced nervously along the corridor. He looked about to protest or refuse.

"Yes or no?" Kelsey demanded. "I can always go back in there"— he jerked his head in the direction of Spedding's office—"and get your boss to send for you, say what I have to say to you in front of him."

Trewin's brow broke into perspiration. "All right, then." His voice was sullen. "I'll be across the road in ten minutes."

"If you decide not to show up," the Chief warned, "we'll be in through these doors again the minute Spedding gets back from lunch. Never you doubt it."

Trewin didn't appear to doubt it. As one o'clock struck from a church tower he came into view, striding rapidly along the pavement. He reached the car and Kelsey flung open the rear door.

"In here!" he commanded. Trewin got in beside him, turning his head from the gaze of any curious passer-by. He sat well back in the corner, with a hand up to shield his face.

"You know why we came here today to talk to Spedding," the Chief began as Lambert set the car in motion.

Trewin nodded.

"You are a friend, a friend of long standing, of Ian Wilmot, Jubilee Cottage, Overmead?"

This time there was a perceptible pause before Trewin again nodded. He looked extremely uneasy.

"You are aware of the existence of a trust set up by the late James Boland for the benefit of his daughter Karen?"

A somewhat longer pause, then again a nod. Trewin shifted in his seat.

"Earlier this year an approach was made to the Wilmots, to see if they would be willing to foster Karen Boland." Trewin sat silent and motionless. "I put it to you that Ian Wilmot immediately contacted you to ask you to ferret out the details of the trust, that you did ferret out the details—highly confidential details—and passed them on to Wilmot."

Trewin's eyes roved about. "That isn't how it was," he said at last in a tone of protest.

"Then how was it?"

Trewin jerked out a hand. "Ian happened to be over here in the ordinary course of his duties. He called in at the pub where I go for lunch. He just wanted a chat, that was all." He came to a halt, he had to be prompted by the Chief before he continued.

"It just so happened that a few days before, the Social Services asked Mr. Spedding his opinion of the Wilmots as possible foster-parents for Karen Boland. Mr. Spedding mentioned this to me, as I've known both Ian and Christine a good many years. He wanted to know what sort of housekeeper Christine was, was she fond of children, what interests they had, that sort of thing. We had quite a chat about it, he wanted to satisfy himself he could recommend them." He fell silent again, again had to be prompted.

"I just happened to mention this to Ian in the pub," he went on with growing reluctance. "And he asked me—very casually—about the trust fund. It was all perfectly harmless, we were just chatting."

"How did Wilmot know there was a trust fund?"

Trewin looked extremely uncomfortable. "I'm not sure," he ventured at last. "It could have been something the Social Services people said to him. Or—" his tone suddenly increased in confidence as if he had hit on a brilliant inspiration—"he could have worked it out for himself. He would always have known from Christine that James Boland had done well in life, he must have left plenty of money. It stands to reason he'd have set up a trust for Karen, she was his only child."

"So you obligingly supplied Wilmot with all the details—in case there was any little point he might not have been able to work out correctly for himself."

"No, not then," Trewin put in defensively. "I don't go round carrying in my head all the details of every trust we've drawn up— and it was some years since we drew up the Boland trust."

"So you went back to the office and discreetly looked up the details for him."

Trewin made no reply, he sat chewing his lip.

"And then what? Did you phone Wilmot?"

He shook his head. "He phoned me at home that evening."

"And you gave him all the details then?"

Trewin drew a long, miserable breath, then gave a couple of despairing nods.

"So the end result of all this casual chat, all this just happening to mention this and that, all this idle inquiry, was that by the end of the same day Wilmot had ferreted out from you, a confidential clerk, the precise details of the Boland trust?"

Trewin's forehead was beaded with sweat. "I suppose so," he conceded after several moments had slipped by.

"I don't want any supposing about it," Kelsey persisted. "Did he or did he not ferret out the precise details?"

"Yes, he did," Trewin was forced to admit. He suddenly darted a glance at Kelsey with the air of a badgered animal. "I saw no real harm in it," he flung out defiantly. "I still see no real harm in it. If Christine had gone to see Mr. Spedding, if she had asked him openly for the details of the trust, he'd very probably have told her —or at least he'd have told her the details that affect her personally."

"Ah!" Kelsey rejoined softly. "But Christine didn't go to see Spedding, she didn't ask him openly for the details of the trust." He stabbed a finger at the lapel of Trewin's jacket. "Instead, Ian went to see you."

14

Shortly before six o'clock Sergeant Lambert drove the Chief out to Overmead. Downstairs lights shone out from Jubilee Cottage as Lambert turned in through the gates. They got out of the car and Lambert pressed the bell. The curtains were not drawn in the sitting-room on the right of the front door. Lambert could see a television set switched on, an announcer giving out the news.

The door opened and Ian Wilmot looked out at them. Kelsey asked if they might come inside for a few minutes. Ian stepped aside at once for them to enter. He didn't appear disconcerted or displeased.

"I'm afraid Christine isn't here," he explained as he took them into the sitting-room where his interrupted meal was set out on a tray in front of the television. An inviting, savoury smell hung in the air. "She's out on her rounds," he added as he switched off the television. "If you'll excuse me, I'll just put my supper back in the oven." His tone was amiable, his manner relaxed. He invited them to sit down and took the tray out to the kitchen, returning a minute later to ask if they'd like any refreshment. Kelsey declined the offer and Ian sat down facing them, settling comfortably back into an easy chair.

"Christine's still pretty upset about it all," he said. "Only to be expected, of course. The doctor advised her to carry on as normally as possible. I'm sure that's the best thing. It does no good to sit around moping—and she doesn't want to let her customers down."

Kelsey responded to these remarks with an abrupt question: "What do you know of the financial situation of Karen Boland?"

Ian's eyes blinked open.

"Did she, for instance, have any financial expectations?"

Ian glanced about the room. He guesses we've talked to Spedding by now, Sergeant Lambert thought, but he doesn't know if we've talked to Trewin—or, more precisely, if Trewin's talked to us.

"I believe she may have had," Ian replied easily. "I have a notion Christine mentioned something about it."

"Are you not at this moment familiar with the exact terms of the trust fund set up by James Boland for his daughter?"

A slight pause before Ian answered in the same easy tone. "Yes, I think perhaps I do recall them."

"Did you raise the matter with Spedding's clerk, Trewin, immediately after you were approached about the possibility of Karen coming to live here?"

Ian moved his head with the air of someone recalling a trifling act. "Yes, I believe Trewin did raise the matter."

"Trewin raised it? Was it not you who raised it with Trewin?"

"No. It was definitely Trewin who raised it. I knew nothing about the trust, I didn't even know it existed, so I could hardly have raised the matter." He sounded mildly injured. "I was over in Okeshot on business. I thought I'd look in at one of my old stamping-grounds, see if I could catch Trewin, have a chat with him. I told him about Karen getting in touch with us. I knew he'd be interested, working for Boland's solicitor." He waved a hand. "He may have said more than he should, strictly speaking, but he knew it would go no further." He grinned. "We're all human."

"You are aware that under the terms of the trust one half of the capital sum comes to your wife as soon as the trust is wound up—which must now be done, as Karen is dead."

Ian inclined his head judicially. "I believe that may be so. But the idea that Christine might actually benefit under the trust never crossed my mind. Karen was a healthy young girl, years younger than Christine."

"Your wife wasn't at all keen to take Karen, at first, but after you talked to Trewin you got to work on your wife, persuaded her to take pity on the girl, give her a chance."

He shook his head vigorously. "Nothing of the sort. You're making all kinds of insinuations. There isn't a shred of truth in any of them."

"Did you pass on to your wife the details of the trust which you had learned from Trewin?"

Ian hesitated, he looked far from comfortable.

"It's a straightforward question. Either you did or you did not pass on the details."

"You're talking about a time months back," Ian protested. "We discussed the possibility of Karen coming to live here from all sorts of angles. We talked about all kinds of old family matters, they came up naturally at that time. I know I told Christine I'd seen Trewin. She was very interested, she knew Trewin quite well over in Okeshot. And I remember telling her there was a trust, but whether she asked me for details or whether I passed any of them on to her, I can't remember now. If she asked me, then it's very likely I told her. I can't honestly say it loomed all that large in my thoughts. I didn't think it was of overwhelming significance."

Kelsey suddenly darted at him from another angle. "Did you phone Karen at the college last Friday evening? To tell her something had cropped up, you had to talk to her, you'd be waiting outside at six o'clock?"

"I certainly did not. I never went near the college on Friday."

The Chief took him back in minute detail over his movements on Friday afternoon. Ian told him the location of the various sites he had visited, the time he had spent at each one, the names of those he had met and spoken to.

He had left the last site—some eight miles to the southwest of Cannonbridge—at around a quarter to six and set off for home. After he had driven a couple of miles it occurred to him that he couldn't recall putting his builder's rule and fifty-metre measuring tape back in the boot of the car on the last site.

He pulled up, got out and looked in the boot. The items were not there. He cast his mind back. He could remember setting them down on a bench outside the site office while he went inside with the foreman to look at plans. They had spent some time in the office, they were still deep in discussion when they came out again. The foreman locked up and Ian walked with him across to the foreman's car, still talking. The foreman drove off and Ian got into his own car, completely forgetting the tape and the rule.

He couldn't simply abandon them, they were the property of the department. By morning some sharp-eyed prowling lad would have spotted them and borne them off. He turned the car round and went back to the deserted site. The tape and measure were there on the bench. He put them away in the boot and set off again for home. He recalled looking at his watch as he did so—the delay had irritated him and there might not now be time for the hot bath and good meal he needed to restore him for the meeting. But it was not too bad, his watch showed a couple of minutes before six. He checked the time again as he opened the front door of Jubilee Cottage; it was twenty-five past six.

He had his bath, put on clean clothes, ate a substantial meal, cleared the table and washed up. He was a little late setting off for the meeting; it had already begun when he arrived at the hall around twenty minutes to eight. He supplied the names of the chairman and various committee members who could vouch for the fact that he had attended the meeting.

Kelsey asked if he always drove home on a Friday afternoon from the last site he visited, if it wasn't more usual for him to return first to his office. Ian didn't answer immediately. "We can check with your boss," Kelsey reminded him.

Ian moved his head. "It depends how many sites there are, what time I finish. If it's early enough I do go back to the office, I make a start on my reports. If it's getting on for five, or later, I come straight home."

"How often in the last couple of months have you driven straight home on a Friday?"

"Once or twice, maybe."

"If at all," the Chief hazarded. Ian made no reply.

On the way back to the Cannonbridge station, as the Chief sat brooding beside him, something stirred in Lambert's brain.

"There's a woman who knows my landlady," he said. "Comes to see her sometimes. They serve together on various committees, charities, good works. The woman's name is Mrs. Sheldrake."

Kelsey came out of his absorption. "What about this Mrs. Sheldrake?"

"She has a daughter, Eunice. I'm pretty certain Eunice works in the Cannonbridge planning office. Clerical or secretarial work."

"Does she though?" The Chief suddenly snapped into sharp concentration. "What kind of person is this Eunice?"

Lambert made a face. "Not my cup of tea. She's a spinster, forty, forty-five, no raving beauty, an acid type. I don't know her all that well. My landlady has the pair of them round to Sunday tea now and again. Eunice teaches Sunday school, they're both strong church people. The mother's a widow, her husband was an insurance broker, they're pretty well-heeled. Mrs. Sheldrake has a very good opinion of herself, very forthright views. I've always made my escape as quickly as possible." In his time he'd had to endure Mrs. Sheldrake's views on the Brazilian rain forest, community policing, the conservation of wetlands, modern methods of education, the preservation of dolphins, and a great many other topics; it hadn't helped to digest his tea.

The Chief struck his hands together. "Just the ticket!" he exclaimed with relish. "Can you get your landlady to invite the pair of them for tea this coming Sunday?"

"I'll see what I can do." The sergeant's landlady was a shrewd, active, naturally inquisitive woman who had trained herself over the years into a necessary degree of restraint and discretion. Since he had become her lodger, Lambert had further trained her to ask him no questions—or, at least, none directly connected with his work. He foresaw no difficulty in persuading her to arrange the tea-party. Nothing the good lady would enjoy more than being allowed, however briefly, however slightly, to stir a finger in any little pie Lambert might be baking.

"And this time," Kelsey added with energy, "there'll be no question of you making your escape."

15

Immediately after briefings on Wednesday morning the Chief set about checking Ian Wilmot's account of his movements on Friday afternoon. They tracked down the foreman from the last site Ian had visited but the man couldn't be exact about the time Ian had left. He did recall that they had had a lively discussion and that Ian had gone with him into the site office to look at the plans. He hadn't noticed Ian setting down his rule and tape on the bench outside the office. Yes, Ian had walked with him to his car. As he drove away he saw Ian walk across to his own car. "I'd put it at around five-thirty when I drove off," he concluded. "But I certainly couldn't swear to it."

Kelsey asked if he had noticed the time when he reached home.

He hadn't gone straight home. He was a widower, living alone, he had stopped, as he often did, at a transport café for a meal. He hadn't checked the time at any stage, he'd had no reason to.

Nor could Kelsey come across anyone who could tell him exactly when Ian arrived at the meeting, though there was no doubt that he had attended the meeting and had gone along afterwards to the home of the chairman. Nothing in his behaviour during the evening had aroused any comment, had appeared in any way unusual or remarkable.

"The whole thing's pretty inconclusive," the Chief pronounced with dissatisfaction as they headed back to Cannonbridge. "That tale about forgetting the rule and the tape could be a complete fairy-story. Ian could have left the site as early as five-thirty, driven straight over to Cannonbridge, stopping on the way to phone Karen at the college, tell her some tale, any tale, something had happened to Christine, some emergency had cropped up, she'd have to get home pronto at the end of classes, he'd drive her home himself, he'd be waiting outside at six."

"That note Karen passed to Lynn Musgrove after she came back from the phone," Lambert said. " 'Can't come home with you this evening. I've got to meet someone.' If it was Ian who phoned her, don't you think she'd have written something like: 'I have to get home straight after class, something's cropped up. Ian's picking me up.' . . ."

Kelsey gave a grunt. "Possibly. But Karen doesn't strike me as a girl who would ever be inclined to spell out any little bit of her business to anyone if she didn't have to." Karen might have started out in life as an outgoing, merry, trusting, little girl, but all the evidence went to show that along the way she had definitely acquired a strong taste for secrecy—as well as a taste for keeping all the compartments of her life separate.

If was after four when they left the station again, bound for Overmead. The afternoon was dark and overcast, lights gleamed from dwellings along the way.

But no lights showed in the windows of Jubilee Cottage. Nevertheless they rang and knocked, kept on knocking and ringing. At last a light appeared in a front bedroom and a few minutes later they heard slow footsteps inside the house.

The door opened to reveal Christine Wilmot huddled into a woollen dressing-gown. Her face was flushed and shiny, her eyes heavy, the skin around them puffy. She looked far from well.

She gazed lethargically out at them. "I was having a rest before I have to go out again," she told them flatly. "I must have dropped off."

Kelsey apologized for disturbing her and asked if they might come in.

She made no move to admit them. "Ian's not here," she pointed out. "He's still at work."

"It's you we want to talk to," Kelsey said. She made no reply but held the door wide for them to enter.

Inside the sitting-room the Chief began by asking if she was aware of the existence of a trust set up by James Boland for his daughter. Christine gave a weary nod.

"When did you first learn of the existence of the trust?" Kelsey asked. "Think well before you answer. I want to know the very first time you ever heard anything to suggest that such a trust existed." She leaned back in her chair. "Ian said something about it when it was first suggested that Karen might come here to live. He heard about it from a friend of ours called Trewin, he's a clerk in Mr. Spedding's office in Okeshot. Ian was over there one day and he ran into Trewin. He told him about Karen and Trewin mentioned the trust."

"Did your husband tell you in detail the terms of the trust?" She shook her head slowly.

"Weren't you interested?"

She gazed at him expressionlessly. "Not particularly. I was pleased that Karen would have some money coming to her, but I always imagined she would have. Her father had done well in business, he always lived very quietly, I thought he must have a lot put by. I took it for granted he'd have made good provision for his only child."

"Did your husband tell you that in the event of Karen's death half the trust capital would come to you?"

She stared at him. "I have no recollection that he ever told me that. If he did, then I certainly paid no attention to it. It would have seemed far too remote a possibility, Karen was less than half my age."

"You're inheriting it now," Kelsey said.

The colour rose in her cheeks. She spoke up with sudden challenge. "I've no idea how much that money amounts to, or what we'll do with it. We certainly never wanted it—and we certainly don't need it. I'd give every penny of it to bring Karen back." The colour ebbed again. She looked pale and exhausted.

"You weren't at all anxious to take Karen in here at first," Kelsey observed. "Why was that?"

She said nothing for some moments, then she answered in a low voice. "When Karen got in touch, it brought back painful memories I thought I'd turned my back on for good. I didn't have a happy childhood, I was never on good terms with my parents." She put a hand up to her face. "They drank. And gambled. Both of them. My father only had a labourer's wages—when he had any wages at all. You can imagine the rest of it.

"I cleared out as soon as I could, I was determined to have nothing more to do with my family, I wanted to make my own way in life. After I was married, when Ian was offered the chance of moving over to the Cannonbridge office, I was the one that wanted the move, Ian wasn't all that keen. I couldn't wait to leave Okeshot, to turn my back on the past."

She gave a long, trembling sigh. "I've never set foot in the town since the day we left. I never even went to the funeral of either of my parents."

She pressed her hands together. "But that doesn't mean you can forget it all, blot it all out. It doesn't mean you don't suffer terrible guilt. You can push it all to the back of your mind, you can kid yourself you've got over it, it's all in the past, over and done with." She made a bleak little gesture. "But it's all there, somewhere, still. It bubbles up sometimes, you can never get rid of it completely."

She put a hand across her eyes. "That was why I didn't want to take Karen at first. I felt as if it would pull me back into the past. The very fact that she wrote to me, just that first letter, started Ian talking to me about my family." She took out a handkerchief and dabbed at her eyes. "It was natural enough. He was interested in Karen, in her background. He knew the bare outlines of my childhood but I'd never really talked about it to him, I always wanted to forget it."

She put her handkerchief away. "Ian took the line that it might be a good thing for me to face the past. If I took a really good look at it it might not haunt me any more. After all, there was no one else left, just me and Karen. Why not take her in? Maybe we could help her. She'd had a rotten time too."

Her tone grew firmer. "I began to think maybe Ian was right, maybe I could help Karen and at the same time help myself. So I agreed to have her to stay for a weekend, see what she was like, how we all got on."

She gave a tremulous smile. "I was so nervous. But the moment I saw her I felt it was going to be all right." She suddenly broke into loud, racking sobs. She lowered her head and gave way to them. Kelsey waited in silence until the sobbing had died away.

She exhaled a long breath, took out her handkerchief again and dried her eyes. She gave him all at once a warm, glowing smile.

"You've no idea," she said in a lively voice, "how much better I feel, just telling you all that." She shook her head. "It's been like a dreadful nightmare since Karen died, I've felt so muddled, so confused. I think now I might be able to come to terms with it."

"Was it your husband who persuaded you in the end to foster Karen?" Kelsey asked.

"No, not really. It was that first moment when I met her. I saw she was just a lovely young girl who'd somehow got herself into a mess. She had nothing at all to do with the bad old days of my childhood, she wasn't even born then. She was just herself, needing a home, wanting a family to love her. We stood there and looked at each other. I knew then I was going to take her—and love her. I knew it would be all right."

She leaned back again. "It was all going so well." Her voice was full of sadness. "She would have had a good life here."

Kelsey asked about her husband's movements on Friday afternoon and evening but she could give them no assistance. She had left the house shortly after lunch, hadn't returned till almost midnight. She couldn't even tell the Chief what time Ian normally came home on a Friday; she was always out herself.

She didn't come with them to the door when they left but remained sunk into her chair.

"There's the other half of the trust money," the Chief said grimly as they got into the car again. "The half that goes to Enid Lorimer. And there's no doubt whatever that Enid knew every last detail of the trust fund."

Victor Lorimer had served his sentence in a prison twenty-five miles to the north-east of Cannonbridge, a large, mid-Victorian building of grey granite, sombre-faced, with a great many tiny, barred eyes.

The Chief had an appointment to see the deputy governor at eleven on Thursday morning. He also spoke, during his visit, to the prison chaplain, and to a warder who had known Lorimer.

According to the deputy governor, Lorimer's attitude when he entered prison had been neutral; certainly not positively cooperative, but he had never displayed any overt rebellion. He had been a very quiet, silent prisoner, obeying all the rules, determined not to lose a single day of remission. He hadn't spent his time protesting his innocence, attempting to get his case reviewed, making appeals to members of staff or prison visitors. He had tried to keep his head down and get through his sentence as best he could. He was given a job in the prison library and had worked well there.

But it was rarely possible for a man sentenced for sex offences to escape the attention of other prisoners, however hard he tried to keep a low profile. Lorimer had been in prison only a few weeks when he was attacked in the showers, slashed about the body. He was moved to the hospital wing. Later, when he had recovered, he asked to be segregated from the other prisoners. He was prepared to serve the rest of his sentence in solitary but that hadn't proved necessary. He was found a job in the hospital wing and remained there until his release.

Nine or ten months after Lorimer began his sentence his mother died. It seemed that her health had broken down under the strain of her son's trial. She had gone steadily downhill and was never well enough to visit Lorimer in prison, although she wrote to him faithfully. According to the chaplain, her death had a shattering effect on Lorimer. "He became seriously depressed," he told the Chief, "but I couldn't get him to talk about it." Lorimer had been offered psychiatric help and counselling, opportunities for group therapy, but he would have none of it. He had somehow slogged his way up through the depression by his own unaided efforts.

"His wife came regularly to see him," the chaplain added. "She never missed a visiting day. She was very concerned about him, very devoted. You don't often see that when a man's committed the sort of offence Lorimer was sentenced for. Very few marriages survive that kind of trauma."

Far from seeking solace in religion, Lorimer had completely turned his back on religion in all its manifestations. "My wife has been a good churchwoman all her life," he told the chaplain with great bitterness. "But that didn't stop her being driven out of all her church groups and activities because of me. She even had to give up attending church services, because of the whispers. What had she done? What crime had she committed? Nothing, nothing at all. That's the true face of religion for you."

Kelsey asked the warder if he could tell him of any prisoner who had known Lorimer and might be willing to talk about him. The warder mentioned an old lag by the name of Barny Pringle who had left prison a week ago. Pringle had worked in the hospital wing, had shared a cell with Lorimer during the final part of Lorimer's sentence. Pringle's address on release was in a town eight miles to the east of the prison.

The address, when they located it shortly before one o'clock, turned out to be that of a shop in a rough area of the town. Double-fronted premises dealing in men's working clothes. Every inch of window space crammed with jeans, corduroys, tweed trousers, flannelette shirts, piles of large, coarse handkerchiefs in dark serviceable colours. The entrance was festooned with heavy boots of tan leather, wellingtons, donkey jackets, string vests. The Chief left the car parked right outside, where he could keep a watchful eye on it.

The shopkeeper glanced up at the clock as they came in. "I'm closing for lunch in five minutes," he warned. The shop was empty except for a couple of girls shrieking and giggling in front of a wall mirror as they tried on a selection of men's cloth caps.

The Chief discreetly disclosed his identity and indicated that he would be happy to wait until the girls had departed and the door had been locked behind them.

"Well, now," the shopkeeper said a few minutes later when the girls had gone on their way, still giggling and shrieking, in their new caps. "What can I do for you?"

The Chief asked if he had a man named Barny Pringle lodging with him. Yes, Barny did have a room at the back, but he wasn't here at present. The shopkeeper couldn't tell them where he was or when he would be back. He had known Barny a good many years, he always let him have a room in between his spells in gaol. "He seemed very nervous this time when he came out," he added. Barny hadn't been very forthcoming, he had given the impression of some kind of vendetta being afoot. After a few uneasy days he had decided to take himself off for a week or two, give things a chance to settle down.

Kelsey assured the shopkeeper that it wasn't Pringle himself they were interested in, merely in what he might be able to tell them about another ex-prisoner; their inquiries concerned the brutal killing of a young girl.

As soon as the shopkeeper heard mention of the death of a young girl, his manner underwent a marked change, becoming on the instant a great deal more cooperative.

"Barny said he'd give me a ring from time to time," he volunteered. "To find out if anyone's come calling here, looking for him, if I've noticed anyone hanging round the shop." As soon as Pringle phoned the shopkeeper would find out where he was and at once ring the Cannonbridge police.

When they left the clothes shop they found a café where they had a bite to eat. Afterwards they drove across country to the Fairdeal supermarket which the Lorimers claimed to have visited on Friday afternoon.

Kelsey produced the garments the Lorimers said they had bought there and showed them to the manager. He was able to tell them that the underwear came from their regular stock and could have been bought any day since the supermarket opened a couple of months ago.

The case was somewhat different with the shirt and sweater. They were part of a consignment of chance-bought merchandise. Such goods were always disposed of quickly, heaped up in open baskets at strategic points along the aisles.

The lot from which Lorimer had bought the shirt and sweater had gone on display first thing last Thursday morning, November 12. The baskets were usually empty by closing time but the manager couldn't take his oath there hadn't been a few garments left on Friday morning, though he was very doubtful indeed about Friday afternoon.

There was no record of any credit transaction or use of a cheque card in the name of Lorimer, with the Furzebank Cottage address, on either Thursday or Friday. Anything the Lorimers bought must have been paid for in cash. And the manager confirmed that the till slips did indeed show the time of day as well as the date.

At the Chief's request the manager produced the menus for teas served in the restaurant during the previous week. Toasted muffins with butter and bramble jelly had been served on Friday afternoon and only on Friday afternoon; a different speciality appeared at teatime every day.

The tea menus were never placed on the tables until three o'clock, after lunch had been cleared and the tables relaid. But when the

Chief strolled round the restaurant it became clear that an obser-
vant customer could have learned of Friday's speciality ahead of
time.

A number of posters were displayed on the restaurant walls, giving gobbets of information: opening times of store and restaurant,
the hours various meals were served, special facilities and discounts
available for large parties, and—for the benefit of the staff—a list
pinned up by the door leading out to the kitchens, setting out the
week's menus in advance, including the daily specialities. This list
was smaller and less conspicuous than the others but there were
some tables nearby and a sharp-eyed customer, sitting at one of
them, waiting to be served, glancing idly about, would have no
difficulty in reading the list, commenting, perhaps, to a companion
on some unusual item.

On the way back to Cannonbridge the Chief sat deep in thought.
As they neared the station he roused himself to say, "That accident
the Lorimers say they passed on their way home from Fairdeal, get
on to the local radio station as soon as we get in, see if they put out
reports of the accident."

It didn't take Lambert long to discover that the radio station had
indeed made mention of the accident, giving details of time, place,
vehicles involved, number of persons injured, in their news bulle-
tins throughout Friday evening, the first mention being made in the
bulletin put out at six-thirty.

16

It was after ten on Friday morning by the time the Chief managed to
get away from the station, bound once more for Furzebank Cottage.
They were three-quarters of a mile or so from the cottage turning

when Kelsey noticed a shop a short distance ahead on the other side of the road.

"Pull up," he instructed Sergeant Lambert. The car slid to a halt opposite the shop, a little general store. They got out and crossed over.

The shop was empty. At the sound of the doorbell a woman came out from the living quarters, a middle-aged woman with a good-natured face and cheerful smile, a friendly manner.

The Chief told her who he was and asked if she knew the Lorimers of Furzebank Cottage, if they were customers.

She answered at once in an amiable, garrulous flow, happy to be of assistance. Yes, she knew the Lorimers, they did come into the shop. "She buys bits of grocery," she added, "and he gets his cigarettes here. They haven't been here long. Very quiet folk, not very chatty. Mrs. Lorimer moved in first. Her husband had been abroad, on some job, he came home about a month ago." A look of concern suddenly flashed across her face. "I hope they're not in any kind of trouble? I wouldn't like to think that."

"No, not as far as we know," Kelsey assured her. "We're making general inquiries about a case we're working on. We have to ask all kinds of questions about all kinds of folk." He grimaced. "Ninety-five per cent of it's a total waste of time but it's all got to be done, all part of the job."

"Yes, I see." She appeared vaguely reassured.

"You may be able to help us."

"Yes, of course, any way I can."

"I'd like you to think back and see if you can tell us the last time either of the Lorimers called in here at the shop."

She frowned in concentration. "Mrs. Lorimer was in here yesterday afternoon, and Mr. Lorimer came in on Sunday morning—I particularly remember that." She looked up at him. "I open later on a Sunday. He came in just after I'd unlocked the door, wanting cigarettes. I made a joke about him waiting on the doorstep."

"And the time before that when either of them called in?"

She put a hand up to her face. "It was Mrs. Lorimer who came in before that, as far as I recall, for some cigarettes for her husband—she doesn't smoke. Now when was that? It was one evening, I know that because it was dark. I went out into the kitchen to attend to something, and then I heard the shop doorbell go and I came back in here." She closed her eyes in thought. "I think it must have been the Friday, a week ago today." She opened her eyes, gave a decisive nod. "Yes, I believe it was the Friday, that was the evening Robin went out to play with the group, they had a booking. Robin's my son. He's still at school but he and some of the other lads got together and formed a group. Robin plays the guitar." She moved her head. "That's probably why I went through into the kitchen, to make sure he'd eaten a proper meal before he went out."

She stopped abruptly. "But then again it could have been the day before when Mrs. Lorimer called in, the Thursday. I know I made a steak and kidney pudding for supper on the Thursday, that could have been why I went through to the kitchen, to make sure the pudding hadn't boiled dry." She clasped her hands. "It could even have been the Wednesday—I don't have any half-closing day during the week. I make a cake on Wednesday afternoon, I might have gone into the kitchen to take a look at that." She gave an apologetic laugh. "I'm getting into a proper muddle. The more I try to puzzle it out, the worse it gets."

"Don't worry about it," Kelsey said soothingly. "I can see you're doing your best."

"I've got so many things on my mind these days—my husband died eighteen months ago and I'm running it all on my own now. You'd never credit how much there is to see to in a business, even one as small as this."

"What time was it, when Mrs. Lorimer called—whatever day of the week it was?"

"That I can tell you," she was delighted to be able to answer with certainty. "It was around five or a quarter past, it had just about got dark."

"Was Mrs. Lorimer on her own or was her husband with her?"

"As far as I know she was on her own. I didn't see her husband and she didn't mention him. If he was with her then he must have been waiting outside. He certainly didn't come into the shop."

"Was she on foot or did she come by car?"

She searched her memory but without success. "I'm afraid I can't tell you that. I can't remember hearing the car." She tried to think of some more positive assistance she might offer. "I can ask Robin

when he comes in from school this evening. He might remember
something.''

"Was he in here when Mrs. Lorimer came in? Did he see her? Or
speak to her?''

She shook her head with regret. "I'm afraid not. But I'll ask him
all the same.''

"I hope the good lady's books are in a better state than her
memory,'' the Chief said to Lambert as they went back to the car.

Five minutes later Sergeant Lambert turned the car in through
the tumbledown gateway of Furzebank Cottage. Enid Lorimer answered the door to them. She was drying her hands on a towel. She
wore a neat nylon overall; her abundant nut-brown hair was covered
in a silky scarf, tied round her head like a turban. She looked out at
them in silence, with a composed, neutral air.

Kelsey apologized for disturbing her when she was busy. He
asked if they might come in; there were a few points he would like to
raise with her and her husband.

In reply she gave a nod. She took them into the living-room, asked
them to sit down. She didn't offer any refreshment. "I'll tell my
husband,'' she said. "He's in the garden.''

She was gone several minutes. She came back into the room alone
and seated herself on the sofa without a word. She looked calm and
unflustered. Kelsey heard sounds coming from the kitchen quarters
and after a further interval Lorimer came into the room. He was
dressed in old gardening clothes but he had changed his shoes and
washed his hands before joining them. Without any word of greeting, barely a passing glance, he went across and sat down on the sofa
beside his wife.

The Chief plunged straight in, asking what Lorimer's financial
position had been at the time of his release from prison, what Enid's
financial position had been before Karen Boland's death, what her
position could now be expected to be. He allowed no vague, hazy
answers, no generalizations, no fudging or shifting ground. He
forced Enid to spell out every detail of her new and immeasurably
improved position, the difficulties and strictures of the immediate
past. Inch by inch he compelled Lorimer to disclose his almost total
lack of funds, the absence of any reasonable expectation of finding a
suitable, well-paid job. Husband and wife both behaved as if every

question held traps, hidden or overt; they took their time about answering even the most straightforward query.

The Chief then switched abruptly to the visit they had claimed to make to Fairdeal on the Friday of Karen's death. He took them once again through their movements that day but they didn't vary their story in the slightest. He asked how often they visited the supermarket. After a slight pause Enid told him they went once a week, on a Friday. He asked if they had ever gone on any other day of the week. This time there was a considerable pause before she answered: No, never. He asked if they always went in the afternoon. An even longer silence followed. Finally Enid told him: Yes, they always went after lunch.

"Today is Friday," Kelsey observed.

For once he didn't have to wait for a reply. It came swiftly, from Lorimer.

"We're not going over there this week. My wife doesn't feel up to it."

"The shirt and sweater you say you bought at Fairdeal." Kelsey produced the garments, each in its official plastic envelope. "Do you still maintain that you bought them on the afternoon of Friday, November 13?"

They both agreed: Yes, that was when they had bought them.

Kelsey asked how they had spotted the garments.

"They were on special offer," Enid replied without hesitation.

"How were they displayed?"

"In baskets along the aisles."

"These particular lots—were there a great many shirts and sweaters, a fair number, or just a few?"

Lorimer slid a glance at his wife as if a danger signal flashed in his brain. Sergeant Lambert saw that she was aware of the glance but she didn't return it. She looked calmly across at the Chief. Working out all the implications of the question? Lambert wondered. Or merely taking her time, showing the Chief—and her husband—that whatever we throw at her, she isn't going to be needled or panicked.

"There were just a few sweaters," she said at last with a judicial air. "Not more than nine or ten, various colours and sizes. There were rather more shirts, a couple of dozen, maybe."

The Chief made another of his swift changes of tack. "I understand," he said to Enid, "that you called in at the local shop, the little general store on the main road, at around five-fifteen last Friday evening, to buy cigarettes for your husband."

She looked surprised. "Then you understand wrong," she retorted with spirit. "I didn't call in at the shop at all last Friday, I'd no reason to. We bought what we wanted at Fairdeal." She thought back. "I did call at the shop the previous evening, Thursday, and I did buy Victor some cigarettes then. That could be what the woman remembers. I went along to post some letters—there's a box in the wall beside the shop. I wanted to catch the last post and that's collected around five-thirty, so it would have been about five-fifteen by the time I got there. It was just getting dark when I left here. Victor was still out in the garden, clearing up. I told him I was going to the post, I asked him if he wanted any cigarettes. He said I could get him a packet, just the one packet as we'd be going to Fairdeal next day." She moved a hand. "He stocks up at Fairdeal. Cigarettes are cheaper there."

"Did he go with you to the shop?"

She answered with an air of manifest patience. "No, I went by myself. I left him clearing up in the garden. By the time I got back he'd finished and gone into the house."

"Did you go by car?"

"No, I walked. It was a fine evening."

Kelsey glanced at Lorimer. "Did you phone the Cannonbridge College of Further Education at lunch-time last Friday?"

"No, I did not," Lorimer answered with vigour. "Why would I want to do that?"

"Ostensibly to try to speak to Karen. In reality to find out from the office what time her last class would finish."

Lorimer uttered another vigorous disclaimer. The Chief transferred his gaze to Enid.

"Did you phone the college at twenty minutes to six on Friday evening?" She began to shake her head in silence but the Chief went on. "Did you speak to Karen? Persuade her to meet you in the car park at six o'clock? Did you assure her you were on your own? All you wanted was to talk to her." Enid said nothing but continued to shake her head.

The Chief glanced from one to the other. "Did the two of you drive into Cannonbridge last Friday evening?"

They maintained with energy that they had not.

All at once Lorimer's air of tightly-lidded control evaporated. He leaned forward. "You're disappointed," he taunted Kelsey. "You'd give anything to be able to pin it on me." He voice was charged with resentment, bitterness, fury, triumph. "I've done time, so I must be guilty of any crime that's going begging, never mind what it is. I'm handy, I'll do, no need to look any further."

Enid placed a quelling hand on his arm and he subsided abruptly. The Chief sat for some moments regarding the two of them. At last he observed in a detached tone, "I notice neither of you has asked me about the findings of the post-mortem." They both sat very still. "We have the results now," the Chief added in the same detached tone.

There was another, longer silence, then Enid asked in a low, tremulous voice, "What do the results tell you?" Almost, Sergeant Lambert thought, as if compelled to speak against her better judgement.

The Chief began to describe in deliberate, harrowing detail the nature of the attack on Karen Boland, the injuries from which she had died, sparing nothing, omitting nothing. If he was trying to provoke a reaction in either of them he was markedly successful as far as Enid was concerned. Lorimer sat throughout with his head lowered, silent and motionless, but long before Kelsey had finished Enid showed signs of distress. She moved in her seat, put both hands up to her face, began to utter whimpering sounds. By the time the Chief reached the end of his chilling recital she was sobbing openly.

"I'll get her some water," Lorimer told the Chief. He went into the kitchen, returning with a glass. Enid took it shakily from him. He stood over her as she drank, looking down at her with angry solicitude. She handed the glass back to him and lay back with her head on the arm of the sofa, her feet up on the seat. She closed her eyes, she seemed ready to sink into oblivion. Lorimer bent over her, slipped a cushion behind her head.

Kelsey got to his feet. Lorimer glanced up at the Chief as the two policemen moved to the door. "I hope you're satisfied," he flung after them in a tone of simmering ferocity. "I hope you feel you've done a good morning's work."

"That teacher," Kelsey said to Lambert as they left the house, "the one Karen confided in, over in Okeshot. We'll pop over to the school this afternoon. See if we can get a word with her."

The school Karen had attended in Okeshot was a church-endowed mixed secondary school, operating for many years now inside the State system. Small, compared with State schools, with a good local reputation, adhering strongly to old traditions.

The woman who had been Karen's form teacher was a grey-haired, motherly-looking woman, plump and amiable. She had heard of Karen's death only on the previous day, was still shocked and horrified.

The Chief took her through the circumstances in which Karen had confided in her about Lorimer. Her account tallied closely with what the Okeshot police had told him. He then asked more general questions, about Karen's earlier behaviour in school, what friends she had made, any contacts the teacher might have had with either of the Lorimers.

"Karen was in my form only during the last year she was with us," the teacher explained. "But I knew her to some extent from the time she came into the school at the age of eleven—I teach art to the lower forms, I knew her through that. She had no particular gift for art though she always did her best, she was a conscientious girl. I thought her work very inhibited. I tried to get her to loosen up, open out, express herself more freely, but I didn't have much success. She always turned out conventional, stilted work, careful and accurate, but no individuality, no freshness."

From early on she had felt a degree of concern about Karen, the girl had seemed so quiet and controlled. She had made it her business to find out something of her family background. When she discovered the way in which Karen's mother had died, the fact that her father was seriously ill, that he had recently remarried, she no longer found it surprising that the girl was so quiet and bottled up. "Then her father died, during her first year here, before she'd had any real chance to settle down. She seemed to get over his death reasonably well."

Karen's stepmother had attended various school functions. "I spoke to her often, though never at any length. I thought her a disciplined, conscientious, serious-minded woman. She seemed to do her best to look after Karen." But on the occasions when she had seen the two of them together she had never observed any signs of deep affection, no real closeness, no warmth.

She made a little face. "Then her stepmother married again, after Karen had moved up into my form. I knew Lorimer slightly, from using the public library." She had quite liked Lorimer, had always found him helpful and obliging, with a pleasant manner. "I thought the marriage had every chance of being successful. I was pleased for Karen. I thought it would be good for her to have a third person in the household, someone used to young folk, who'd take an interest in her schoolwork, be a second father to her." She sighed and shook her head. "It only goes to show how wrong you can be."

After the marriage Lorimer often came along to school functions with his wife. "He spoke to me several times about Karen's work and general attitudes," the teacher said. "He'd noticed, for instance, that Karen wasn't interested in any kind of sport, he wondered how that might be improved. And he mentioned that she didn't seem to have any hobbies. I thought he took a genuine interest in her. I thought everything was working out well for the three of them."

Had she been astounded when Karen spoke out against Lorimer? She looked thoughtful. "Yes and no. My first reaction was tremendous surprise, and shock. Then a moment later I began to think: Yes, he is always so very interested in Karen. I began to wonder if maybe that was why he'd married her stepmother."

Kelsey asked if she knew of any particular friends Karen had made at the school.

She gave a reflective shake of her head. "She wasn't one to make friends. She didn't join any of the school clubs or societies." She pondered. "There was one girl, in the same class, they sat together. I suppose Karen was as friendly with her as with anyone. Becky Ayliffe, the girl was called, she was by way of being a bit of an outsider. A coloured girl, big and strapping, about as different in looks from Karen as you can imagine.

"Becky's left school now. She was several months older than Karen, she left school last summer. She wasn't as clever academically as Karen but she was a hard worker. One thing she was good at was art, I thought she had a real gift for it. I had the impression the friendship, such as it was, was more on Karen's side than Becky's. Becky always seemed just to tolerate Karen. Becky came from a pretty rough part of town. We don't get many pupils from that area but Becky's mother was very anxious she should come to us. The mother's a very decent sort of woman, a strong churchwoman, very keen Becky should make something of her life. I never saw any sign of a father. I gather he took himself off years ago."

She tilted her head. "Looking back on it, I suppose that could have been one of the things that drew Karen towards her, the fact that Becky didn't have a father. Karen could have felt they were in the same boat. And Becky didn't have any brothers or sisters, either, another point in common." She had no idea if the two girls had kept in touch after Karen had been taken into care.

Kelsey asked if she could give him Becky's address. "I can give you her home address, here in Okeshot," she told him. "But I don't think you'll find her there. The last I heard of her, she'd been accepted for a training course." She didn't know the details but she had an idea it had taken Becky over to the other side of the county. "You could call round and get her address from her mother," she suggested.

And that was what they attempted to do, but without success. Becky's home address turned out to be the end house in a crumbling terrace of flaking, pock-marked brick, the district every bit as seedy and run-down as the teacher had intimated. There was little sign of life about the streets, the area seemed sunk into afternoon somnolence.

The Ayliffe dwelling stood out from its fellows by virtue of bright, clean curtains, fresh paintwork, glittering windows. Sergeant Lambert pressed the doorbell and went on pressing it, but no one answered. He tried next door, with no better result. At the third house he caught the whisk of a curtain at an upstairs window as he approached, but repeated rings brought no one to the door.

As he worked his way in this fashion to the seventh dwelling the Chief strolled along to join him. No reply at the seventh house, either. Not a neighbourhood, apparently, where folk were disposed to open the door to any kind of authority figure, debt-collector, council official, employee of the gas or electricity board. Or maybe they could recognize a policeman when they saw him walking up the street, however discreetly dressed, however harmless and un-threatening his posture and expression.

Lambert had by now got the bit between his teeth. He marched doggedly up to the eighth—and last—door and jammed his thumb on the bell. This time he was in luck. He could hear a slow, shuffling sound from within. The door opened a fraction to disclose a wrin-kled segment of face, a pale, watery eye, a few straggling wisps of white hair.

By now Lambert had almost forgotten what he was doing here at all, why he was ringing all these bells. After a second or two he recalled his mission and inquired about the lady in the end house, Mrs. Ayliffe. When might she be expected home? Or perhaps he might be directed to her place of work?

The door began to inch inexorably towards closure. An ancient, croaking voice—male or female, Lambert was at a loss to decide—informed him that the owner knew nothing about anyone and, fur-thermore, had no wish to know. The door clicked shut.

Lambert acknowledged defeat. He rejoined the Chief with the look of a man who knows when enough is enough.

The Chief had no difficulty in recognizing the look, it was one he had worn himself more times than he'd had hot dinners. I don't suppose it matters, he told himself with a resigned shrug, I doubt if we'd have got anything from Becky Ayliffe—but an instant later he brusquely dismissed that easy, treacherous notion. If there was one lesson to be learned in the force, to be learned and relearned, slowly and painfully, over and over and over again, it was this: there was no possible way of knowing which tiny, apparently insignificant detail among a myriad of details, related or random, might turn out to be the one to point the way out of the labyrinth.

The Ayliffe house might be on the phone; if not, a constable could be despatched from the Okeshot station to call round during the evening, and, if necessary, to call again and again over the weekend. One way or another they would in the end get Becky's present address; sooner or later, with or without any fruitful result, they would talk to her.

Six o'clock in the evening found the Chief sitting at his desk over yet another cup of coffee, yet another canteen sandwich, mulling over the results of the investigation so far.

There had been no useful response to radio and press appeals, asking for any sighting near Overmead Wood at the relevant time. Nor had anyone come forward with fresh information about seeing Karen in the college car park; no one had noticed her in conversation, getting into a vehicle, or being driven away.

As he ploughed through the reports, the files, the Chief suddenly remembered that they hadn't yet made any contact with Desmond Hallam, absent from Hawthorn Lodge since shortly after the murder. He picked up the phone and rang the lodge but there was no reply. He rang the Overmead postmistress but she knew of no signs of life at the lodge over the past few days, nor had she had any kind of communication from Hallam or his aunt.

Kelsey then rang the college principal and was told no, Hallam had not yet returned to the college, nor had there been any further message from him. Kelsey replaced the receiver and wrote a note, explaining nothing, merely asking Hallam to contact him at the station as soon as he got home. He sent a constable off to push the note in through the front door of Hawthorn Lodge.

When the door had closed behind the constable the Chief sat contemplating with acute distaste the mountains of paperwork requiring his attention. He felt drained after a week of unremitting effort, flat, stale, despondent, bogged down in a quagmire of detail, all momentum lost.

He knew of old it was useless to attempt to struggle on in this frame of mind. The remedy was to turn his back on it all, get off home, eat a decent meal for a change, take his mind off the case, get an early night. Nothing like a good, solid, eight hours' sleep for restoring energy and lifting spirits.

In the event his good resolutions fell away somewhat. The decent meal turned into a couple of tins picked up in the neighbourhood store—he couldn't even be bothered to buy one of the excellent ready meals in the freezer cabinet, for that would have meant reading the instructions, heating up the stuff, paying attention to the timing, and he was well beyond all that, exhausted and ravenous.

He despatched the contents of the tins cold, just as they were, standing at the kitchen sink spooning them out, gulping them down. He well knew how dearly he would pay for it later but he had his indigestion tablets at the ready. He was never without them, he bought them several packets at a time, in case by any horrid chance he might suddenly find himself without them, in the middle of the night, perhaps, all shops closed.

He finished off his repast with a cup of milk, downed ice-cold from the fridge in a few shuddering swallows. No washing-up to bother about. He went into the living-room and switched on the television, selecting a lively, popular quiz show. He dropped into a chair and stared at the screen, hoping for distraction. He felt like death warmed up, he had to struggle against a dull headache that aspirins wouldn't shift. Try as he might, his mind kept slipping away from the jolly cavortings, the engineered comradeliness and gaiety, back to scenes and faces from the case.

He switched channels, with no better result, switched again. After an hour or two he abandoned the effort and took himself off to bed. He fell at once into an uneasy, troubled sleep in which he wandered ceaselessly about in an unknown town, couldn't remember where he was staying or what he was doing there, encountered only hostile or indifferent strangers.

When he finally surfaced again to full consciousness he switched on his bedside lamp to discover it wasn't yet three-thirty. He threw back the bedclothes and pulled on a dressing-gown. He went along to the kitchen, thankful to be released from the disturbing disorientation of the dreams. He set a pan of milk on the stove, paced about the room as he waited for it to heat.

Down on the road the local community midwife drove by, on her way home from delivering yet another Cannonbridge citizen, red-faced and bawling, into the dark November morning. As she went by she glanced up at the light, the shadow moving, up and down, up and down, behind the blind, and thought, by no means for the first time: The Chief Inspector's at it again.

Shortly after eight he was sitting slumped at his desk, unrefreshed and irritable, the remains of the headache still with him. Before him the phone shrilled. He stretched out a hand and picked up the

receiver. It was a call put through from the desk: Desmond Hallam
on the phone.

Hallam and his aunt had got back late last night, had found the
Chief Inspector's note. No, he had no idea why the police should
wish to see him. No, he had spoken to no one in the village. He
sounded completely baffled.

The Chief's weary, deflated mood fell away, vanished utterly. He
felt wide awake and cheerful, briskly energetic. The whole bag of
tricks was bursting open again.

17

Fifteen minutes later the Chief sat beside Sergeant Lambert in the
car, headed for Hawthorn Lodge. When he had informed Hallam of
the murder over the phone, Hallam had offered to drive into Cannonbridge, to help in any way he could, answer any questions. No,
you sit tight, the Chief had told him, we'll be out right away to see
you. An interview with a man on his own stamping-ground was a
thousand times more valuable and informative than one conducted
within the confines of a police station.

Hallam's reaction to the news of Karen's death was very much
what might have been expected from a man who had recently passed
through a time of change and shock in his own life, a time of
bereavement, stress, anxiety. He couldn't at first take in the fact,
couldn't believe it. He had then begun to cry.

They drove past Overmead Wood, silent and peaceful in the hazy
sunlight, and took the next turning on the left. If they had continued
along this course it would very soon have led them to Jubilee Cottage, but a turning on the right, some hundred yards short of the
cottage, brought them instead, a minute or two later, to Hawthorn
Lodge.

As they drove in through the gates Kelsey spotted a man he took to be Hallam some little distance away in the garden, stooping, with his back to them, over a border still brilliant with yellow and crimson, bronze and gold. A Transit van was drawn up at the far side of the house.

At the sound of the car Hallam straightened up and came over. A spare, active figure, sprucely groomed and dressed; his face looked pale and anguished. He introduced himself and asked them to come inside.

An enticing odour of percolating coffee drifted out as he opened the front door. A woman came hurrying along from the kitchen quarters to greet them. A stout little woman with a busy air, trimly dressed in a crisp nylon overall. Her thick, curly, white hair looked as if it had been freshly washed and set, her pink-and-white skin glowed with health; behind the lenses of her spectacles her pale blue eyes were quick and shrewd. She held out a hand with a friendly smile as Hallam introduced her: his aunt, Miss Ivy Jebb.

"This is a terrible business." Her smile was replaced by a look of sympathy and concern. "I didn't know the poor girl, of course. I never came across her, I didn't even know she existed." She ushered them into a sitting-room furnished with a considerable degree of comfort and good taste. "I've just made some coffee, I'm sure you won't say no to that. And there's some of the fruit-cake left that I made a couple of days before we took our little trip—we went off in something of a rush." She smiled. "It's a very good cake, though I say it myself, one of my best. You'll both have a piece, I know—you won't disappoint me." She went bustling off, returning shortly with a laden tray. Hallam sprang forward to relieve her of it.

Sergeant Lambert, ever hungry, wasn't at all disposed to disappoint Miss Jebb in the matter of the fruit-cake; he could easily have despatched the lot, unaided. It was excellent, like the coffee. Even the Chief, after his sketchy breakfast based largely on aspirins and strong tea, accepted a second slice, commenting—most unusually for him—on how good it was.

Miss Jebb and Hallam had not long stood up from a proper breakfast but Miss Jebb poured coffee for herself and her nephew, for the sake of friendliness. Hallam, the Chief observed, couldn't manage so much as a sip; he raised his cup in a hand that visibly trembled. After a moment he set the cup down again, untasted. He still looked shattered by the news. He sat gazing down, with an exhausted, apathetic air.

Kelsey asked how well he had known the dead girl. Not very well, Hallam told them in a low, expressionless voice. He had met Karen when he started classes at the college in September. They both attended a play-reading class on Tuesdays. He was very interested in the theatre. He had inherited his father's collection of theatrical items and had enlarged it himself. He had spoken of it to Karen and she had said she'd like to see it. On the last Tuesday that he had attended the class—the Tuesday before Karen died—he had given her a lift back to Overmead at the end of the afternoon. Miss Jebb's head came sharply round at that. She looked very surprised but made no comment.

"It was about half past four when we got here," Hallam went on. "We both finished early on a Tuesday. My aunt didn't come in till getting on for six." Karen had stayed about half an hour, then she walked home to Jubilee Cottage. He had given her a lift from the college on a number of occasions, perhaps seven or eight. He had never driven her right up to the door, she had never seemed to want that. On the first occasion, as they neared the turning off to Hawthorn Lodge, she had asked him to pull up there, she would get out and walk the last short stretch; she had offered no explanation. Subsequent occasions had followed the same pattern, with him halting just before his own turning to let her out.

On that last Tuesday, during her visit to the lodge, she had asked if she might borrow a scrapbook. She had returned it on the Friday she died, over a cup of coffee during morning break. That was the last time he had seen or spoken to her. They had chatted for a few minutes; she had appeared much as usual.

Kelsey asked if he would give an account of his movements from, say, five till seven-thirty on Friday evening, adding that this was purely normal routine. In spite of this assurance Hallam looked even more distressed. But he raised no objection and gave his account in the same low, expressionless voice, with a certain amount of stumbling and hesitation.

His last class had finished at five. Afterwards he had gone to the common room and sat reading papers and magazines, chatting to a student. He had left shortly before six, had driven off alone. He had seen nothing of Karen in the car park. It would have been five or ten to six when he drove out through the college gates.

He stopped for petrol at a garage on the edge of Cannonbridge, where he always bought his petrol. The garage operated a vehicle-hire service and he asked the owner about hiring a van for the trip up north. His own car was too small to bring back his aunt's belongings. He had spent some time talking to the owner.

No, he hadn't made a firm booking at that time. He hadn't in fact definitely decided exactly when he would make the trip, or if indeed he would make it at all; these were merely preliminary inquiries.

Kelsey asked what time he had arrived home. Hallam tilted back his head, half closed his eyes. He had left the garage at around six-twenty, six-twenty-five, he hadn't particularly noticed the time.

"I can tell you exactly when he got home," Miss Jebb broke in. "He was on the late side and I'd started looking at the clock, wondering what was keeping him. I was in the kitchen, looking at the supper in the oven, making sure it wouldn't spoil. I had the radio on and they were reading out the news headlines at seven o'clock when I heard the car."

Kelsey frowned. "Seven o'clock?" He glanced at Hallam. "Why did it take you so long?"

Hallam waved a hand. "I had a puncture on the way home. I had to change a wheel."

"You should have seen the state he was in." Miss Jebb made a face of distaste. "He was soaked through, covered in mud."

Hallam gave an apologetic smile. "I'm not very good with anything mechanical, never have been. I slipped and fell a couple of times while I was changing the wheel. I'm afraid I did get into a bit of a mess."

"A bit of a mess indeed!" Miss Jebb confirmed with a snort.

Kelsey asked if he could see the clothes Hallam had come home in.

"Indeed you cannot!" Miss Jebb asserted with energy. "I wouldn't have them in the house!" She made a face of even greater distaste. "They'd got something worse than mud on them, I can tell you."

Hallam's grin was even more apologetic. "I pulled off the road into a gateway, to change the wheel. It was only after I'd slipped and fallen that I discovered it was a farm gateway, the entrance to a field where cattle are kept."

"Where exactly was this gateway?"

Hallam described the spot: on the main road, a mile or so out of Cannonbridge—and a good half-mile before Overmead Wood.

"I went to the door when I heard his car," Miss Jebb enlarged. "When I saw the state he was in, I wouldn't let him come right into the house. I made him stand in the back porch while I went to get some plastic bin bags from the kitchen. He took off his filthy things, there in the porch: shoes, socks, jacket, trousers, gloves."

"Gloves?" Kelsey echoed.

"Yes, his driving gloves."

"I always wear driving gloves," Hallam explained.

Kelsey asked him to hold out his hands. Very well cared for, the skin soft and smooth.

"Do you look after the garden here yourself?" he asked.

Hallam nodded. "I always wear gardening gloves."

"He's very fussy about his hands," Miss Jebb put in. "Worse than any girl."

Kelsey returned his attention to her. "I interrupted you just now. Please continue."

"I put all his dirty clothes into the bin bags," she resumed. "Then I took them straight out to the dustbin."

"Could they not have gone to the cleaner's?"

She shook her head vigorously. "No cleaner would accept garments in that condition. And even if they would, none of it would ever really have been fit to wear again." She made a face. "It wasn't as if any of it was special, there was nothing he was very fond of. None of it was new, or particularly good."

The dustbin had been emptied while they were away. As for the rest of what her nephew had been wearing, shirt and underwear, she had put those into the laundry basket while he went upstairs to have a bath. They had set off on their trip early next morning, before she had time to attend to any washing. She had dealt with that this morning, as soon as she had got up, she had put the clothes into the machine, together with the dirty laundry they had brought back from their trip.

"I'd like to take a look through your wardrobe," the Chief told Hallam. Miss Jebb opened her mouth as if to utter some question or protest but Hallam directed at her a glance that, although mild, effectively silenced her.

"By all means," he said to the Chief and led the way up to his bedroom.

By now they had the results of Forensic's examination of the fibres caught up on the bark and twigs of trees, brambles, and undergrowth in Overmead Wood, marking the headlong passage of Karen and her killer. Apart from those ripped from Karen's clothes, there were fibres of a lightish-coloured, blue-grey, marl-mix, woollen tweed, fibres also of a dark grey worsted gabardine. But nowhere among the contents of Hallam's wardrobe could the Chief come across any article, snagged or unsnagged, corresponding with those fibres.

When they were all downstairs again Kelsey observed to Hallam, "You could have locked your car, left it safely on the verge, walked home and gone back to deal with it next morning. You could have changed the wheel in daylight, in dry weather. Or you could have phoned the garage, got them to come out and do it for you."

Hallam gazed helplessly back at him. "I suppose I could, but it simply never occurred to me."

Kelsey asked Miss Jebb exactly when her nephew had told her that they would be making the trip on Saturday morning.

"More or less right away when he came in on Friday evening," she answered without hesitation. "While he was standing there in the porch, taking his muddy things off."

Hallam made an apologetic gesture. "I felt so mean about it. I'd been thinking entirely about myself, whether the trip would be a great bother, all that driving, and so on. Then when I came in soaked through, there Aunt Ivy was, rushing out to help me, seeing to everything, with a good hot meal ready and waiting, the table laid. I thought what it would have been like coming back to the house in that condition if I'd been on my own. I felt really ashamed of myself. I knew what Mother would have thought of me, treating her sister like that, after she'd been so good to both of us." A tear glinted in his eye. "I made up my mind there and then, I'd do what she wanted, we'd go first thing next morning. I'd phone the garage and fix it.

Aunt Ivy was so pleased, absolutely delighted. There was no trouble getting the van at such short notice. They told me I could pick it up at seven-thirty, leave my own car to be serviced, have the tyre attended to—and they'd give the car a thoroughly good clean, inside and out. I'm returning the van this morning, picking my own car up at the same time."

Kelsey asked how long he had booked the van for.

"No particular length of time," he answered. "I told them I didn't know how long we'd be away." His aunt had originally wanted to go up north just for the night, but in his mood of gratitude he had decided to give her a little break, make a jaunt of it, a few days perhaps. "I thought we could see how it went. If she was enjoying going back, seeing old friends again, then we could stay on; if not, we could come home."

In the event they had both thoroughly enjoyed the trip. The town where she had worked wasn't far from the village where she and his mother had lived as girls. She had taken him round many of the old haunts, introduced him to people who had known his mother as a child. "It made me feel very close to Mother again," he told the Chief. Tears shone again in his eyes.

The garage-owner had raised no objection to the indeterminate booking. The vehicle-hiring trade was always slack at this time of year. A few days, a week or longer, Hallam could suit himself how long he kept the vehicle.

"To get back to your relationship with Karen Boland," Kelsey said with one of his sudden switches.

"It was no more than friendship." Hallam's voice held a note of mild protest. "Even calling it friendship is stretching it, it was just a slight, friendly acquaintance. We had something in common—we both felt alone to a certain extent, we were both doing our best to make a new life. And we both knew what it was to feel the loss of parents."

Had Karen spoken to him of her past life?.

"Not to any extent. I knew her parents were dead and that she was living with her cousin in Jubilee Cottage after some time in foster care."

"Did you never ask about her past life?"

Hallam shook his head with vigour. "I would never have dreamed

of probing. I guessed it must have been an unhappy past or she
would have talked about it."

"Did she ever speak of any trouble in Wychford over a married
man?"

Again he shook his head. "She never mentioned Wychford."

"Or Okeshot?"

He shook his head once more.

Karen had never mentioned that she had a stepmother, let alone
the fact that the stepmother had remarried. The names Lorimer and
Clayton, in connection with Karen, meant nothing to him.

Kelsey got to his feet and went across to a shelved alcove by the
fireplace where a number of family photographs were ranged on
display. In pride of place stood a large, handsomely framed wedding
group of Hallam's parents. The Chief picked it up and studied it.

The bridegroom, in his middle or late thirties, showed a strong
resemblance to Hallam. The bride, ten or fifteen years younger,
looked scarcely out of the schoolroom. Short and slight, with soft,
delicate features, large expressive eyes, a smoothly rounded forehead.

Kelsey returned the photograph to its place and turned to face
Hallam who had sat in silence watching him.

"What about your relationships with other women?" Kelsey
asked.

Hallam slid a nervous, embarrassed look in the direction of his
aunt who was paying the keenest attention to everything that
passed. She registered the look but showed not the slightest intention of removing herself.

"I'm sure you have a great deal to attend to," Kelsey observed to
her. "We wouldn't want to keep you."

She levered herself up out of her chair with marked reluctance
and walked to the door. On the threshold she halted and threw at
Hallam a glance of supportive encouragement. "If I'm wanted," she
announced, "I shall be in the kitchen."

The moment the door closed behind her Kelsey repeated his
question.

Hallam jerked out a hand. "I can't say I've ever had any relationships with women." His manner showed greater ease and freedom.
"Not of the sort you mean."

"Have you never been in love?"

He shook his head. "No, never." He smiled slightly. "I've always been baffled by the fuss they make over it, in literature and poetry. I've always wondered if anyone ever really feels like that, if it isn't all some universal fiction, and people feel they have to go along with it in case they appear abnormal."

"Were you never in love when you were young?"

He moved his shoulders. "I suppose I had my crushes when I was a lad, the same as everyone else. But that's all they were, crushes, very mild and passing." He gave a half-laugh. "I couldn't tell you now the name of any of those girls, or what they looked like."

"These are young girls we're talking about?" Kelsey queried.

Hallam's manner altered abruptly. He sat up in his chair, frowning. "Yes, of course they were, it was when I was at school, sixteen or seventeen. If I had a crush at that time it was bound to be on a young girl. But I'm not sixteen years old now." His tone was a good deal sharper, more peremptory.

He appeared to recollect himself and sank back into his chair. "I'm not looking for love," he went on in a restrained, explanatory tone. "Not of the kind you mean. All I want is peace of mind, a quiet, harmonious life, friendship, companionship, some shared interests." He looked directly at the Chief. "Not to be lonely—that's the important thing."

"Were you to any degree at all in love with Karen?" Kelsey pressed him.

His manner was firm and unshaken. "No, I was not. Not to any degree whatsoever."

"Did you fantasize about her?"

"I most certainly did not. I'm not given to fantasizing about women—or, indeed, about anything." He sat silent for a moment, looking levelly at the Chief. "I'm not in the least interested in sex. I'm simply not given that way. I can't see why it's taken for granted these days that everyone has to be. No one supposes everyone is passionately interested in the theatre or football or anything else you care to name. In the old days people accepted that. No one raised an eyebrow when someone went off to be a monk or nun, or if someone remained a bachelor or spinster, never married. But now, we all have to have our heads full of sex all the time or we're objects of suspicion, highly unnatural." He struck his knee. "I am the way I am, the way I was made. It's my nature and there's nothing in the slightest degree unnatural about it."

Kelsey looked stolidly back at him. "Let me put this picture to you. A man in middle age, emotionally immature, leading a settled, comfortable life. Then, out of the blue, a series of distressing, deeply disturbing events: redundancy, the death of a much loved mother, a nervous breakdown, anxiety over the future. Such a man must be in a vulnerable, susceptible state, his sound judgement, his sense of proportion, all affected. It would be easy for such a man to mistake kindness, friendly interest, for something more, to clutch at it, hoping it might be a lifeline, to pull him out of despair."

Hallam shook his head but Kelsey went on.

"Such a man might easily make an approach that startled or frightened the girl, caused her to jump out of the car and run off. What more natural than that he should run after her? To reassure her, perhaps, to bring her back to the car."

Hallam continued to shake his head.

"She catches her foot and falls. She lies there, unable to move. Something sweeps over him."

Hallam gazed dispassionately at him. "Karen was never in my car at any time that Friday. I drove away from the college alone, I was alone the whole way home." He raised a hand to his chin. "I can see the way you have to operate. It isn't very agreeable to be on the receiving end, but I can understand it."

As they left, the Chief walked round to the back of the house and lifted the lid of the dustbin. It was empty.

Miss Jebb didn't reappear, but as Sergeant Lambert opened the car door he glanced up and caught the quick drop back into place of the edge of a curtain at one of the upstairs windows.

On the way back to Cannonbridge they were able to identify without difficulty the farm gateway where Hallam said he had changed his wheel. Certainly the entrance bore clear and abundant evidence of its regular use by cattle.

A few minutes later Lambert ran the car on to the forecourt of the garage from which Hallam had hired his van. Trade was brisk and the Chief had to wait some little time before the owner was at liberty to speak to him. Kelsey had come across the owner once or twice before in the course of other inquiries. The garage was a highly reputable concern and the Chief had always found the owner and his staff more than ready to be of assistance to the police.

But this morning the owner certainly didn't fall over himself to be helpful. It was plain he didn't relish answering questions about a valued customer of long standing. His manner all the time suggested the question: What is all this in aid of? But Kelsey didn't enlighten him.

The Chief's questions did however produce clear, straightforward answers, however reluctantly given. Hallam had phoned earlier in the morning to say he would be returning the van and asking if his car was ready for collection. He said nothing about any police inquiries into his movements. As far as the hiring of the van was concerned, what the owner had to say tallied pretty exactly with what Hallam had told them. The owner was able to be precise about the time Hallam had arrived at the garage that Friday evening. He employed a number of part-time workers; this demanded a nice dovetailing of duty rotas so that the forecourt was never for a moment left unattended. On Friday evenings one of his workers, a married woman, always left on the dot of six, and the owner himself always came on duty a few minutes before six to take her place. On that particular Friday, as he came out of his living-quarters and walked over to the forecourt, he saw Hallam drive in and halt by his usual petrol pump. He nodded at Hallam as he went by on his way to the office. A minute or two later Hallam came into the office to ask about hiring a vehicle. Hallam was definitely alone in his car; there was no sign of any girl anywhere about.

He put the time at which Hallam had left the garage at around six-twenty or six-twenty-five. Towards the end of his conversation with Hallam another customer had come to the office door and glanced in, had stood there, waiting to speak to him. Hallam observed this and brought his own conversation to a speedy conclusion. He left the office, presumably to get into his car and drive off, but the owner hadn't actually seen him go; he had remained in his office for several minutes, talking to the other customer.

He showed them Hallam's car, standing waiting to be collected. A small saloon, dark grey, seven or eight years old, in excellent condition, now immaculately clean.

They got back into their car and Lambert began to drive off the forecourt. He was compelled to halt, to wait for a gap in the traffic. He turned his head and glanced up the road. A short distance away, fifty yards or so, a group of folk stood by a bus stop. Lambert sat pondering.

"That Friday evening," he said to Kelsey, "when Karen went over to a car in the college car park, suppose she didn't get into the car, she just stood there chatting for a minute or two, then she went off to get her bus. But for some reason she didn't go to her usual stop. Instead she went to that stop along the road there. But she misjudged it. She missed the bus, she saw it moving off as she came running up.

"Hallam is sitting there, in his car, waiting to pull out. He sees Karen come running along, sees her miss the bus. Easy enough to recognize her with that light-coloured shoulder-bag, that yellow cap and scarf. He gives her a toot on his horn, leans out, waves and calls. She catches sight of him, she knows the car. She's delighted. She comes running up. Hop in, he tells her, I'll give you a lift home. She doesn't hesitate. She jumps in and he drives off."

Kelsey grunted. "Possible, I suppose. But why would she take it into her head to use this bus stop? If she was late enough to miss the bus here, then she'd have stood a far better chance of catching it if she'd gone to her usual stop. It's a good deal nearer the college."

Lambert sighed. "Yes, you're right. It was just a thought." A gap appeared in the traffic and he slipped into it.

18

Sergeant Lambert's landlady managed easily enough to arrange her little tea-party for four o'clock on Sunday afternoon, giving Eunice Sheldrake time, after teaching Sunday school, to drive home and pick up her mother.

Mrs. Sheldrake was still handsome enough in her way, a tall, commanding-looking, amply upholstered woman, corseted with elegant restraint, dressed with expensive provincial chic, her white hair beautifully cut and set. Her manner towards the world in general was patronizing and dominating.

Eunice was shorter and several stones lighter, with a face that might at best be called plain. Her clothes were every bit as expensive as her mother's but succeeded only in appearing dowdy and old-fashioned. With her skinny, slightly stooping, almost bosomless frame, she looked an acidulated spinster.

Lambert was waiting in the sitting-room when they arrived. His landlady brought them in and Mrs. Sheldrake gave him a lofty nod. "Are you working on this horrible case at Overmead?" she asked as she graciously took her seat. Lambert murmured something noncommittal in reply and she at once abandoned the topic and launched into a discussion with his landlady—more of a soliloquy on Mrs. Sheldrake's part than a discussion—about fund-raising events to mark the centenary of a ladies' guild, the committee of which they both adorned. Eunice sipped her tea and toyed with her food in silence and for several minutes Lambert was able to devote his attention to his landlady's excellent scones and superb walnut cake. Then his landlady took Mrs. Sheldrake off to another room to look over a provisional programme of events she had drawn up.

As soon as the door closed behind them Eunice's manner underwent a marked change. She looked across at Lambert with a matey, conspiratorial smile. "I could see you didn't want to talk in front of Mother." She made a coy little face. "I realize you have to be terribly discreet—but you know me, I'd never break a confidence or say anything out of turn. You are working on the Overmead case, aren't you?" Lambert admitted as much with a movement of his head.

Now she was off, in full flood, getting it all out before the others could return. "I never actually met the poor girl that was killed," she said in rapid tones. "I knew she'd gone to live with the Wilmots, of course, Ian mentioned it. And I saw her in town once or twice with Christine." She leaned forward. "I know the Wilmots quite well. Christine often calls in at the office to have a word with Ian. And I've been out to Jubilee Cottage a couple of times." She gave a mischievous grin. "I can't say I was ever actually invited but I couldn't resist finding an excuse to call in once or twice at a weekend when I was out that way in the car. I wanted to see what they'd made of the cottage."

She jerked her head in a knowing fashion. "They've made a very fair job of it. Of course they got every possible grant from the local authority. Ian knows his way round every nook and cranny of the system, I'll give him that." She raised a hand. "Not that I'm for one moment suggesting anything not strictly legal—and no question of any outright queue-jumping, either—but it certainly never hurts to know your way around." She paused and gave him a meaningful glance. "Do you happen to know how the Wilmots came by the cottage in the first place?"

Lambert shook his head. Eunice put her elbows on the table, linked her hands under her chin and fixed him with her light green eyes.

"The pair of cottages belonged to an old lady. She lived in one and let the other to an old man, that had been the situation for years. Both the cottages were pretty run-down. The old man got very strange towards the end and wouldn't let anyone in to do repairs and then the old lady started to let her own place go downhill as well, it all got to be too much of a bother.

"Then the old man died. She realized something would have to be done or both cottages would fall down. By this time, of course, the cost of repairs, particularly repairs to period dwellings, had shot sky-high. She got a terrible fright when she started making inquiries. One of the builders she went to told her she might qualify for a repair grant, so she came wandering into our office to see if we could help her.

"Ian Wilmot took her under his wing. He ran her back to the cottages and had a good look round, then he went into her financial situation with her." She removed her elbows from the table and sat back in her chair with an air of satisfaction. "The upshot was that in no time at all he and Christine moved into the vacant cottage— they'd been living in rented accommodation, no great shakes."

She raised a hand again. "Not that I'm suggesting anything irregular or out of order. Ian arranged for the grant, the repairs, and all the rest of it. And he and Christine kept an eye on the old lady for the rest of her days. She died a year or two later." She directed at him a look heavy with significance. "She left both cottages to the Wilmots. It seems she had no relatives. She left the Wilmots her savings as well—and they amounted to a good deal more than you might have supposed."

She pursed her lips. "Christine had been working in a supermarket ever since they moved to Cannonbridge. She gave her job up right away and started her mail-order and sales-party business. And Ian lost no time either. He had plans drawn up and passed, further grants applied for and approved. Before you could turn round he had the two cottages knocked into one. And a very comfortable, handsome house they've made out of it, worth a small fortune these days."

She sat regarding him with her green eyes glinting. "They're very well suited, Christine and Ian. It might look on the surface as if she's the one who wears the trousers but that isn't the case, believe you me. Underneath all that charm, that hail-fellow-well-met manner, Ian's as tough as old boots, as hard as nails. He's got an eye to the main chance all right, just as much as Christine. He means to get on, one way or another, he's every bit as ambitious as she is."

She waved a hand. "They both came from nothing. Give them their due, they've managed to make something of themselves. But the trouble with people like that is they never know when to stop, where to draw the line, they're compensating all their lives for their humble origins. They're always in a hurry for money and what it can buy."

She inclined her head judiciously. "Christine's a very good saleswoman. Most of the women and girls at work are customers of hers, quite a few of the men, too. She doesn't come selling in the office, of course, she's far too professional for that. She calls on them at home, in the evenings or at weekends." She shook her head. "Ian hasn't got the brainpower to get to the top and by this time he knows it. The old boss liked him, he was an easygoing sort of man. But he died six months ago and the new man's a very different kettle of fish, a good deal younger and sharper—not so easy by a long chalk to pull the wool over his eyes."

She put a hand up to her face. "Ian hasn't talked about Karen Boland's death in the office. I don't know how he's taken it, he hasn't said a word to anyone." She shook her head again. "Terrible times these days, when a young girl can't walk home without being attacked and murdered by a sex maniac."

"We don't know that," Lambert objected. "The investigation's still very open." Across the hall he heard a door open and close, voices, returning footsteps.

"But that's what it's sure to turn out to be," Eunice declared with total conviction. "It's all sex these days." She gave a refined little shudder. "Sex and violence."

Both Karen Boland's parents had been cremated in a town fifteen miles the far side of Okeshot and the Wilmots elected to have Karen cremated there too. Monday evening was cold and dark, with a lingering, clammy fog. This, together with the distance from Cannonbridge, ensured that there were no mere curiosity-mongers present in the little chapel attached to the crematorium. And the type of case, a young girl brutally done to death, was too common these days to have summoned reporters from the national newspapers to the funeral.

A female member of staff had driven over from the college, bringing with her a representative party of students, among them Lynn Musgrove; the floral tributes included a handsome wreath from the lecturers and pupils. In a nearby pew the Chief spotted the young woman social worker and her boss. Both the Wilmots were close by, dressed in dark mourning clothes, Ian calm and composed, Christine again looking as if she were under sedation.

Behind them sat the Roscoes, Karen's former foster-parents, neither appearing upset or agitated, Mrs. Roscoe glancing freely about with unrestrained interest and curiosity.

Miss Jebb was there, sombrely attired. She had an alert, cheerful air as if determined to relish every moment; it was clear that she dearly loved a funeral, any funeral. There was no sign of her nephew. As she told Sergeant Lambert on her way into the chapel, he couldn't by any manner of means be persuaded to attend. He couldn't bear to sit through the ceremony, was sure he would break down. "I suppose he felt it would bring back memories of his mother's funeral," Miss Jebb conjectured. In the end he had agreed to drive her over, drop her off at the chapel, meet her again afterwards to run her home. How he intended to pass the interim he wouldn't say; she guessed it would most probably be spent wandering through the local park.

Neither of the Lorimers was present. And neither of the Claytons. Nor, as far as the Chief could ascertain, had any one of the four of them sent a single flower. From first to last of the proceedings Lambert saw tears shed for Karen Boland by only one person— Lynn Musgrove, a girl Karen had known a bare two months.

Afterwards Sergeant Lambert drove the Chief back to Cannonbridge. A woman was sitting in the reception area of the police station, drinking a cup of coffee, waiting to see the Chief; she had, it seemed, called in twenty minutes earlier, asking to speak to the officer in charge of the case.

Kelsey went over and introduced himself. She was a pleasant-looking, comfortably built countrywoman, fifty or so. She seemed quite at her ease, calmly drinking her coffee, explaining herself to the Chief.

She was a Mrs. Dyson, a widow working as resident housekeeper to an aged clergyman, long retired, living in a village a few miles to the north of Cannonbridge. In the late afternoon of Friday, November 13, having concluded her arrangements for ensuring that the vicar would be well looked after while she was away, she got into her car and set off on holiday. She was driving to the house of a woman friend sixty miles away to the east, where she would spend the night; next morning the two of them were going off on a coach tour of Europe.

Mrs. Dyson had got back from her holiday yesterday evening and had heard for the first time of the murder in Overmead Wood. She was told there was a full account of the crime in the regional Sunday paper but she didn't look at it then; she was tired after her journey and took herself off to bed. This morning, over breakfast, she read the paper and learned of the police appeal to passing motorists. She realized she had been in the Overmead area herself, had actually driven past the wood during the relevant period. And there had been a little incident. She couldn't see how it could have been in any way connected with the crime, but the timing was pretty exact, so in the end she decided to call in at the station, at the risk of being told she was wasting police time.

Kelsey assured her there was no question of her wasting his time

and asked what it was she had seen. Much encouraged, she em-
barked on her story.

A mile of two after beginning her journey she had entered a side
road that would drop her down on to the main thoroughfare running east out of Cannonbridge. This was the same side road which
ran past Jubilee Cottage, past the turning off to Hawthorn Lodge,
past the eastern edge of Overmead Wood, before joining the main
road.

The evening had grown wild and stormy, it was raining heavily as
she approached the junction. A short distance before the junction,
some twenty yards or so, she saw a stationary car facing her, on the
other side of the road, its headlights full on, both near side doors
wide open. The car had halted in the roadway, not on the verge. It
was dark, her windscreen wipers were going full blast, the car's
headlights dazzled her—but she did manage a glance in at the car as
she drove past, already slackening speed for the junction. Her impression was that there was no one inside the car.

Over on the verge, by the edge of the wood, she caught sight of a
woman. In the moment in which she glimpsed her she had the
fleeting impression that the woman had just ceased from rapid
motion.

Mrs. Dyson slowed her car to a crawl, wound down her window
and called back to the woman who stood motionless in the drench-
ing rain, looking across at her. "Are you all right?" Mrs. Dyson
shouted against the gusting wind. "Do you need any help?"

In reply the woman gave an energetic shake of her head. She
raised both hands, waved them in a vigorous gesture of refusal, and
shouted back, "No, thanks, I'm all right."

Reassured, Mrs. Dyson set off again for the junction; she didn't
glance back. Within a minute or two the little incident had dropped
from her mind.

Kelsey took her along to an interview room and settled down to
closely detailed questioning. She was an admirable witness, detached, shrewd, sensible—and, finest quality of all, in no way sug-
gestible.

She had seen no other person anywhere about, had received not
the vaguest impression of any other person being there. She had
noticed nothing lying on the verge—but that didn't mean there

might not have been objects scattered about. She hadn't glanced down at the verge, and, even if she had, she very much doubted that she would have been able to make them out, what with the rain, the dark and the dazzle.

The woman she had seen wore a light-coloured jacket, a light-coloured headscarf; whether trousers or a skirt she couldn't say, but whatever the lower garment was, it was dark in colour. When the woman raised her hands Mrs. Dyson saw that she wore dark-coloured gloves.

As to the woman's age, she would put that in the thirties or forties. Certainly not a young girl and quite definitely not elderly. The woman had not worn spectacles.

The Chief then tackled the matter of the car, getting Mrs. Dyson first to give him her recollection of the vehicle and only then showing her silhouettes and outlines in an effort further to prompt her memory.

The final results were neither clear nor sharp but by no means to be despised. She would set the vehicle down as large rather than small, old rather than new; an estate, station-wagon or hatchback type. With a rack on the roof. She was quite certain about the rack. When she slowed and looked back she glimpsed the rack, white or pale in hue, against the dark colour of the car. She couldn't specify the actual type, whether ladder-rack or roof-rack, though she unhesitatingly dismissed the notion of an octopus-style contraption.

The Chief threw at her an abrupt question: At the time she drove off again, what impression had she formed, what guess had she made, as to what the woman was doing there on the verge in the pouring rain, no one else about, but two, repeat two, of the car doors open?

She gave him a relaxed smile. "I was brought up in the country, we always had dogs. And the vicar I work for has a couple of dogs. It flashed through my mind that she could have been driving along with a dog in the back, that he'd let her know he wanted to get out to relieve himself, wouldn't take no for an answer, whining and agitated, pouring rain or not. So she pulled up, jumped out, threw open his door, and away he bounded. Afterwards he couldn't resist the wood, the undergrowth, maybe a rabbit in the brambles. She shouted and called but he wouldn't come back. She had to jump out herself, run up and down, calling, trying to spot him." She grinned. "I wish I had a five-pound note for every time that's happened to me." After her brief exchange with the woman she had been perfectly satisfied, she had in no way felt the woman was in any kind of real trouble.

The Chief then took Mrs. Dyson very carefully over the matter of the time this encounter had taken place. Mrs. Dyson was in no doubt at all about this, could in no way be shaken. She had been a little late in setting out and had therefore particularly noticed the time. The road was one she often used and she knew how long it took to reach the junction, allowing for the rain and the time of evening. But over and above all that, she had actually looked at her watch as she halted for the junction. She had given her friend a definite time of arrival and there would be a hot meal waiting; she never liked to be late.

Her watch had shown six-twenty. "It's an excellent timekeeper," she assured the Chief. Kelsey compared the time it gave with that on his own watch which he knew to be reliable beyond question; both were identical.

"That woman on the grass verge," the Chief said to Sergeant Lambert when he returned from escorting Mrs. Dyson from the building. "What's the first name that springs to mind?"

"Mrs. Clayton," Lambert replied promptly. "She could have found out, one way or another, that her husband was still seeing Karen. The first phone call to the college, at lunch-time, could have been made by Clayton, trying—and failing—to get hold of Karen, to tell her he'd better not see her for a while, his wife was growing suspicious. The second call could have been from Mrs. Clayton, demanding that Karen meet her after class, or she'd go to the Wilmots and the Social Services. The note Karen scribbled to Lynn Musgrove: 'Got to meet someone.' That's always sounded to me like someone she didn't want to meet, someone she was forced to meet, rather than a lover or a relative she was on good terms with." He grimaced. "Only one thing doesn't square—the car. Mrs. Clayton drives a family saloon, cream colour. There's no way anyone could call that car dark, however bad the light. You couldn't call it large, and you couldn't call it old. And it doesn't carry any kind of rack."

Kelsey waved a hand. "The car's no problem. Mrs. Clayton said she was out collecting jumble that afternoon and early evening. I can't see her using her own car for that, she'd be much more likely to borrow a vehicle from her husband, one of the firm's cars. I'll bet you any money there's an estate car—or something similar—among them. Oldish, darkish, largish. And with some kind of rack."

19

Mrs. Clayton had just finished a meagre lunch when they called. She looked tense and drawn. She didn't appear surprised to see them, she seemed to have gone beyond a point where surprise could touch her.

She took them into the kitchen and began to clear her lunch things from the table with a mechanical air. Her lunch appeared to have consisted of coffee and biscuits. She didn't offer them anything, didn't ask them to sit down. The Chief said nothing but stood waiting for her to speak.

She turned suddenly from the sink and flung at them in an agitated, distracted fashion: "Paul isn't here, he never comes home to lunch on a weekday. You'll have to ask at the office where he is. He could be in the works or he could be out seeing a customer, I've no idea." Still Kelsey said nothing. She seized the back of a chair with both hands and pressed heavily down on it in a fierce grip. "I don't know why you keep coming after him. He didn't kill her. I know he didn't."

Kelsey sprang on that at once. "How do you know he didn't?"

She fell silent. "He's not that kind of man," she said at last in an exhausted tone. "He wouldn't hurt anyone."

"It isn't your husband we've come to see," Kelsey told her. "It's you." She stared up at him. "Why don't we all sit down?" he suggested.

She drew a little sighing breath and removed her clenched grip from the chair.

"That Friday evening," Kelsey began when they were all seated. "You told us you were out collecting jumble for the PTA." She gave a nod. "What vehicle did you use?"

She seemed disconcerted. "Vehicle?" she echoed, frowning. Kelsey waited in silence while she cast about in her mind. "I used one of the firm's cars," she eventually decided. He asked her to describe it, he had to keep prompting her with subsidiary questions before she finished the description: an estate car, eight or nine years old, on the large side, medium grey in colour. Yes, there was a rack, made of chromium, the metal unpainted; whether a ladder-rack or roof-rack she couldn't say, she didn't know the difference between the two. She had never made use of the rack itself.

The Chief asked what clothes she had worn that afternoon.

Again she appeared disconcerted. When he repeated the question she told him she couldn't be sure, after the lapse of time. He continued to press her. What would she be likely to wear for that kind of job, on an afternoon of intermittent rain? Most probably slacks, she answered after further hesitation. And a jacket of some kind. She couldn't be sure which one, she had several. Would she have covered up her hair? Yes, she might have worn a headscarf, she couldn't say which one.

Yes, she did normally wear driving gloves. She had only one pair and produced them at his request. Black leather, in very good condition, almost new; no cuts or rips, no stains. He asked if he could look through her outdoor clothes and she complied without reluctance. He took his time, looking carefully through everything—including her half-dozen headscarves—without result.

He asked her to hold out her hands, to turn them over, although there was little point at this late stage. Her hands were fairly well cared for, although some of the nails were deeply bitten. Here and there the skin showed a tiny, half-healed cut, the mark of a little scald or burn, as might be expected of any housewife.

"Did you phone Karen Boland at the Cannonbridge college at twenty minutes to six that Friday evening?" he asked abruptly.

There was no hesitation now. "I did not," she retorted with force.

"Why should I phone her? I never phoned her, I never had any occasion to."

"To ask her to meet you after class, you wanted to talk to her."

"Why should I want to talk to her? I didn't want anything to do with her. I was very glad to see the back of her."

"To tell her you knew she was still seeing your husband. To threaten her that if she didn't stop seeing him you'd go to the Wilmots, to the Social Services."

A brilliant flush surged in her face. "That isn't true!" she burst out. "I had no idea Paul was still seeing her."

"It started to rain as she came out of the college," Kelsey continued imperturbably. "Did you tell her to get in the car? You'd run her home, say what you had to say on the way."

Her face was still fiery red. She struck a fist into her palm. "There's not a word of truth in that! I never laid eyes on the girl since the day she left the Roscoes." All at once she broke into unrestrained sobs. She dropped her head into her arms, leaning forward on the table, her shoulders heaving.

It was some time before the Chief could proceed. He took her through her account of the way she had spent that Friday afternoon and evening, in particular through her timings. She appeared drained and fatigued, she answered his questions flatly, without protest.

She had collected her last load of jumble from the house of a couple named Havergill, an address on the western edge of Cannonbridge. They were completely unknown to her. Mrs. Havergill had phoned a few days previously in response to an advertisement Mrs. Clayton had put in the evening paper, asking for jumble for the PTA sale, offering to collect.

The Havergills were moving house and had a quantity of bric-à-brac they would be happy to give. Mrs. Clayton didn't make a definite appointment. Both the Havergills went out to work; she could call at any time after five-fifteen. In the event she reached the house around six and left about half an hour later. She then drove straight to the hall where the sale was to be held, as she had done with her other loads. Several mothers were at work in the hall, unloading, sorting, pricing; she supplied the Chief with names. As soon as her load had been dealt with she drove off home, arriving there around seven.

The Havergills told her they were moving the following Monday to a town seventy miles away to the north. She didn't have the address.

But the new owners of the house the Havergills had just vacated did have the address and later in the afternoon Sergeant Lambert drove the Chief north. The Havergills were expecting them; Kelsey had spoken to Mrs. Havergill on the phone. He hadn't told her what information he was seeking or what case he was working on, merely that he believed she and her husband might be able to help in some inquiries. The result was that when Lambert halted the car outside the brand-new, up-market, detached house on the exclusive estate where the Havergills now lived, he and Kelsey were received with an air of mystification, baffled and inquiring looks.

The Chief still didn't enlighten them. He apologized for disturbing them at a busy time. He accepted their offer of coffee and at once began to ask about the events of that Friday.

The Havergills were a childless couple in early middle age, both employed by the same prosperous, rapidly expanding firm; Havergill had been transferred to manage a new branch.

They both remembered clearly the events of that Friday. Mrs. Havergill confirmed that they had had no previous acquaintance with Mrs. Clayton, that the offer of jumble had been made in response to an advertisement, and that no particular appointment had been made; Mrs. Clayton was to call during the early evening. She had arrived just as the weather forecast was coming on before the six o'clock news.

It was raining heavily as all three of them went to load the car, so Mrs. Clayton backed it up to the side door. They were both able to recall the vehicle Mrs. Clayton was driving, not in precise detail, but well enough: an estate car, largish, oldish. About the colour there was a difference of opinion, Mrs. Havergill inclining towards an indeterminate blue, her husband plumping for a middling shade of green. They were both positive there was a rack, though neither could describe it. They were certain of its existence because there had been a discussion about whether everything could be got inside the vehicle or some of it might have to go up on the rack. In the event it had all been stowed inside.

When they had finished, Mrs. Havergill made tea and the three of them sat in the kitchen drinking it. They chatted about their move, Havergill's promotion. It must have been at least six-thirty as she drove off into the blustery downpour.

Mrs. Clayton's manner had been in no way unusual, she had not appeared at all agitated. She had struck them as a quiet, rather reserved woman. As to what she had been wearing, they both agreed on a light-coloured jacket, dark trousers and a headscarf. Mrs. Havergill thought the scarf was pale blue, her husband described it as whitish.

Kelsey got back into the car in a deflated mood. It only remained now to check with the mothers about the time of Mrs. Clayton's arrival at the hall but he was already sure that they would confirm her account. "Looks as if she's in the clear," he observed moodily as Lambert set the car in motion.

He sat for some time in silence, staring despondently out at the thickening traffic. It would be late by the time they got back to Cannonbridge. A bite to eat, a hot bath and straight into bed.

"Christine Wilmot," Sergeant Lambert said suddenly on a flash of memory: that first Saturday morning at Jubilee Cottage after they arrived there from Overmead Wood, himself crossing the hall of the cottage, going into the kitchen to make tea. A woman's jacket lying over a chair, a light grey jacket of some waterproof material. On the table beside it, a shoulder-bag, a pair of navy blue woollen gloves. And a headscarf, of some silky, flowered stuff, pale lavender in colour. He said as much to Kelsey.

"We only saw the one car at Jubilee Cottage," Lambert added. "Ian Wilmot's car." A smallish saloon, claret-red, roughly four years old. "But Ian said he always gave Karen a lift in the mornings. If he takes the car to work then Christine must have another for her rounds."

Shortly after eight-thirty next morning Lambert drove the Chief out to Jubilee Cottage. With luck Ian Wilmot would already have gone off to work but Christine would still be in the house.

And luck was with them. Christine was alone, dealing with chores before setting out on her rounds. They heard the drone of a vacuum cleaner as they stepped out of the car.

Lambert gave a long, steady press on the bell and the drone ceased. Christine came to the door, giving them a calm, wary look. She seemed a good deal better, alert and energetic. She was neatly dressed, well groomed.

The Chief wasted no time in preliminary chat but at once asked her what vehicle she used in her business.

"You can see for yourself," she answered without hesitation. "It's in the garage." She took them round to the back of the house and over to the far side of the garden. A double garage stood behind a tall, carefully trimmed screen of Leyland cypress.

Inside was an estate car some twelve years old. Showing its age but in fairish condition. A nondescript colour between khaki and dark beige. A roof-rack painted a toning shade of putty several years ago, the paint flaking here and there.

"I use this during the week," Christine explained. "I take Ian's car on Saturday mornings." She didn't ask why they wanted to see the vehicle; she didn't ask any questions. Kelsey asked if they might go into the house, there were one or two matters he would like cleared up. She turned without a word and led the way back to the house.

In the sitting-room she remained standing, didn't ask them to sit down. She turned her head with a deliberate movement and looked at the mantel clock.

"We won't keep you long," Kelsey assured her. "I'd like to take you back over your movements during the afternoon and evening of Friday, November 13. This time we'd like a little more detail."

She gave an impatient nod and without further prompting launched into an account of her catalogue round, the two sales parties she had attended, supplying names and addresses, approximate times. After finishing her round she had driven back to the cottage to take a quick shower and change before going on to the first party. She hadn't stopped to eat anything, there were always plenty of refreshments at such parties. It was about a quarter to eight when she returned to the cottage to change, about a quarter past when she left again.

Kelsey asked what she had worn during her catalogue round.

She frowned. "Probably jeans or slacks, a sweater, a jacket." She certainly couldn't remember which. Yes, probably a headscarf against the wind and rain. And yes, she did always wear driving-gloves. He looked at her hands. Exceptionally well cared for, though their shape was far from elegant, large and broad, the fingers thick and blunt-ended. A legacy from her father and grandfather, Sergeant Lambert thought, a modified female version of the powerful hands of a building labourer.

She showed him her outdoor clothes, her headscarves, driving-gloves, all without result. Downstairs again Christine gave another open glance at the clock but Kelsey waved her into a chair and sat himself determinedly down opposite her.

He plunged in at once. "Did you phone Karen that Friday at twenty minutes to six at the college?"

"I did not," she replied with force. "I had no reason to phone her."

"Perhaps you told her you were in the vicinity, it looked as if it was coming on to storm, you could give her a lift if she was going straight home after classes."

"I was nowhere near the college at that time," she declared. "I was on the council estate, I'm always there at that time on a Friday. I've already told you." The estate was large, on the south-western outskirts of Cannonbridge. She always covered it on Friday afternoon, from two-fifteen till seven-thirty. "I couldn't possibly have offered Karen a lift home at six o'clock, I had another hour and a half of calls to make on the estate after that."

Kelsey darted off at a tangent. "Were you jealous of Karen?" he fired at her. "Did you feel your husband was paying her too much attention? Were you suspicious of her? Did you think she was making up to him?"

"This is ridiculous," she answered with angry contempt. "There was never anything like that between them."

"With the best will in the world," Kelsey observed, off at another tangent, "the situation you found yourself in, Karen being placed in your care, put a great deal of temptation in your way. You knew about the trust, you knew you stood to gain a considerable sum of money in the event of her early death. You knew your husband wasn't likely to get any further in his career. You do well enough in your business but you can never make a fortune at it, never make any large capital sum—and it involves you in never-ending work." She flung out a dismissive hand. "We were very comfortably off as we were, we had no need to go looking for capital sums." She took out a handkerchief and dabbed at her eyes. "The money will make no difference to the way we live."

"How did you see Karen?" the Chief pressed her. "As a stranger determined to insinuate herself into your family, your home? As the child of a man you'd been brought up to envy and resent, the successful uncle who would never stretch out a helping hand to your father, who'd made nothing of his own life?" He leaned forward. "Or did you see her as an immoral, delinquent teenager, bringing trouble with her wherever she went, not entitled to normal human rights?"

She looked steadily back at him. "I know you have to do all this, say all this, it's all part of your job. Neither Ian or I had anything to do with her death. Neither of us would have hurt a hair of her head." She suddenly broke into shaking sobs.

When they left the cottage a few minutes later they drove straight to the council estate Christine had spoken of. Lambert rang the bell at the door of the little semi-detached house she claimed to be visiting around six o'clock that Friday.

The door was opened by a spry, cheerful old man somewhat hard of hearing. He leaned forward, cupping his hand behind his ear, straining to catch the Chief Inspector's words. His wife came briskly along from the kitchen. "I'll deal with it," she told her husband with a crisp, smiling nod. She listened to the Chief's deliberately vague spiel. Yes, certainly they might come inside. Yes, she and her husband would be delighted to offer any assistance they could. She clearly recalled Christine Wilmot's visit that Friday; she had a particular reason for recalling it. Her husband had had a modest endowment insurance policy reach maturity and pay out a couple of days before and they had decided to splash out, treat themselves to some new, smart clothing for the coming winter, some extra items for the house. Christine had called at around half past five and they had all three settled down to an engrossing study of the catalogue. Shortly after six their granddaughter called in on her way home from work —she lived close by and looked in every weekday evening.

On that Friday she stayed longer than usual, joining in the poring over the catalogue, offering advice and opinions. Eventually decisions were made, orders placed. The granddaughter went off home and Christine departed to the semi next door. That would be at about a quarter to seven. Some ten minutes or so later the old lady had second thoughts about the colour of a cardigan and went next door to see if she could catch Christine.

Christine was still there. The old lady apologized for intruding, asked Christine to change the colour on the order form and returned to her own house. That would be around seven o'clock and Christine had by no means yet finished her dealings with the neighbours.

Kelsey heaved a long sigh as he got into the car again and directed Lambert back to the station. No question about it: from half past five to seven Christine's movements were indisputably accounted for.

He found a message waiting for him at the desk: the owner of the clothes shop had rung to say that Barny Pringle, the old lag who had shared a cell with Victor Lorimer, had phoned to ask if the coast was clear. The shopkeeper assured Pringle he could safely return but Pringle had hummed and hawed, he would give it another few days, to be on the safe side. The shopkeeper, mindful of his promise to the Chief Inspector, managed to winkle out of him the address of the place where he was now staying—a doss-house in a town forty miles to the north-east of Cannonbridge. The shopkeeper said nothing to Pringle about the police wanting a word with him.

Half an hour later the Chief was on his way.

20

It was close on twelve-thirty by the time they located the doss-house in a dismal, dilapidated quarter of the town. They left the car parked at a discreet distance and walked round to the building, a very rough and ready place but clean enough, run with some attempt at discipline and humanity by a down-to-earth married couple by the name of Cochrane.

Yes, they had a Barny Pringle staying there. He was sure to be in, he displayed a profound reluctance to leave the premises for any purpose, was under the fixed impression there were men waiting for him outside. Cochrane didn't know if Pringle could be persuaded to talk to them, he would probably at once conclude his worst fears had been realized, his pursuers had caught up with him.

It was very nearly lunch-time. Mrs. Cochrane always served up a hot meat stew with chunks of bread and mugs of tea at this time of day and the line of men was already forming outside the dining-room. Cochrane offered to find Pringle, reassure him, persuade him to come and talk to them; they could use the Cochranes' private sitting-room for the purpose. He found Pringle firmly ensconced in his position near the head of the line of hungry men. It took him some little time to detach Pringle from his place in order to speak to him on one side in comparative privacy, the word "police" not being one to utter too audibly in that company. When he finally managed to get Pringle out of earshot of the others—on the sworn promise that his place would be kept for him—it was only by the exercise of considerable diplomacy and the guarantee that Mrs. Cochrane would save an extra large helping of stew for him, that he agreed to see the two detectives at all.

Cochrane lost no time in taking Pringle along to where Kelsey and Lambert sat waiting for him. As soon as the door opened Kelsey got to his feet and approached with his hand held out, his most affable and fear-allaying smile plastered to his lips.

"Well now, Barny," he began, adopting the matey, semi-jocular tone he always used with old lags who might conceivably be disposed to help him. "It's very good of you to spare us five minutes, we really appreciate it." He cast a rapid eye over Pringle. A skinny, nimble-looking little man of seventy or so, who gave the impression that he might still be able to call up a turn of speed, might yet be capable of outdistancing a pursuer. Dressed and groomed fairly presentably—by doss-house standards.

Pringle suffered his hand to be grasped and shaken. Cochrane was about to take himself off again but Pringle darted at him a glance of alarm that halted him on the threshold. "It's all right, Barny," the Chief said with massive benevolence. "Mr. Cochrane can stay if it makes you any happier." Pringle gave a quick nod and Cochrane sank into a chair near the door.

When the Chief managed to persuade Pringle to sit down he chose an upright chair, perching on the edge, leaning forward with his hands splayed out on his knees, ready for flight. The Chief explained that he had no interest whatever in any aspect of Pringle's own behaviour. All he wanted was to ask him what he knew about a former cell-mate. Still Pringle gazed warily and uncooperatively back at him. Kelsey went on to say that his inquiries were in connection with the brutal death of a young girl and that the name of the cell-mate was Victor Lorimer, though the Chief was scrupulously careful not to let slip the information that the dead girl was Lorimer's stepdaughter, the girl in the case that had put Lorimer behind bars.

Pringle's attitude underwent an abrupt change. Suspicion and wariness dropped away. He sat back in his chair, moved his hands into a more relaxed position. He invited the Chief to fire away, he was ready to tell him anything he knew, help in any way he could. Indeed, before the Chief could open his mouth to get out his first question, Pringle launched into an energetic appraisal of Lorimer.

He had never liked the man, couldn't stomach the kind of crime Lorimer had committed. He couldn't blame the prisoners who had attacked Lorimer in the showers, Lorimer had only got what was coming to him. Men like that knew what to expect if they landed up in gaol.

Not that Pringle himself had ever openly quarrelled with Lorimer. Pringle would have the Chief know he regarded himself as a peaceful man, avoiding all forms of violence whenever possible. He certainly wouldn't have run the risk of adding to his own sentence by having a go at Lorimer—who was in any case a good deal younger, taller and fitter than he was—when they were assigned a cell together. He had simply made it his business to get along with Lorimer without friction, keeping his critical opinions to himself.

He couldn't in all honesty say that Lorimer had been difficult to get along with. He had kept his head down, complied with all the regulations, maintained an iron grip on his temper, offered no hostility to staff or inmates. He spent much of his time reading, talking little, hardly at all about himself, displayed no interest in Pringle, no wish to hear the story of Pringle's life.

Although Lorimer religiously worked through a daily programme of physical exercises he often lay on his bed doing nothing at all, staring up at the ceiling in silence. Some nights he would be unable to sleep, and then he would get up and pace up and down, up and down. "I've always been a first-class sleeper myself," Pringle told them with pride. "If it woke me up, him pacing about like that, I never let it bother me. I just used to turn over and close my eyes again, let him get on with it."

He grimaced. "These educated men, prison's a lot rougher on them—even when they're not perverts—than it is on ordinary blokes like me. They seem to feel pent up all the time, can't seem to settle down. The longer they're in, the worse they get. Lorimer's mother died while he was inside and he got even quieter, more shut up inside himself, after that. It really did knock the stuffing out of him for a while. He was like a wooden dummy for a long time afterwards, just going through the motions."

No, Lorimer had never talked to him about the case that had sent him to gaol. He had never uttered one single solitary syllable on the matter to Pringle, who would in any case—or so he averred in virtuous tones—have instantly shut him up if he had tried to broach so unsavoury a topic.

"But Lorimer's missus did talk to me about it once," he added, jerking his head with an air of self-approbation as if at the mention of some signal honour bestowed on him. "It was one visiting time," he enlarged, catching the look of sharp interest in Kelsey's green eyes. "An old mate of mine had been in to see me but he couldn't stay the full half-hour, he had to get off, a bit of business to attend to. I stood up to go back to the cell. I was walking past the table where Lorimer was sitting with his missus. A very tidy-looking woman, very ladylike, very neatly dressed, nothing showy.

"As I went past she touched my arm. She said, 'Please excuse me. I hope you don't mind me speaking to you but I'd like to introduce myself.' Lorimer was sitting there not saying a word. You could see he didn't like her speaking to me. She said, 'I know you share a cell with Victor, I asked him to point you out to me.' She asked me what I was in for."

He made a face. "I was a bit surprised, her coming straight out with it, like that, but I didn't take offence. I told her I was in for housebreaking. She said, 'Did you actually do it?' Very serious." He gave a laugh of genuine amusement. "I wondered what was coming next. I told her, 'Well, I may have done. The judge certainly seemed to think so.' But she never smiled.

"I didn't sit down. She did ask me to, right at the beginning, but I didn't like to, not with Lorimer sitting there with a face like a hanging judge." He tilted his head back, half closed his eyes. "I can see her now, looking up at me, talking low and fierce, as if she meant every word. She said, 'My husband never did the terrible thing they charged him with. He was pressured into pleading guilty. One day the truth will come out and his name will be cleared. That's what keeps me going, what keeps both of us going. They took the word of a deceitful, jealous girl against an honourable, upright man. It was a gross miscarriage of justice.' " He widened his eyes at the Chief. "Her very words, I've never forgotten them. She looked really wound up, as if for two pins she could have burst into tears."

A little later, as they came out again into the bleak street, Kelsey said, "That girl, the one Karen was at school with—"

"Becky Ayliffe," Lambert supplied.

"She's working not all that far from here, if I recall."

Lambert cast his mind back to what the Okeshot constable had told them over the phone. "It'd be about twenty miles from here, by my reckoning. Over to the north-west." The constable had called round to the Ayliffe home a couple of times, had finally found Mrs. Ayliffe in. She was horrified at the news of the murder, anxious to be of help in any way she could. Yes, Becky was working away from home, apprenticed at a pottery. She couldn't afford to come home often for weekends but she rang her mother faithfully every Sunday.

Kelsey looked at his watch. Back in Cannonbridge the paperwork would be rising, mound upon mound. He moved his shoulders. What would another hour or two signify against that silent, inexorable progress?

"Right," he said with cheerful decision. "We'll nip over there now, see if we can get a word with Becky. We'll find a bite to eat on

the way. It should be a nice little run." He glanced about at the grey
street, the disheartened buildings. "Make a pleasant change from
this."

And it did make a pleasant change, a very nice little run indeed,
taking them into tourist country, through pretty villages immaculately groomed, along the path of a noble river, past wooded slopes,
gold and amber, across stretches of common land clothed with
gorse and bracken, through twisting lanes, brightly berried.

The pottery where Becky worked was a small, privately-run concern, on the outskirts of a picture-postcard village much frequented
by holidaymakers in the season. A well-organized, thriving set-up,
with a comfortable dwelling-house attached, where Becky lived with
the owners of the enterprise, a married couple, both potters, and
their two school-age children.

The husband answered the door to them. A slender young man
with a gentle, amiable face artistically fringed with golden sideburns
and a short, curling beard. He wasn't surprised to see them. Becky
had told them in some distress, after her phone call home on Sunday, of the appalling news her mother had just broken to her—and
the fact that the Cannonbridge police might at some time be in
touch with her. They had all three of them later in the day read a full
account of the case in the regional Sunday paper.

His wife was busy in the pottery, at a crucial stage of operations.
He would have to get back there himself, but Becky could be spared
for half an hour. He took them into a sitting-room and sat them
down, vanished briefly, returned to say that Becky wouldn't be a
moment, she was washing her hands, vanished again.

Becky appeared a minute or two later. A tall, well-built girl, strong
and active-looking. Pleasant enough appearance, honey-coloured
skin and large brown eyes, thick, shining, black hair simply and
becomingly arranged. She wore trim working clothes.

Her manner was composed as she greeted them; she looked like a
girl it wouldn't be easy to fluster. She seemed older than her years,
with an air of lively awareness, shrewd common sense. She answered the Chief's questions readily.

She had had no contact of any kind with Karen since the day
Karen spoke to the teacher about Lorimer. Becky had first met
Karen when they were both eleven years old, on the day they walked

in through the doors of the secondary school in Okeshot. Karen had latched on to her at once, had made a point of sitting next to her in class, always seemed to regard her as some kind of protector. "She was a very quiet girl," Becky said. "She always seemed very lonely."

Karen was never at all eager to talk about herself but with perseverance Becky managed to piece together a few details of her background. She learned that Karen's father was very ill, that he had recently remarried. "She was very locked up inside herself," Becky added. "Very worried about her father. After he died she got quieter than ever."

She looked levelly at the Chief. "We were never close friends. She just hung on to me. She was never any bother. I was always rather sorry for her, she didn't have any other friends at school. She never invited me to her home and she never came to mine." She smiled slightly. "We came from very different backgrounds."

"Do you know how she got on with her stepmother?" Kelsey asked.

"She hardly ever talked about her. I saw her stepmother at school sometimes. I had the impression Karen thought she did her best for her, did her duty by her, but that was all it was, duty, nothing more. I never got the impression they were really fond of each other."

Kelsey asked how Karen had taken her stepmother's remarriage.

"She never said a word about it to me till it was all arranged. There was something on at school one Saturday morning, some sports fixture. I asked her if she was going to it and she said she couldn't, she had to be at her stepmother's wedding." Becky made a little face. "That did rock me back on my heels. I always knew she was pretty secretive, but not to say one syllable about the wedding until a couple of days before—and then only when she was forced to —that really did take the biscuit.

"Of course I wanted to know all about it, who the man was, what did he do, did Karen like him, and so on. She didn't want to talk about it but I kept on at her." She grinned. "I'm rather nosy, and I can be pretty persistent when I want to be. And the situation did strike me as very interesting, most unusual—Karen would be living with two step-parents after the wedding; I'd never come across that before. In the end I did get her to open up a bit."

She paused. "She told me that the man her stepmother was going to marry fancied her, Karen, that he'd fancied her all along, but he wasn't getting any change out of her and he wasn't going to get any change out of her. She sounded quite vicious when she said that. Of course when she told me who he was, Mr. Lorimer from the library, I was more interested than ever. I used to go to the library a lot. I'd often seen him, I'd talked to him sometimes. I always thought he was very nice, kind and friendly.

"After what she told me, of course, I used to stare at him whenever I went to the library." She smiled. "But he didn't look any different. I used to think she could have made it all up, lonely people often do make things up. Right at the start, when she first told me about the way he was behaving, I asked her why she hadn't said anything about it to her stepmother, why she was just standing by without a word and letting the marriage take place."

"What did she say to that?"

"She said it would be no use saying anything, no one would believe her, Lorimer would simply deny it. She hadn't wanted her father to marry her stepmother and now she didn't want her stepmother to marry Lorimer—it would look like pure jealousy on her part, trying to throw a spanner into the works. Her stepmother certainly wouldn't believe her, the marriage would still take place, but from then on Karen would be living under a black cloud. So why speak up? What good would it do?" She jerked her head. "I couldn't think of any answer to that."

"And after the marriage?"

"She got more locked up inside herself than ever. I asked her sometimes how she was getting on with Lorimer, if he was behaving himself. She still wouldn't talk about things, she never did, all the time I knew her. Anything she ever told me I had to prise out of her. She gave me the impression things were just the same, Lorimer was still trying it on, she was still freezing him off, still keeping her mouth shut. Her stepmother was still crazy about Lorimer and still hadn't noticed anything. I used to mention sometimes that I'd seen Lorimer in the library, that I'd spoken to him. I'd say he looked all right to me, ordinary, normal, very pleasant."

"What would she say to that?"

"She'd just shrug and say, 'That's how he seems to everyone.' I did ask her once outright if she'd invented the whole thing because she hadn't wanted her stepmother to marry again." Becky sighed. "She didn't answer that at all. She just gave me a look and turned away. I can see that look now, as if she was saying: Even you don't really believe me."

"But in the end she did speak out," Kelsey said. "Did that surprise you?"

Becky hesitated. He repeated his question but still she hesitated.

He frowned. "Is there something you know? Something apart from what came out at the time?"

Still she made no reply.

"Karen died a hideous death," Kelsey said. "The girl who sat next to you in school. Unless everyone tells us everything they know we may never find her killer."

She moved a hand. "I don't really know anything, not actually know. It would only be guesswork on my part."

"Tell me," he urged. "We won't take it for any more than it is."

Still she hung back. "I wouldn't want to appear in court."

"You won't have to," he assured her. "Courts of law don't deal in guesswork."

She studied him in silence, then suddenly shrugged. "Oh well, she's dead now, and the boy's over at the other side of the world. I don't see it can make much difference to him now." Once her mind was made up she launched rapidly into what she had to say.

"There was this boy—I don't know his name, I never did know it. He was about eighteen months older than Karen. His dad was a right martinet, a warrant officer in the army, serving in Germany. The lad was an only child, he'd been moved about a lot, his father being in the army. At the time I'm talking about he was at some boarding-school near London. His father was coming to the end of his time in the army and his mother took a house in Cannonbridge, rented it, furnished, for a year. She went to the same church that Karen and her step-parents went to.

"Karen and the lad saw each other at church when he came back to Cannonbridge for his school holidays. One day they came across each other, just by chance, in the park; they were both watching the tennis."

She cast her mind back. "This would be around the time Karen's stepmother and Lorimer were courting, getting married." She paused. "The way I know all this is because one day in the holidays I happened to see Karen and the lad together, otherwise Karen would never have said a word to me about him, you can bank on that. I was in the park with some other kids, playing some game, and it came on to rain. I dashed into one of the shelters and there they were, Karen and a boy, tucked away in a corner. I was so surprised I couldn't say anything, not even hello—Karen was the last girl I'd ever expect to find sitting there with a boy. I just dashed off out again, to another shelter.

"After the holidays, when we were back at school again, I asked her about him and she told me what I've just told you." Becky grinned. "Of course when I say she told me, I mean I had to worm it out of her inch by inch. That time in the park was the only time I ever saw them together. She never mentioned him again and I forgot about him.

"Then one day months later, I happened to think of him and I asked her if she still knew him. She sounded very non-committal. She said his father would be leaving the army very soon, the family was emigrating to New Zealand. The father had an uncle out there, a widower with no children. The uncle had pots of money, he owned a big sheep station. He'd told them he'd leave them the whole lot if they came out to join him. The father jumped at the chance, they were all dead keen to go. I thought no more about it.

"Some time later I noticed something was wrong. Karen seemed quieter than ever, not at all well. I asked her if she was all right but she said she was. She was quite short with me. But I still wondered. The form teacher noticed it too. She asked Karen a couple of times if there was anything wrong but Karen always told her no, everything was fine.

"Then not very long after that Karen opened her mouth." She shook her head, still astonished at the speed of it all. "She was there in the morning, sitting beside me in class as usual. By the end of the afternoon she'd gone. I never saw her again, never spoke to her again. It was just as if she'd been snatched from the face of the earth.

"It was several days before the rest of us in school knew anything at all about what had happened, and then for a long time it was mostly rumours. Afterwards, when it was all over and Lorimer had been sent to gaol, I did sometimes think about getting in touch with

Karen again, writing to her, trying to find out where to send the
letter." She stared out of the window. "I started a letter once or
twice, but I could never think what to say. The longer I left it the
harder it got. In the end I never did write to her."

"To get back to this bit of guesswork on your part," Kelsey
prompted. "What did that amount to?"

She gazed earnestly at him. "You must understand I didn't work
all this out at the time. It was only afterwards, when I began to grow
up a bit, that I started trying to figure it out.

"What really puzzled me, when I first heard about the accusations
she'd made was how Karen had come to let such things happen.
She'd been able to handle Lorimer all right for long enough, how
come she hadn't been able to fend him off to the end?

"I started thinking. I remembered the boy I'd seen her with. I was
sure it was all very innocent between them, just boy and girl, both of
them lonely, looking for affection. When the lad started talking
about going off to New Zealand I dare say he was full of excitement,
a new country, a new life, new friends. But for Karen it was probably
a terrible blow. Going off all that great distance away, knowing she'd
never see him again. When the time came to say goodbye, maybe
she lost her head, got carried away. Then very soon afterwards, she
discovers she's in trouble. She's terrified, worried out of her wits.

"What can she do? Who can she turn to? She's absolutely desper-
ate. The boy's on the other side of the world. His father would half
kill him if he found out. And they were both under age—she's
terrified she'll land up in court if anyone discovers what she's
done."

She struck her hands together. "Then, out of the blue, she sees
the answer." She threw a glance at Kelsey. "It looks like a brilliant
inspiration—she's not much more than a kid, worried half out of her
mind. Her stepfather—he's the solution! He's still trying it on with
her, she still has to keep him at bay, though by this time it's automatic, she doesn't think about it much. All she has to do is stop
giving him her regular get-lost signal. Just that, no more—for sure
she can leave the rest to him.

"She acts out of impulse and panic. It wouldn't cross her mind
that her stepmother would stand by Lorimer, that she'd be the one
to be sent away. And I don't for one moment suppose she worked it

all out, that she realized everything it would mean for Lorimer. If any thought of that does bother her she tells herself he's asked for it, it serves him right. He's an adult, on the other side of the fence, he can look out for himself."

She tilted her head back. "I don't suppose Lorimer ever really knew what hit him. For long enough she's resisted him, then all of a sudden one day her manner changes." Becky spread open a hand. "He takes the bait." She snapped her fingers into a clenched fist, like a springing trap.

She moved her head. "There could have been something else in it too, a bit of getting her own back on her stepmother. She may have told herself: She took my father, now I'll take her husband." She grimaced. "Even in the middle of all that worry, all that panic, that notion might still have appealed to her."

21

A huge gold sun hung low in the sky as Chief Inspector Kelsey and Sergeant Lambert set off at a quarter to eight next morning for Furzebank Cottage. The greater part of the journey was made in almost unbroken silence.

As the road straightened after a bend Lambert saw the little general store come into view on the other side of the road.

"The shopwoman's son," he said. "I'd forgotten about him." The Chief made no reply, sunk deep in his own thoughts.

"Robin, she said his name was," Lambert went on. He allowed the car to slacken pace. "I wonder if he remembered anything. She was going to ask him."

The Chief registered the car's loss of speed. He gave the sergeant an abstracted glance.

"Bit of a long shot," Lambert added. "Robin wasn't even in the

shop when Mrs. Lorimer called in for cigarettes." He let the car slow
almost to a halt. "Still, one never knows." He directed a questioning
glance at the Chief.

Kelsey gave an irritated grunt. What was uppermost in his mind
was pressing smartly on to Furzebank Cottage, tackling the
Lorimers—in particular Enid Lorimer—yet again. The last thing he
wanted right now was to find himself submerged in a stream of
inane chatter from a woman who had difficulty identifying the day of
the week—and her no doubt equally exasperating son.

He opened his mouth to instruct Lambert to drive on. But old
training and long habit were too much for him. "All right," he
conceded with deep reluctance. "Pull up. Let's get it over with."

The shop was empty but the woman came promptly through from
the domestic quarters at the sound of the bell. The Chief had no
time to utter a syllable before she burst out: "Good morning, Chief
Inspector! I wondered if you'd be calling in again." She gave him a
broad, delighted smile. "I did talk to Robin as soon as he came
home after the last time you were here. I asked him if he remembered anything about Mrs. Lorimer coming in for the cigarettes, as I
promised you I would." She gestured towards the doorway at the
rear of the shop. "You can speak to him yourselves. He's eating his
breakfast before he gets off to school. You'd better come through."

She took them into a cosy, comfortable kitchen where her son sat
at the table attacking a plateful of bacon, sausage, egg, fried pota-
toes, baked beans, tomatoes. A rack of toast stood close by. An open
textbook was propped against a jar of marmalade.

Robin glanced up as they came in and at once set down his knife
and fork, pushed back his chair and sprang to his feet. A tall, thin lad
in school uniform, very clean and neat, very well groomed. An
intelligent, studious face, a courteous, friendly manner.

His mother had barely made the introductions when the ping of
the shop bell summoned her back to serve a customer. "Give the
officers some coffee," she instructed her son as she left the kitchen.

The Chief declined the coffee and waved Robin back into his seat.
"We don't want to delay you any more than we have to," he said as
he sat down facing him. "You can get on with your breakfast as we
talk."

Far from breaking into a tiresome stream of confused chatter,

Robin answered his questions simply, sensibly and concisely—while contriving at the same time to tackle his breakfast with efficiency and despatch.

When his mother told him of their previous visit, of her difficulty in deciding if it was on the Wednesday, Thursday or Friday evening that Mrs. Lorimer had called in for cigarettes, Robin had sat down there and then and given the matter concentrated thought.

His recollections were clear and he wrote them down without delay, in case the Chief Inspector should call again. He excused himself while he went to fetch his notes from a desk in the sitting-room.

"It was definitely the Friday evening when Mrs. Lorimer came in for the cigarettes," he told them on his return. "Friday, November 13."

Kelsey sat back in his chair. "Tell us exactly what you recall," he said easily. "You can show me your notes afterwards."

"It was around a quarter past five," Robin began. "I know for certain it was the Friday, I was going out to play with the rest of the group at the Folk Club." The group only ever played there on a Friday evening, once every four weeks.

He was studying hard for his exams, he went out little in the evenings. He had been out only one other evening that week, on the Tuesday, and that was at a later time, around seven-fifteen; he had attended a practice session at the home of one of the group. Both the Tuesday and Friday dates were recorded in his pocket diary; there was no possibility of his having confused the two evenings.

Furthermore, at the time he saw Mrs. Lorimer he had just wheeled his motorcycle over to the open doorway of the shed attached to the side of the shop, and Friday was the only evening that week that he'd used the motorbike—on the Tuesday a member of the group called for him, gave him a lift in his jalopy to the practice session.

The Folk Club meeting was held in a neighbouring village hall. It started at seven and the group normally arrived at six-thirty. On that particular Friday, however, they arrived earlier. They had written some new numbers, had decided to include them in the programme at the last moment and wanted to get in a final run-through. They arranged to meet at the hall at five-thirty. Robin produced his diary for the Chief's inspection. Kelsey gave an approving nod as he looked at the entries; everything set down in a clear, businesslike fashion, times carefully noted.

"I'd just stepped outside to take a look at the weather," Robin continued. "I was standing under the canopy." This was a wooden overhang running along the entire frontage of the premises, providing a degree of shelter for both shop and shed. "I could see out along the road, as well as the front of the shop.

"I heard the shop door open and I saw Mrs. Lorimer come out, I saw her clearly in the light shining out from the shop. She turned in the doorway and called something back to my mother, some remark about the weather. She didn't see me, she didn't glance my way. She went off in the opposite direction and got into the car."

"Car?" Kelsey echoed.

"Yes. It was parked a few yards off, facing my way. It started up and a minute or two later it came past me."

"In the direction away from Furzebank Cottage?"

"That's right."

"Going towards Cannonbridge?"

"Yes. Mrs. Lorimer was in the passenger seat. Her husband was driving."

Kelsey jerked up in his chair. "You're certain of that? Lorimer was in the car with her?"

"Quite certain. I saw them both clearly. The car hadn't had time to pick up any speed."

"Did either of them see you?"

He shook his head. "I'd stepped back into the doorway. They were both looking straight ahead."

His mother came back into the kitchen and sat down nearby. The Chief barely registered her presence. "You're certain about the time you saw the Lorimers drive past?" he pressed Robin.

"Quite certain. It was going on five-fifteen. I looked at my watch as I went back into the house to pick up my crash helmet. I didn't want to be late getting to the hall."

"We had a bit of an argument when Robin came back in," his mother put in with a smile. "I asked him if he didn't think he'd better take a torch, in case they had another blackout."

"Blackout?" Kelsey queried.

"Yes, we've had quite a few in this area over the last three or four months. The Electricity Board say it's a fault in a substation. They don't seem able to trace it properly, though they keep on trying." She jerked her shoulders. "Mostly it's of no consequence, it only lasts a few minutes, but once or twice it's lasted well over an hour, and that can be pretty inconvenient when you've got a business to run."

"And there'd been a blackout on some previous occasion at the Folk Club?" Kelsey directed his question at Robin but his mother answered before he could speak.

"Yes, the time before. The electricity didn't come on again for some time and there they all were, stumbling about in the dark, looking for matches and candles, flicking cigarette lighters—a good way to have a nasty accident. That's why I wanted Robin to take the torch with him, in case it happened again."

She shook her head. "But he didn't want to take it. He said it would be a bit too much of a coincidence if they had a blackout two Folk Club Fridays on the trot." She grinned. "In the end he did take it, though, to humour me, so he could get off."

The Chief asked if either could recall what Mrs. Lorimer had been wearing that Friday evening. The woman couldn't remember but Robin answered at once. She had worn a jacket and trousers, a headscarf. Further pressed, he thought the jacket and scarf were light in colour, the trousers dark.

The Chief asked if he could describe the car he had seen. He gave a description that tallied with the vehicle Kelsey had seen at Furzebank Cottage. "It was definitely the Lorimers' car," Robin added. "I know it by sight." He recollected another detail. "It has a rack." Kelsey sat motionless. "A white ladder-rack."

"Does the car normally carry a rack?"

"It always used to. It certainly did that evening. But the last few times I've seen it, there isn't any rack."

His mother couldn't say if the car usually carried a rack or not. "But you can bank on what Robin tells you," she added stoutly. She made a face. "Mr. Lorimer's been getting through a lot of cigarettes lately. One or other of them's in every day now for cigarettes, sometimes twice in the one day."

She glanced up at the clock and the Chief got to his feet. "We won't keep you any longer," he told Robin. He expressed his gratitude to them both, adding that there was one last favour he'd like to ask. He had a number of phone calls to make. Would it be possible to use their phone? Certainly it would. The woman took them into the sitting-room. "You'll be quite private in here," she assured them as she went out, closing the door behind her.

22

The crows had vanished from the field opposite Furzebank Cottage but the four donkeys had been joined by an old spavined horse. At the sight of the car he came hobbling over to the hedge in the vain hope of a titbit.

Enid Lorimer answered the door to Lambert's ring. Her appearance showed marked deterioration since their last visit. She was thinner than ever, pale and haggard, her manner subdued and strained. She looked as if she hadn't slept properly for several nights, as if she were desperately drawing on fast-diminishing reserves of nervous energy.

She had been engaged in ferociously scrubbing the kitchen floor when the doorbell rang. She stood gazing out at them in silence, drying her hands—red and puffy from the scrubbing—on a towel. She wore a rough apron over an old jumper and skirt. Strands of her thick nut-brown hair, no longer lustrous or freshly washed, had strayed loose from a careless knot.

The Chief told her he would like to speak to both her and her husband. She made no reply but stepped out of the house and led the way round to the garden. Lorimer was hard at work some distance away, slashing with an air of grim determination at straggling shrubs, stubborn tangles of rank undergrowth. In the brief time before Lorimer became aware of their approach Sergeant Lambert had a snapshot impression of him: battered, sunk into himself, tense and nervous, but nowhere near any point of collapse.

The moment he registered their presence he froze into immobility, in the act of stooping to gather up an armful of looped boughs. The Chief spoke to him as they came up, repeating his request to talk to them both. Lorimer slowly straightened up. He didn't look at them, didn't glance at his wife. He turned without a word and walked with an air of casual unconcern towards the back door of the house, with the others following.

Inside the kitchen Lorimer ignored the bucket of cooling, sudsy water, the scrubbing brush and cloth lying abandoned on the floor which was still sloppily wet. He went into the living-room, still in silence, and dropped on to the sofa. He lit a cigarette, inhaling deeply. His fingers were stained with nicotine almost to the knuckles.

The other three followed him into the room and Enid took her place on the sofa beside her husband. It was plain that the two policemen might have to wait a long time before they were asked to take a seat so they sat down without invitation.

Kelsey plunged at once into the business he had come about, taking them both in minute detail yet again through their account of the day of Karen Boland's murder; neither was shifted in the slightest degree from what had been said before. Lorimer looked straight ahead as he answered, alert and composed. Enid sat with her head lowered, rolling and unrolling a corner of her apron between her fingers.

"I ask you once again," Kelsey said. "Did either of you call in at the little general store down the road at any time that Friday?"

Enid didn't glance up, she merely shook her head without speaking, but Lorimer was loud in his denials. "You keep on asking us and we keep on telling you: No, neither of us was anywhere near the shop at any time that Friday."

"The lad at the shop," Kelsey persisted, "is positive you were both over there at around five-fifteen, that the two of you drove off in the direction which could take you to Cannonbridge."

"Then he's mistaken," Lorimer retorted with confident challenge. "You surely can't pay serious attention to what a chattering, gossiping widow and a guitar-strumming schoolboy tell you about what they think they might remember about something they fancy might have happened the best part of two weeks ago."

Kelsey pushed back his chair and got to his feet. "We'll take another look at your car," he said abruptly.

Once more Enid led the way in silence, out to the open shed that housed the estate car. Kelsey scrutinized the vehicle with minute care.

"Was this car new when your first husband bought it?" he asked Enid.

"Yes, it was."

"Did either he or you ever lend it to anyone?"

She looked baffled by the question. "No, never."

"Does it have a rack for the roof?"

She shook her head.

"Has it ever had one?"

Again she shook her head.

"I am given to understand that the car has frequently been seen round here carrying a rack."

Again she shook her head, answering in a low, faltering voice, "It hasn't got a rack."

"The lad at the shop states quite categorically that until very recently the car carried a white ladder-rack. Furthermore he says the rack was in place when he saw the car over by the shop that Friday evening."

Lorimer gave an angry snort. "All that lad's interested in is publicity, attention. He'd agree to any statement you cared to feed him. What he says is totally and utterly untrue. He's either mistaken, or lying—for God knows what silly reasons of his own. The car doesn't have a rack, it has never had a rack, it didn't carry a rack that day, the car was nowhere near the shop that evening. Neither my wife nor myself were anywhere near the shop that evening."

Kelsey walked round the vehicle, pausing here and there to point out slight indentations, traces of rust. "These marks definitely indicate that the car has at some time carried a rack."

Enid twisted her hands together. She said in a little stumbling rush, "Now I come to think about it, I believe it may have done. I seem to remember now that my first husband did sometimes use a rack—though I certainly never have." She stared down at the ground, biting her lip. No, she couldn't recall the type or colour of the rack, she had no idea what had happened to it.

Kelsey led the way back to the house, into the living-room where they all resumed their seats. He began to question them again about their visit to the Fairdeal supermarket. Lorimer did all the answering, smoking ceaselessly, repeating with an air of dogged determination the substance of his earlier account. Enid appeared only too glad to leave it all to him; she sat in unnerved silence.

"You had tea in the Fairdeal café, you left at around five," Kelsey said. "You're absolutely certain of that?"

"Quite certain," Lorimer replied.

"And you?" Kelsey asked Enid. "Are you equally certain?"

"Yes, I am." She didn't look at him. She pressed both hands to the sides of her head.

"You would both take your oath on that?"

"We certainly would." Lorimer sat back. His face relaxed, his manner became more open, tinged with exuberance. "I particularly remember because the girl asked if we wanted anything as the kitchens were closing. The restaurant closes at five."

"You clearly recall the girl telling you the restaurant was about to close?"

"Yes, I do. We had quite a chat with the waitress, she was a pleasant, friendly sort of girl. We told her we didn't want anything else. We paid the bill, left and drove straight back here."

The Chief glanced at Enid. "Do you confirm all that?"

She kept her gaze lowered. "Yes, I do."

"Now I find that odd," the Chief observed in a detached, conversational tone. "While I was over at Fairdeal the other day I made a list of the opening and closing times of both the store and the restaurant." He dug into his pocket.

"Friday," he said as he consulted the list. "Now it very definitely was Friday you were at Fairdeal, Friday you had tea there, Friday you chatted to the waitress as the restaurant was about to close?"

Lorimer had lost his air of relaxed exuberance, he looked tense and watchful again. After some moments he gave a nod. There was a further brief pause before Enid also nodded.

"Now this is what I find odd," the Chief went on in the same easy tone. "On Monday, Tuesday, Wednesday, Thursday and Saturday

the store closes at five-thirty and the restaurant closes at five. But
Friday is late-night closing. On Friday the store closes at eight-thirty
and the restaurant closes at eight. Eight o'clock, not five." He gazed
blandly across at Lorimer. "It was on the Thursday that you went to
Fairdeal, not on the Friday. You've never been there on a Friday."

Lorimer looked back at him unabashed. "You're wrong there," he
said lightly. "The girl simply made a mistake. She was very young,
inexperienced, she must just have forgotten for the moment about
the late-night closing. Understandable enough. It was her first job,
and a temporary one at that—she told us about it when we were
chatting. She'd only been working there a couple of days. They use a
lot of temporaries at Fairdeal, it seems, for illness, holidays, and so
on."

Kelsey switched tack. "This film you say you watched on TV—did
you watch the whole of it? Right through from start to finish?"

They both agreed that they had.

"I understand," The Chief continued, "that there is an intermittent fault at a local substation, it causes occasional interruption to
the electricity supply."

They both agreed, with manifest wariness, that this was so.

"Was there a failure of supply, a break in transmission, during the
screening of the film that Friday?"

Neither spoke. They sat in frozen silence.

"A straightforward question," Kelsey said. "Either there was a
break or there wasn't."

Sweat broke out on Lorimer's brow. "Yes," he said suddenly. "I'd
forgotten that. There was a break during the film."

"Do you confirm that?" Kelsey asked Enid. She gave a silent nod
but he refused to be content with that, he insisted on a spoken reply.
She gave it in a voice barely audible: Yes, she did confirm it.

"What time was this break in transmission?"

"Difficult to be sure," Lorimer answered in a tone grown relaxed
and confident again. "I remember the film hadn't been on very
long." He glanced at his wife. "What would you say? I'd guess
around six-fifteen, six-thirty, somewhere in that region."

Again the Chief insisted on a spoken reply from Enid and again
she gave it in a low voice: Yes, she agreed with her husband. She
didn't look at Lorimer.

"How long did the break last?"

Their replies followed the same pattern: Lorimer answering, looking at Enid for confirmation, the Chief demanding an unequivocal response from her. Their estimate for the length of break was five or ten minutes.

Lorimer relaxed visibly in his seat, his manner again took on a tinge of exuberance. "We were quite disappointed, because of the film, not knowing how long the break would last. We looked out a torch, candles and matches."

Again Enid agreed that this was so. Her tone and manner had grown even more hesitant. "You're certain about all this?" Kelsey pressed her. "You clearly recall looking out the candles and matches?" She twisted her hands as she answered: Yes, she clearly recalled it.

"This is where we have some difficulty," Kelsey said. "Earlier this morning I phoned the local Electricity Board. They were one hundred per cent positive in what they told me: There was no interruption to supply anywhere in this area that Friday."

Enid began to utter little whimpering sounds. Lorimer stared stonily ahead.

"You were neither of you here around six-fifteen or six-thirty that evening," Kelsey continued. "You were both at Overmead Wood. We have a first-class witness, a woman motorist, who saw a car by the wood. She spoke to a woman on the grass verge. She gives a good description of the car, a good description of the woman."

Enid began to weep. Tears ran down her cheeks, her face was contorted. "He couldn't rest till he'd seen her, talked to her, made her see how his life had been ruined." The words came out in rapid gushes, she sat wringing her hands. "He thought if she would just take some of it back, he might have some sort of chance, some sort of hope."

Lorimer suddenly sprang to his feet, his features twisted in savage anger, pouring out at them a torrent of words.

"Have you the faintest notion what it was like? No one would have anything to do with us, family, friends—even shopkeepers. It sent my mother to her grave. Take a look at this!" He flung aside his old gardening jacket, ripped off his shirt. He was very thin, his ribs stood out. "That's what they did to me in gaol!" He jabbed at his body, at the scars plainly visible against the dead-white skin. He swung himself round, displaying other scars on his back.

The gabble of words ceased abruptly and he dropped back on to the sofa. He sat slumped forward, cradling his head in his arms, shaking and shuddering.

Enid had stopped crying. She stared up at the Chief, her face puffy, stained with tears.

"She'd never have got in the car if she'd seen him. He was lying down in the back, under some rugs." She pressed her hands together. "On the way out to Overmead I kept trying to talk to her, to get her to see how his life was in ruins but she wouldn't listen." She flung out a hand. "He jumped up and started shouting at her. She was terrified, shrieking and screaming. She grabbed the door handle. He reached over to grab her. I stopped the car. She jumped out and ran off. He went after her. I jumped out and ran after them. A car came by and the woman called out to me. I said something to her and she drove off again.

"Victor came running back, shouting at me to get back in the car. Karen had fallen and struck her head. She was dead."

She made a helpless gesture. "It was like a terrible nightmare. I didn't know what to do, I couldn't think. We ran back to the car and drove back here." Her voice trailed off into trembling silence, she drooped her head.

Kelsey stood up. "We'll take another look round," he said into the silence. Neither made any response, offered any objection. He went up the stairs and thrust up the lower sash of the landing window overlooking the lane. He leaned out, signalling to the men waiting below.

They carried out the search with thoroughness and despatch, upstairs and down, inside and out. Throughout, Enid remained seated on the sofa, leaning back in collapsed stillness, her eyes closed, her face pale. Beside her, Lorimer sat crouching forward, frowning, endlessly smoking, watching intently through the open door of the living-room the to and fro of the searchers. From time to time he got to his feet and crossed to the window, staring out at the men going back and forth across the yard and garden. He and Enid never spoke, never exchanged a word or a glance.

Upstairs in the third bedroom, when the men began shifting the stacked furniture out on to the landing, they came, half-way into the room, upon a rug laid down over the floorboards. The edges of the boards showed fresh chisel marks. As the men prised up the boards a rank odour of mould rose up at them. In the space underneath a number of bundles had been stowed away. They carried the bundles downstairs and out into the yard. Lorimer stood by the window watching, smoking, as the bundles were opened out and the contents examined.

Mildewed clothing, male and female, put away soaking wet; all the garments of good quality, some of it bearing maker's labels. A man's jacket of lightish blue-grey, marl-mix tweed, trousers of dark grey worsted gabardine; both garments ripped and snagged, the trouser ends deeply muddied, the knees heavily stained. A pair of men's leather shoes, thickly caked with yellow-ochre mud. Embedded in the mud blades of grass, slivers of twigs, thorns, leaves.

A woman's light beige jacket, black trousers, walking shoes, driving gloves of dark brown leather, a patterned headscarf, cream-coloured. The shoes and trouser ends muddied and stained, some ripping and snagging on the lower part of the trousers, none apparent on the jacket, on the gloves or headscarf.

In the final bundle, dismantled into two long tubes and four curved endpieces, a white ladder-rack for a car.

It was a clear, sparkling morning as the vehicles set off for Cannonbridge a little later.

In the field opposite the cottage the four donkeys barely glanced up before bending their heads once more to the pasture, but the old broken-down horse, incurably hopeful, came hobbling over again to the fence, still looking for a carrot or a lump of sugar.

ABOUT THE AUTHOR

Emma Page is a British mystery writer whose skillful plots have won her a considerable following among connoisseurs of the classic detective novel, who rightly regard her as one of its most gifted exponents. *A Violent End* is her third novel for the Crime Club.